The Burning Bracken

Morgan Davies

www.victorinapress.com

Typesetting and layout: Jorge Vasquez
Cover design: Triona Walsh

British Library Cataloguing in Publication Data
A catalogue record for this book is available from the
British Library.

ISBN: 978-1-9169057-9-5

Typeset in 11pt Garamond
Printed and bound in Great Britain by 4edge Ltd

For my parents

1

When he was gone, Sarah held the mug of coffee away from her and began to tip its contents out slowly onto the living room floor. It spattered loudly on the carpet, forming a brown spume and spitting at the nearby sofa. She noticed the flecks of spray appearing on her dressing gown and stopped. Instead, she threw the mug and what was left of the coffee at the far wall. The porcelain shattered, leaving a dripping broth of liquid and coffee grounds and a satisfying rupture in the plasterboard. She reached a bare foot out in front of her and began to grind and smear the mess she had made, feeling the soggy warmth between her toes and working the stain deep into the thick and expensive pile of the formerly cream-coloured carpet.

She stood still for a moment, taking in the silence. The house was full of him. Whatever they were together, she was breathing it in now, in this room. Their lives had soaked into the walls.

She made her way upstairs to the bedroom and removed a large suitcase from under the bed. Unzipping it, she took out the plastic folder of documents from within. This was to be the fourth and final check she would make of them. She knew that her passport, her driving licence, her birth certificate and everything else she needed was there, but she could not help herself. Though she felt calm, almost detached, she was conscious of the significance of what she was doing, and if she suspected that anything were missing, she would take it as a terrible omen. Satisfied, she replaced the folder within the suitcase and set about packing it, folding each item of clothing neatly on the bed before tucking it in with the rest. She chose very carefully, weighing up how necessary each item might be and how much it reminded her of him. When she was finished, the suitcase held most of her jeans and T-shirts and some of her shoes, together with her underwear. The blouses, pencil skirts and maxi dresses were left still hanging in the wardrobes. With the case full, she pulled out the roll of bin bags she had secreted under the bed and stuffed them with the bulkier coats and jumpers. Taking another bag, she moved on to his clothing, selecting the most expensive shirts and cramming them in, together with his suits. When this bag was full, she took it downstairs and into the kitchen. She emptied the clothing into the sink and made sure that the plug was secure, then chose a large bottle of bleach from the cupboard under the sink and poured the stinking, viscous liquid out onto his best clothing.

He had left late that morning, annoyed with the replacement phone he was having to use and pressing her lips with the usual kiss.

'You look like shit,' he said. 'Stay and have a sofa day.'

In the night she had got up to go to the toilet and dabbed under her eyes with her darkest eye shadow until they were dull and ill-looking. It was unlikely he would have taken the care to notice but it gave Sarah a satisfaction in the assiduity of her plan.

For Sarah, the time for emotion had passed. That day came when she first found out, three days previously. She had lain on the bathroom floor for what felt like hours, seeing the tiles blur then clear, then blur again through the rising tears. Retching into the toilet, she had dragged her fingers across her scalp until her nails were filled with freshly harrowed skin. When she finally stood up and washed her face, that was it; the last nine years were gone. She had left the bathroom determined to cut him away from her and discard him, as coldly and precisely as a surgeon.

She grabbed the nearest chair from under the kitchen table, holding it up with both hands, before striking at the window above the sink. The glass trembled but did not crack. She tried again. Frustrated, she jammed the chair into the wall above the tiles instead. Pleased at the puncture it made in the plasterboard, she moved down the length of the kitchen and into the hall beyond, punching a chain of wounds into the wall. When she came across the picture of the two of them, hanging in the centre of the hall, she stopped and threw down the chair. She remembered the beach in Ireland. They were both smiling. Her red winter scarf was bunched beneath her neck and his head was close to hers, his forehead shape just beginning to change as his hairline receded. She wrenched it from the wall and made a tour of the rooms, gathering any other pictures she could find. She took the old memory cards from the desk in the box room and removed the one in use from the digital camera. Returning to the kitchen, she put on her slippers and carried her bundle out into the garden.

It was late autumn and the morning sky was predictably, stubbornly, uniformly grey. From somewhere unseen, a jet could be heard making its way through the gloom, the sound reverberating between the houses. The tall slats of the fence which blocked out the other gardens had turned the colour of apricot flesh. Sarah went over to the shed and dumped the pile of pictures onto the grass next to the rotary airer. A lone spider was working its way across the washing lines, struggling amongst the glassy spheres of dew. She carried the barbecue out of the shed and went back to rifle through the shelves until she found the matches and lighter fluid. The barbecue was greasy and beginning to rust. She filled it with the pictures and the memory cards and gave them all a liberal soaking with the lighter fluid. The fire burnt with a foul black smoke and was soon over. She went back into the shed, leaving the shrivelled and sooty remains still smouldering. Emerging with a toolbox and hand saw, she returned to the house.

At the foot of the stairs, Sarah readied the saw and began to drag it backwards and forwards across one of the rungs of the bannister. It was harder work than she had expected, and she gave up after the first rung, feeling a trickle of sweat running down her upper arm inside her dressing gown. She took the heaviest of the hammers from the toolbox and went into the living room to work on the television set instead. It left the screen with a crazing of savage and oddly beautiful cracks that reminded her of frozen puddles. She went back into the kitchen and took out the flour, sugar and the jars of pulses and scattered them around, opening a few tins of beans and chopped tomatoes and adding them to the mess. She threw the plates and bowls at the worktop one by one, where they smashed and spread across the floor in jagged white shards. She finished by upturning the cutlery drawer over the confused and multi-coloured landscape she had created. On her way up to the bathroom, she passed the toolbox and noticed the utility knife sitting amongst the screwdrivers. With a few gratifying slashes, the three piece suite was ruined and the snowy innards bulged out like some strange and alarming fungus.

When she had showered and wrapped her hair and body in twin towels, Sarah switched on the mirror light and began to cleanse her face.

How long had it been? It was his phone that had given it away. He was spending too long texting, always saying it was for work, never once leaving the phone alone and taking it with him to the bathroom at night. It was only when he came back from a night drinking with friends and passed out on the sofa that she was able to ease it from his pocket without disturbing him. He was too careless to have changed the code and too drunk to have noticed the sobbing from upstairs. Looking back, there must have been times when he had slept with both of them on the same day.

She smoothed her eyebrows with the brush and began applying her mascara. When she was dressed, she sat on the bed and opened her laptop. Her gym membership was already cancelled, and she had taken care of all the bills and the council tax. The gym she hated anyway. Her accounts were a worry but there was nothing set to arrive at the house for a good while. The rest of her phone contract had been paid off and it was set to close at the end of the week. It was lucky the rent was in his name. Her manager had been startled when she had handed in her resignation and she felt bad about feigning illness whilst she worked out her notice period. She did not want to think about her colleagues and friends. Gill had sent her a message that morning asking if she was feeling any better, to which she had not replied.

4

Now she set to work on her online self, deleting her social media accounts and changing her email password just to be sure, whilst blocking him and his work address. When she was finished, she packed the laptop away with the rest of her things and collected her belongings from the bathroom, pausing only to tip his aftershave and the stink of him down the sink.

She vaguely remembered the girl from one of the office parties he had made her attend. She could not remember much, having spent her time as she usually did at such events, feeling uncomfortable and self-conscious in one of the cocktail dresses Michael liked her to wear and being led around the room for him to show her off to each of his colleagues. She had not slept well these last few nights, lying awake with him asleep next to her, thinking of the evenings they had spent in each other's arms on the sofa, his free hand texting just out of sight.

With the last of her things by the front door, Sarah hunted through the desk for a pen. She chose the chunkiest black marker she could find and pulled off the lid. There was an adequately pungent smell of solvent. As she walked down the stairs for the last time, she held the pen against the wall and dragged out a thick and wavy black line. Downstairs, she selected an untouched section of hallway wall and wrote 'Fuck you Michael' in large and jagged letters. She then extracted his phone from where she had hidden it behind the corner cabinet and switched it on. It was still working. She had lied to him, telling him that someone had texted her saying they had found his phone and that they were coming round to drop it off with him this evening. Scrolling through the lurid messages to the girl listed only as K, she located the picture she was looking for. It seemed the girl had taken it herself for Michael. She could only be eighteen or nineteen. She was pouting at the camera, her eyes heavily made-up and her free arm cupping her exposed breasts. Sarah attached the picture to a new email and addressed it to Michael's work email group, along with his manager. With the picture sent, she fetched the hammer from the living room and thumped at the phone on the hallway floor until the screen disappeared in a web of cracks and the frame began to warp.

Sarah's Nissan Micra was parked outside in one of the numbered bays. She loaded her things into the car, stopping when she noticed a figure watching her from a window across the cul-de-sac. She stared back until the figure retreated from view. When she was ready, she closed the heavy plastic front door, slipping the key from her keyring afterwards and posting it through the letter box. Once inside the car, she adjusted the seat and rear-view mirror, out of ritual rather than necessity; she was the only person who ever drove it. As she pulled away from the houses and signalled to join the road beyond, she turned over her preparations in her mind. She was anxious not to have missed anything. Her body operated the car unconsciously. She was vaguely aware of a roundabout, some other cars, a set of lights and then another roundabout. When she became truly aware that she was driving, she was already moving at speed amongst traffic along the dual carriageway. She watched the underside of a jet flying low over the road and began to count the concrete arcs of the bridges passing overhead. There was the familiar noise of the car engine and something else. There was another noise, seemingly louder and closer to her. Like the flooding back of awareness upon waking, she suddenly understood that she was crying.

When she was seventeen, four years on from her grandma's death, her grandpa had followed her grandma to the grave. Michael was twenty-three at the time. He was her first real, proper boyfriend. It seemed so natural considering; he made it all so easy. She never spent another night in her grandparents' house after her grandpa died. It was Michael who held her as her grandpa's casket was led away. It was he who threw her mother out of the house when she traced them through the Samaritans and turned up at their doorstep in tearful contrition, only to be later found upstairs in the bedroom, pocketing what valuables she could find. It was Michael who could deal with her one cold aunt – whom she despised – better than she was ever able to.

Turning on to the motorway, she felt it all beginning to grip her. For the first time, she felt doubt tugging at her like a snagged thread. She wanted to go to him. She asked herself what she was doing with a car full of clothes and a sleeping bag, going who knows where. She drove on, moving closer towards no real destination but towards something else, something old and half-remembered.

Sarah climbed the uniform grass slope of the bank until she could see out onto the motorway. The cutting pulsed with the movement of vehicles streaming left and right. The air was sour. Giant lorries were churning the grey sediment at the roadside into convulsions of dust. Nearby, directions were suspended from an overhead gantry above the passing traffic, and she read the names of the cities of the north and west which were picked out in white lettering on the blue boards. London and the Home Counties were behind her now. She stood for a while, watching the unknown faces moving in and out of her life, seeing the families seated together and imagining the words they were speaking. It was all too big to even begin to try and take in. She watched the cars passing instead.

Sarah had never lived anywhere other than the garden city in which she had been born. She and Michael had taken a year out to go travelling, but otherwise her only experience had been administrative work at the same firm of consultants for whom she had worked since she was eighteen. She had planned to go to university but her grandpa's death came just before.

Looking out over the moving traffic, she waited for it all to fit into place, to have a way written clear and safe in front of her. She closed her eyes, trying to see it, but nothing came, just an arbitrary memory of the estate she had lived in as a child and the passageway between the houses, echoing with her footsteps and sprouting with the sunburst heads of dandelions.

Back down the slope behind her, a woman was sitting at one of the picnic benches with her two children, the three of them wrapped tightly in coats and scarves. Sarah was aware of the woman glancing over occasionally. Seeing Sarah climb the slope must have set off some sort of maternal warning signal in her. It made Sarah uncomfortable, and she headed back towards the building.

She was at one of the service stations on the motorway through the Midlands. Intending only to use the facilities, she had found herself unable to continue and had lingered there for what had now been over an hour. It felt as if it were all some sort of bluff; that she was just waiting for someone to break through, to tell her everything was fine and she should come home. She checked her phone again but there had been nothing from Gill since the message that morning.

They had been seeing less of each other recently. Gill worked in an office two streets away from Sarah and they used to meet regularly for lunch or coffee after work. Six months ago, Gill had met Tony on a night out. He was a manager at one of the units at the business park on the edge of town, was a good number of years older and had a richly toned voice that sounded to Sarah as if he were advertising desserts with every sentence. He and Gill were gripped by the first flush of love and had become inseparable. Every conversation she now had with Gill would return eventually and inevitably to him. She was happy for her though. At first the four of them had gone out together at weekends but Michael would always drink too much and fall asleep at the pub table, while Gill and Tony, uninhibited through drink, would start to kiss and touch each other until the barman would say something to them. In the end she made excuses not to go out. When she found out about the affair, she instinctively wanted to go to Gill, but it felt wrong somehow, as if she would be soiling Gill's good fortune with her own unhappiness. What once would have been natural now seemed awkward and intrusive. She did not want to burden Gill with it all, to have the three of them sharing a bathroom, to be sleeping each night on their sofa. It was better to leave them alone.

The concourse was crowded, and the automatic

doors were kept open with a constant file of patrons coming in or going back out to the car park beyond. The place was as brightly lit as if it were midnight. The tables in the cafés and fast food outlets were mostly full. Those unoccupied were piled with used coffee cups and empty sandwich packets. Long, disgruntled queues of people stretched from the counters, and half-complete families waited outside the toilets, their children running between them or swinging from their parents' arms. Unable to feel any hunger but conscious of the need for food, Sarah entered the one over-priced convenience store where she picked up a basket and joined the milling crowd of shoppers. Barely conscious of her decisions, her hand reached for each item and placed it into the basket.

Gill was easily Sarah's closest friend. They had known each other since the early years of secondary school, infuriating her grandpa with the many hours they spent on the phone. They had shared their first packet of stolen cigarettes together, the two of them had vomited Archers and lemonade across the patio at Dan Withershaw's house party and they had both lost their virginity within a week of each other. Gill had been with her in the hospital as they watched her grandma slip away and had called the ambulance the day her grandpa collapsed. She was as much family as Michael was. It had not been easy these last few days, trying to keep what had happened from her. Without Gill, there was little worth salvaging. Better to scrub it out, to wipe the slate clean and start again.

'Can I interest you in a loyalty card?' the man said.

'Sorry?' she replied. She was at the checkout and already had her purse in her hand.

'Can I interest you in a loyalty card?' the man repeated. He smiled kindly at her. She could not remember getting to the checkout. A woman waiting next to her tutted loudly.

'No,' she said finally. 'No, thank you.'

When she was back at the car, she placed the plastic bag of shopping behind her seat and called Gill again. There was still no answer. She sat for a while, fiddling absently with the indicator stalk. London had been the obvious destination. She could lose herself there and still feel safely within reach of Gill and her other friends, but London was too familiar. She wanted something else, not just another place in her life. That was how the idea of travelling to Wales had returned. As a child she had holidayed there a few times with her grandparents, staying at the same caravan park, right in the heart of the country. They were happy times, and she vividly remembered the brown pony they kept there, the walk to the waterfall and the honey ice cream they sold at the park shop. Now, sitting alone in her car by the side of the M6, the idea of driving out to Wales based on a few holidays she had had as a child seemed ridiculous. She was anxious to be moving somewhere, though, and was thoroughly sick of the service station. Feeling that she had no choice but to continue, she reached over for the road atlas to double-check the junction she needed for the route west. Driving out of the car park and onto the slip road, she checked the fuel gauge again and began to pick up speed, ready to re-join the motorway.

She travelled on with the flow of traffic, trying the radio briefly before deciding it was too strange having voices in the car with her. The thin trees which lined the banks either side eventually gave way to rows of saplings standing neatly in their guards. Once, the road passed close to a line of pylons where wires sagged between towers of latticed steel. Buildings began to appear and soon the motorway rose above a sprawl of streets and suburbs. The houses cleared for a moment to reveal a cemetery crammed with the headstones of what must have been thousands of souls. As she drove above the city, tower blocks protruded from the mass of buildings and looked out at her across the many rooves. The road became busier, and the traffic slowed. Before the motorway headed to Manchester she turned off at her junction and drove on past the colossal hulk of a gasometer. When the city was gone and the land returned to winter fields, her phone finally sounded in her handbag next to her. She pulled it quickly from her bag and read the message, holding it out in front of her so that she could glance between it and the road.

Hi hun. How you doing? Sorry for not answering. We've had clients in all day. Will call you when I get out tho could be a bit late. Speak to you soon. Love you. G xxxx

The relief spread through her until her fingers trembled on the steering wheel. She would pull over as soon as she could. She could decide exactly what she would say whilst she waited for Gill. She could turn around then and head back. What did it matter if she had to stay with Gill awhile? The whole idea of leaving had been absurd. This was the end of it; she was going home.

2

The annual race from the clock tower at Hen Gaer to the summit of the Fan was older than living memory, which for the people of the surrounding valleys, meant it was as old as a thing could be. Held during carnival week, the race took its runners from the valley floor, over the river and across the fields of Maesteg Farm, before climbing steeply through the woods up the side of the mynd to the trig point on Fan summit and back. Evan's father had run it and his father's father and that was all the reason he needed to join in every year without fail. At his age, the men had grown used to being beaten by their sons and the young men all sped past him now. Of the farmers of his generation, he was the last from his valley still to run. He was unbeaten by the mynd itself at least, and in any case, he had no son who could run in his stead. Though it was many months until the race next year, Evan would make sure that he was ready.

The hills around were pale and chilled with the season's light. The bracken had fallen into rust, leaving only the broken stalks still standing, covering swathes of the hillside like embers raked across the land. A cold wind was blowing from the mountains to the north. The flowers on the gorse clung brown and papery to their hosts like the moulted remains of insects. As he ran, Evan breathed bursts of vapour into the cold air. He was following his standard route up the bryn which served as a training run and which gave him the gratifying experience of being able to survey most of his land. His father had taken the same route when he trained. He remembered being carried some of the way on his father's shoulders when he was small. More often he remembered him running with one of the lambs slung over his shoulders instead, the two sets of legs gripped in each hand like the straps of a rucksack. Nearing the summit of the hill, Evan felt his throat sore with exertion, as if a piece of the gorse had been crammed down his windpipe. Farmers were not as fit as they were, he thought. Everything was done on quad bikes these days. Reaching the smooth roof of the hill, he felt the relief in his legs as the gradient slackened. To his left, the moor stretched blankly and steadily away into the distance. Looking out and across the valley, he could see the old castle mound, bare and silhouetted against the sky. Built by a king the people had long forgotten and whose name he could not pronounce, it held no interest for him, though it had looked down on his farm forever.

He began his descent, feeling the strain in his knees and the pressure building in his lower back. Hafod Farm opened up beneath him. He kept a close eye on the ground in front but afforded himself the occasional glance over and across to the clustered buildings of his fiefdom. The farm was dominated by two great sheds, whose mighty corrugated frames overshadowed the smaller and older buildings opposite. At the head of the courtyard was the farmhouse proper, a thin curl of wood-smoke leaking almost invisibly from the aged chimney above it. On the other side from the sheds were the old barn and stables, at the end of which, plastic-wrapped bales of silage had been stacked high against the brickwork. At the far end of the farmyard was the track which led away from the farm and to the valley road below. A little way from the gate, under the shelter of the drovers' pines, was a small white cottage that had once been the original farmhouse.

When he drew near the steep bank that dropped into the farmyard, the collies ran out and up the slope to meet him. Excited by his running, the two dogs kept pace at an even distance from him, their bodies keen and alert for his command. He slowed as he drew level with the farmhouse and finally stopped, leaning against the wall with his palms pressed against it. His shoulders flexed with the force of his breathing, but he resisted any urge to sound his relief. He did not want Sioned to hear him exhausted; it was not worth the bother. The dogs watched him as he felt the stretch, deep and painful within his legs. He left them waiting and went into the house.

Flushed with the exercise, the house felt uncomfortably hot to him at first. Sioned was busy loading the washing machine. The door was open to the utility room and he could see her at the other end of the corridor on her hands and knees. In the dim light of the windowless room, he could make out the length of her back rising and falling as she pushed each armful of clothes into the machine. She was a full inch taller than Evan, with slender but deceptively powerful limbs. Her hair retained some of its colour so that in certain lights it seemed youthful and flaxen and in others it was white with age. Strands of it had worked themselves loose from where she had tied it back and she was having to brush them behind her ears as she bent over to scoop up the clothing. She glanced up at him for a moment, then carried on with her work. He steadied himself against the coats hung up in the corridor and pulled off his trainers.

'Are you having a shower?' she asked, directing the question into the drum of the machine.

'Is there water enough?' he called back.

'Should be.'

Evan went into the kitchen. Two places were laid at one end of the long wooden table. A bowl of fruit broke up the unused space at the other end, its contents slightly withered. He picked up a couple of logs from the stack by the hearth and opened the door to the range. There was wood enough aflame in the hot, blackened compartment but he threw the logs in anyway and closed the door. Sioned had wanted the range converted to oil and it was true that this would likely work out cheaper and would certainly be more practical. Evan was too attached to how he had always known it however, and besides, he liked to feed its belly of fire. It seemed to him like the beating heart of the house, of the farm even. It always kept on going, burning without rest as they slept. Many a cold newborn lamb had been saved in the warm womb of its lower compartment. The fire filled the pipes with hot life and the water pulsed though the rooms of the house.

Sioned came into the kitchen.

15

'The Renault won't start again,' she said.

'Oh,' he said.

She filled a glass with water from the tap and handed it to him.

'I'll start it from the landy now,' he said.

'It needs a new battery. Can you get one from Elwyn?'

'They're pricey.'

'I know they're pricey,' she said, her tone changing. 'Do you know why they're pricey? It's because the car's so old they don't make them like that anymore.' She leant against the worktop and faced him across the table. 'Evan, that car costs us more in repairs than a car twice the price would've done.'

'We can't afford a new car,' he said without thinking. She stared back at him, and he looked away and at the fruit on the table instead.

'Well, you know what I think,' she said. 'There could be easy money there.' She nodded towards the window, which looked out towards the cottage. 'Talking of which, I've got some paint off Siân; it's a nice enough colour.'

'All right,' he said. 'It's still a waste of time. Who's going to want a cottage up here?'

'Well no one with the state it's in. It could be a holiday let or something with some work. Where are you going?' she asked him. He was making his way out.

'To have that shower,' he said over his shoulder. She called to him as he climbed the stairs.

'Evan!'

'Yeah, yeah,' he shouted. 'I'll go and have a look at it in a bit.'

What light there had been was fading now. Above him, the trees were quiet and still and the branches looked down at him darkly from the pines. The cottage was a low, stone-walled building that had been set into the slope of the hillside so that the chimney was barely the height of the levelled out farmyard above it. Its rough, whitewashed walls glowed coldly under the trees. Evan picked his way down to it until he was out of sight of the farmhouse and its one illuminated window where Sioned was preparing the dinner. At the doorway of the cottage, he drew out a long, old-fashioned key from his coat pocket and let himself inside.

He knew how bad things were with the farm, but he could not see past the way he had always known it. It was Sioned that always came out with the ideas: renewable energy, free range eggs, or a stall at the farmers market in the Marches. Some were working well, others had never got off the ground. In her mind the cottage was an untapped opportunity for extra income, sitting unused and gathering damp at the bottom of the farm. The place had been unoccupied for many years now. There had been little interest since it had first been advertised. One or two individuals had been up to look around, but none had returned. Evan's nain was the last to have lived in it. She had died a few years back, well into her nineties. They had wanted to take her back into the farmhouse, but she would not leave the cottage.

He stopped just inside and stared into the blackness, half expecting her to emerge lovingly from the ancestral dusk of the hallway. The lightbulb burst into life with the thump of the heavy switch next to him. It was colder than he remembered it. Age had turned the primrose patterned wallpaper into a smudgy, custard mess which was now lifting from the walls.

Ever since the farmhouse had been built, generations of the Bowens had retired to the cottage. Each inheriting son had brought his new bride to live at the farmhouse until gradually, as the space grew cramped with the coming children, the elder farmer and his wife would move out and into the cottage below. Much had changed in the lives of the Bowens since this rite was fist established. Engines had arrived, new breeds had been embraced and the old language had vanished from their tongues. That the original builders had buried a horse's head beneath the cottage doorway was remembered by no one. Evan's nain had died knowing that this tradition of the generations had at last been broken. The knowledge of this returned to Evan now, certain and painful, as he stood there in the gloom. He needed to get out of the cottage. He would make an excuse, another one. The yellow corridor moved swiftly past him, and the key turned once more in the lock. He came away from the building preoccupied, his mind working through what he would say when asked. He knew he could not hold out indefinitely, but for now at least, he was determined he would not go back inside.

The following afternoon was calmer. The hawthorn on the hill's summit was still, holding out its bare boughs and showing the wind-written curves of its branches. Ewes were grazing along the open slopes, feeling the first stirrings of this year's young inside them. Evan was busy repairing one of the farm's many fences. The old wire lay next to him, deformed and useless, rolled loosely together and sprouting locks of captured wool, like the cotton-grass which flowered on the moorland above. He had driven in a fresh line of fence posts and was squatting in front of one of them, hammering in staples to secure the final section of wire. He heard a mewing high above him and looked up. A kite was wheeling slowly through the still air, its crossbow-shaped body dark against the sky. He watched it for a while, gliding silently, making only the faintest of movements with its forked tail. Kites did not bother him. They took mostly carrion and the occasional rabbit kit, which was always a favour. A kite would often have to wait its turn to feed, needing the raven and its dagger-beak to break open the flesh of anything larger. Ravens were a different matter; he would shoot them on sight. A raven would set to work on a lamb or even an upturned ewe, starting always by pecking out the eyes. A further two kites now appeared. As he watched the first pass overhead, he leant back to steady himself, forgetting the handful of fence staples in his fist. He gave a yelp and scattered the contents of his hand. One of the staples remained, embedded in his finger. He pulled it out and the blood ran bright and smooth into his sleeve. Making a fist again, he watched the blood seep out from between his fingers and waited for the bleeding to stop. He finished pinning the rest of the wire, using only the thumb and forefinger of his injured hand.

When he got back, the kitchen was hot and steamy with the savoury smells of boiling vegetables and roasting meat. His insides began to fidget with hunger. Sioned looked round from the sink and at his hand.

'What have you done?' she said. She was first to notice his injuries, sometimes even before him.

'My hand,' he said and held it out for her. She dried her hands with a tea towel and took down the green medical box that was kept on top of one of the cupboards. They both sat down. The fruit bowl was gone, and the table was fully laid. He opened his hand for her, and she began to silently clean the wound.

'Smells good,' he said. She was deep in concentration and did not answer. Her fingers looked pink and raw, and the backs of her hands were mottled lightly with age. She selected a dressing from the medical box and then there was the sound of a car stopping at the gate.

'They're here,' she said, brightening. He tried to look out, but the windows were too steamed to see them arriving. She wound a bandage hurriedly round the dressing. He began to protest but there was the slamming of car doors and the high, insistent voice of a child out in the farmyard. The door opened without a knock.

'Hiya, Mam, Dad,' Ceri called from the hallway. Rachel ran into the kitchen, not yet table height, carrying a scruffy soft toy that had once been the shape of an animal but had since been worn unrecognisable. The kitchen was suddenly filled with greetings and kisses. Richard came in behind them and nodded.

'All right,' he said.

'All right, young Richard,' Evan said. 'I've got some cider for you. The good stuff.'

'Cheers, Evan.'

'What have you done now, Dad?' Ceri asked.

'I've . . .' Evan looked down at his hand. 'What have you done, woman?' His finger was now obscured in a thick sock of bandage. Sioned giggled.

'Your dad's got himself a piercing,' she said. 'Thinks he's trendy now.' Evan held up his injured finger.

'And just how am I supposed to get any work done with this comedy bandage on?'

The four of them laughed and Rachel looked up at the swollen, white finger. Evan wagged it at her. Sioned smiled at him. It seemed easier somehow with everyone here. They sat down to eat, and Evan carved from the joint as Sioned served the vegetables, his bandaged finger sticking out at an angle, unused.

When the meal was over, they left Richard in the kitchen to drink his cider. He was a scrawny young man with an olive complexion that made him look more Italian than Welsh. Evan had never guessed his daughter would marry one of the Powells; the boys were known to get themselves into a bit of trouble every now and again. Richard was the better-looking one and could certainly turn on the charm when he needed to. Evan knew he'd had a good hiding once or twice from a few lads and he could guess the reason why. The Powells had a good farm though, and Ceri seemed besotted with him, which, as Sioned said, was all that mattered.

Sioned sat down in the living room and lifted her granddaughter onto her knee. She opened a book with her, and Rachel pointed at the animals inside and told Sioned their names.

'Let's have a dance then, Dad,' Ceri said. He complained, but she ignored him and went over to the record player. It was old and chunky, with a heavy lid made of grey plastic.

'You haven't heard of iPhones then?' she said, flicking through the worn records on the shelf.

'Rubbish,' he said. 'Those records are older than you and they're still going.'

'I know,' she said. 'How much was this one, two shillings and six pence?' She pulled out the record and set it turning on the record player. Evan groaned.

'Not Spandau Ballet.'

'Come on, Dad,' Ceri said and took hold of his waist. 'I wish I'd never bought this all those years ago,' he said.

'Slow dance,' she said and mimed the lyrics exaggeratedly in front of his face. She was his brother's build, ruddy and plump, but her eyes were her mother's.

The book had not lasted long, and Rachel was now wriggling and chittering on Sioned's lap as she tickled her. Ceri rested her head on his shoulder as they danced. Her hair gave off the same fresh sweetness that had gone from her room upstairs. He felt the struggle go out of him, as if he needed nothing, only the nearness of her. All things became good and right in the farm, and the farm was the world. He pushed everything else away and went on holding her, warm and happy in his arms.

3

Sarah tore open the sandwich packet and bit into the chilled bread. She could not remember being hungrier. Her phone was out and ready on the seat next to her. She had stopped the car not far from the motorway, next to a line of railings demarking what looked like the grounds of a country estate. Beyond the rows of black iron were smooth contours of grass and the neatly spaced trees of an avenue leading gently away. As she ate, she imagined how Gill was going to react. However kind and thoughtful she was, her temper was legendary and anticipating her fury gave Sarah a quickening thrill. She played out the conversation in her mind, planning how she would relay each detail and picturing how Gill would respond. When the sandwich was finished, she tilted back her seat and closed her eyes, willing the call to come soon. It was quiet but for the distant boiling of the motorway behind her and the vehicles that passed occasionally, rocking the car with their closeness. Maybe she could still go to London. Work would be relatively easy to find there. She wondered how she might get a reference for a place of her own. She was forming an image of what her flat might look like when the phone finally rang, making her start even though she was expecting it. The number was Michael's temporary phone. She ended the call immediately, but the number called again.

'Shit,' she said aloud. She had never had to block a number before and she tried searching how it was done, but the number kept calling and interrupting her. She switched off the phone and watched the screen go blank. Her throat pulsed with the quickening of her blood. She drank some water and tried to calm down, counting out seven minutes on the clock on her dashboard. When she was ready, she switched on the phone. Several missed calls and an answerphone message came up in red, but it did not ring. She blew out her cheeks and wound down the car window for some air. A minute later, Gill rang.

'Oh, thank Christ,' Sarah said. 'Hi.'

'Hiya, hun, how you doing?' Gill asked. Sarah felt herself welling up at the sound of her voice.

'Not so good,' she said.

'Oh, sweetheart, are you really unwell? Have you been to the doctors? Do you want me to come round?'

'No, no, no. I'm fine.'

'You don't sound fine. Where's Michael, is he looking after you?'

Sarah drew in a deep breath. 'I'm not at home,' she said. The phone was quiet for a moment.

'What do you mean you're not at home?' Gill asked.

'I'm in Telford, or Shropshire I think.'

'You what? Shropshire?'

'Yeah.' Again, there was a pause.

'What are you doing there? Is Michael with you?'

'No.'

'But . . . what . . . why?'

'I drove here. I'm . . . moving out.'

'Moving out, why? Is it Michael?'

Sarah waited a moment before replying. 'He's been seeing someone else.' She expected the words to linger for a moment, like a bell reverberating, but Gill replied immediately. 'That what's-her-name from his work?' she said.

'You knew?'

'No, no, I didn't know. So, he has been. The bastard. The little shit. I knew it.'

'What do you mean? You did know or you didn't know?' she asked.

'Well, I had my suspicions. Oh, Sarah, I'm so sorry. After all this time.'

'What do you mean your suspicions? When? How?'

'Just something Tony said. Why are you in Shropshire? Why there? Why haven't you come over?'

'What?' said Sarah. 'What did Tony say? When? Why didn't you tell me?' Her voice was high and desperate.

'Oh, nothing,' Gill said. 'He just thought he saw

something. That girl. God, have you got your stuff? What's happening?'

'Why didn't you tell me?' Sarah asked.

'What, there was nothing to tell, I just thought–'

'You just thought what?' she interrupted.

'Well, I didn't know for sure.'

'It doesn't matter. It doesn't matter. Whatever Tony saw, whatever it was, you should've told me!'

'Sarah, I didn't know anything. It could've just been nothing.'

'But why didn't you tell me? What did Tony see? When?'

There was silence for a moment, then Gill began to mumble a reply. 'It was just . . . I just thought I didn't want to upset you if it was nothing.'

'Well, did you find out? Were you going to tell me anything at all?'

'Yes, yes. Sometime. If I found out more. It's just we've been so busy. I thought it might all be nothing. What was the point in worrying you if it was just nothing? Sarah? Sarah?'

She had already taken the phone away from her ear. Slowly, mechanically, she switched it off and put it away in her bag, then sat there, very still. Twilight was coming. Rooks were clattering among the branches of the naked trees. It was some time before she restarted the car and drove away back to the motorway. She continued on her miserable course, aware only of the lights of the cars ahead, not noticing the knurled border of hills beginning to take shape in the distance. Before long the motorway came to an end and the road crossed a great river, moving coolly under the alders below. With the light fading, she passed close to the town of Penbury, and in the chain of roundabouts surrounding it found the road she needed into Wales, signposted simply to Powispoole.

Having spoken to Gill, she felt she understood now. It was a malicious and comprehensive betrayal, planned and carried out by those closest to her. Everyone was lying to her; they were two-faced cowards, all of them. Those moments when she felt most lonely, they were the truth. She did not need them, any of them. She knew if her grandpa were here, he would say you have to look after yourself in this life. From now on, that was all she was going to do. The dream of her father, whoever he was, riding in on his white charger and scooping her up, was long, long, long dead. Her mother was the last person she wanted to see and was probably dead anyway, a needle hanging out of her arm or something similar. She understood now: she was alone.

Ahead of her, the land had distorted into long swellings of hills, standing blue and cold above the fields. A group of them had clustered together to form a ridge like the knuckles of a giant hand. The road was leading her towards them and began to undulate softly as the pastures folded themselves into ever higher mounds. The sun had passed out of view and the sky blushed behind the risen ground. When she came close to the cluster of hills, she saw woods like darkness painted onto the slopes, and the road turned away and began to descend towards a broad valley. She was surprised to see the road signs had changed. Each of them now appeared with what looked like an arbitrary cluster of consonants. She must have crossed the border and missed the sign. She had expected something more obvious. On the far side of the valley glowed the lights of Powispoole. Before it was the river, just visible. It had spread itself here and there across the floodplain, covering the fields and leaving trees stranded in pools of quicksilver.

Sarah drove on for another half hour or so until the valley narrowed, and she found herself squeezed amongst the traffic of Marcherton. She made her mind up to stop and turned off for the town centre, parking under the lights of the main street to pore over the road map. The caravan park they had stayed in when she was a child was called something like Reedy Bennock. She had tried searching the internet for it, days earlier but had found nothing like it. The road map she had was too small a scale and when she tried searching for it again on her phone it loaded the same results, only very slowly. From a pub across the street came the regular thump of a house beat. A pair of teenage girls clopped past her car in high heels, the bare flesh on their legs blotchy with the cold and their arms folded tightly across their chests. A group of boys dressed nearly identically in jeans and check shirts followed close behind. She got out of the car and went into the one convenience store that was open. What she wanted was a drink. As she had no choice but to drive, she bought some cigarettes and a lighter instead. The man serving was not what she expected. He spoke in a thick West Midlands accent and had the letters W.B.A. tattooed in fading ink on his forearm.

'Sorry, do you know where Reedy Bennock Caravan Park is at all, please?' she asked.

'No,' the man said, simply.

'Okay, thanks.'

Outside, she unwrapped the cigarettes and lit one. She had not smoked for years and would only occasionally get a craving, usually after a glass of red wine. The taste and sensation were both vile and not at all as she remembered. She carried on, but by the time she was halfway through had already begun worrying about cancer. She stubbed it out and threw the nearly full packet into the nearest bin. A man was eating chips in the open doorway of a kebab shop a few doors down. He paused for a moment to watch her cross back over the street, then went back to his chips. Except for the man, the street was deserted. The place seemed no different from any of the smaller towns back in England. It was just as dreary, only colder. She got back into the car and turned the heater to maximum. There had not been any hotels as she drove in, and it did not look like the sort of place that would have a youth hostel. Bed and breakfast was a possibility but she could not face going into a stranger's home. As she drove out of town, over a bridge and into the night, she felt she could not even cry. It took energy to be sad and she had none. There was nothing there save for the taste of stale tobacco in her mouth and the hedgerows at either side, lit by the sweep of the headlamps.

Spending the night in the car was far more uncomfortable than she had imagined and much, much colder. She tried lying on the back seats but got a cramp in one of her legs. Instead she took to slouching in the driver's seat in her sleeping bag. The pedals and steering wheel were a nuisance, but she found she needed to switch on the engine occasionally for a blast of warmth from the fan heater. She made it a rule to do this only when she could see her breath again in the light from her phone. The road map was somewhere in the passenger footwell, thrown there in annoyance when she had grown tired of looking up the names of the villages. They were mostly long, yet somehow all similar. After an hour or so of driving in the dark she had given up and had just continued on aimlessly. The roads had become smaller, the villages fewer and the last turning she remembered taking had been signposted 'narrow mountain road'. They were all around her now, the mountains. She could feel them more than she could see them. In the end she had parked in a gravel car park, next to a concrete block of toilets. Hers was the only vehicle there.

At twenty to midnight she could not hold on any longer and made a dash to the toilets again by the light of the phone. They were dismal and stinking and cobwebbed with daddy longlegs. When she emerged, she stopped to take a few breaths from the thickening mist. It was cool and sweetly moist in her nostrils. A fox called somewhere further down the valley, then something else that she did not recognise. She clambered back into the car and shivered in her sleeping bag until she was warm again. They had reached the caravan park via a long mountain lane; she remembered that much. She tried to picture the turnoff leading to it, but her tired mind remembered only a vent full of flies near the floor of their caravan and Grandpa spraying something into it until the buzzing stopped. Exhausted, and with the heater still running, she finally fell asleep.

When she woke it was not as dark. In the ashen light, her sleeping bag seemed to have changed colour. She touched her cold face with the back of her hand. Her nose and mouth felt like they belonged to someone else. She went to turn the key in the ignition. Nothing happened.

'Oh no, no, no!' she said, turning the key quickly forward and back and stamping at the accelerator through her sleeping bag. 'Oh God, Christ!' The battery was utterly flat. She pressed her face into her hands. Joining a breakdown service had not crossed her mind. They had never had one in the past, as Michael was good with engines and liked to think he could do without one. She checked her phone. It simply said 'No Service'. Refusing to cry, she thumped the door next to her instead and reached down for her boots.

The mist had thickened overnight. She could only see a short distance ahead before the view dissolved into white nothingness, and from looking at it, there was nothing to suggest that the road beside her continued. Her fleece felt damp as she zipped it up. Before she locked the car, she stuffed a few cereal bars, a water bottle and some other items of food into her coat pockets. Wherever help was to be found, she was sure it would be a long while. She set off up the road, picking up from where she had stalled her journey last night. There was no sound, only the scuff of her boots on the tarmac. To the side of her, the bank was steep and split open in places to expose rock faces, moist and crumbling with the wear of water. The road climbed steadily, and a crash barrier appeared on its far side. She went over to it and peered into the drop of blankness beyond. There was no way of telling how far down it went. The mist seemed to be brightening, though she could see little further. With the road still ascending, she came eventually to a cattle grid and had to pick her way carefully over the greasy rungs. The crash barrier had by now been replaced by a stone wall and as she stopped and leant against it there was a sudden change in the air. The mist lifted a little, just for a moment, revealing before her the black and angular form of a colossal structure of stone. She was so startled, and the sight so incongruous, that it took a few seconds for her to understand. Drawing closer, she could just make out the water, pale and still behind the monstrous body of the dam. The mist crept slowly along its surface. She felt suddenly unsafe; there was something inhuman about the dam. It was so vast and silent and seemed more like the work of a god than any group of people. Gripped by an unexpectedly urgent desire to get out and above the mist, she came away from the reservoir and continued along the road. Not far away, there was a wooden signpost that said *Llwybr Prydferth - Scenic Trail* which pointed a finger up the bank. She crossed over the stile and followed the path upwards that had been worn into the grass. It was hard going and more than once she had to stop and rest, leaning forward with her hands on her knees. At last, the mist began to disperse, and the blunt summit of the slope became visible against the dawn. When she was finally clear of the vapour, she turned to look back at the valley from which she had escaped.

'Wow!' she said out loud. She was looking out upon an ocean of white. The mist spread out below her in a billowing, spectral blanket, broken only by the humpback peaks of the mountains that rose like islands from the swell. The horizon was split with coloured strata, layers of fleshy pinks bleeding into the blue canopy above. She took some photographs on her phone, then stood for a while to eat something and to watch the mists moving under the island-hills. The air made the food taste good. She felt a little different, though the thinking part of her knew she was deeply, deeply hurt. All the bitterness of yesterday was still there, but there was a tinge of something else. Here on the mountainside, it did not seem so bad, though she did not know why. As she thought about it, she stroked the back of her own hand. She turned away from the view and continued along the trail.

When the sun had finally cleared the last of the mists from the land, Sarah had been walking for some time. She had left the marked trail of the mountain walk and was now following a footpath that descended through woodland. There was still no signal on her phone and she had not yet met one person along the way. The path was strewn with a russet slick of mouldy leaves. To her side, a stream cut a jagged course between the trees, the water sounding over stones then quietening again into shallow pools. Looking ahead, she slowed her pace. A short way from the path she could see the outline of a person, standing quite still with their back turned to her, apparently absorbed. As she came closer, she could make out that it was a woman wearing a pair of baggy combat trousers, her long hair hanging loose and red against the green of her anorak. She seemed to be running her hand over the trunk of the oak tree, caressing the hairy moss and the rough bark above it. Sarah stopped a short way from her.

'Excuse me,' she said. The woman made no sign that she had heard her. 'Do you know where the nearest garage is?'

At last, the woman turned, very slowly, and revealed her freckled face spread with a blissful smile. She said nothing, continuing to smile at Sarah.

'Sorry to bother you,' Sarah said. She turned away annoyed, then noticed that there were other people in the wood with them. A man was standing in the water, further along the stream. She saw him reach down to scoop out a cupped handful of the water, letting it run through his fingers before bending down again to take another. Another woman had hold of one of the bald branches of an oak and was rubbing it back and forth between her fingers. Taking up the path again, Sarah passed close to her. As she did so, the woman brought the branch up to her face to smell it. She felt she must have walked into some sort of collective drug-taking session. Perhaps they were all tripping on mushrooms together. She was glad to be away from them when the trees came to an end, and the path ran instead along a hedgerow towards a group of houses. For the first time that day, her phone displayed a signal. Civilisation at last, she thought, and began searching for a garage. The nearest was a disappointingly long distance away, so she tried searching for taxi numbers instead. The footpath joined a road and she walked on past a pair of pebble-dashed bungalows. A Jack Russell ran out to bark at her as she passed one of the gates. She found a road sign that gave her a name and sat down on a nearby grit salt bin to call a taxi firm. The woman answering asked her to read the name out again.

'Oh, Neuadd Clywedog. That's a fair while away mind. Can you wait?'

'I'll wait,' she said.

The taxi driver was a thick set man who drove with one hand loosely on the steering wheel, showing the chunky gold rings on all four of his fingers. At least three gold chains were visible where his shirt opened, and a crest of grey chest hair rode up between them.

'Where to then?' he asked as she got in beside him. The car smelt strongly of aftershave.

'Can you take me to a garage please?'

The driver thought for a moment.

'I can take you to Elwyn's place at Hen Gaer,' he said. 'Don't know if he'll be in today though, love.'

The journey took a lot longer than she expected but the driver seemed nice enough. He told her the numbers of each of the roads and named the places they led to as they crossed from one valley to another. She asked him whereabouts he was from.

'Oh, I'm from Berriew originally. I live in Llanbadarn now.' She nodded, having no idea where these places were. 'Needed to be closer to my wife's family see.'

'Is she from there?' she asked.

'No, she's from Dolau. That's why she's mental.' He laughed. 'They're all mental down there.'

Taxi rides were commonplace for Sarah, and she and Gill had become adept at getting their fares reduced. Gill used a combination of haggling and outrageous flirtation, but Sarah had developed a tactic of asking each driver about their employer, or if that did not work, their families. It usually took just a few well-placed questions before they were reeling off a lengthy spiel of how unjustly they were treated by their bosses or how their children did not respect them. Having let off steam, there were many occasions when the driver would reduce her fare when the time came for her to pay. On this occasion, getting the man onto the subject of his wife had set off a protracted monologue. She continued to nod as he bemoaned her ill-treatment of him.

'It's my own fault for marrying the daughter of Gavin the Glonc. He's dead now but everyone had heard of him. Used to bite the ear of his horse to make it go faster.' Sarah giggled. 'He had a dog. Called it Fire. Imagine it right, all through the village this man's shouting "Fire, Fire!" whenever he's calling for him!'

When they arrived at Hen Gaer, she was pleased to find that the story of Gavin the Glonc had saved her three pounds fifty from the fare.

A bell rang as she stepped into the garage office. It was a small room with no seating and a counter at the far side where another customer was already waiting. The walls had a few shabby posters for car parts and several large charts with tediously long lists of numbers for something. She went over to stand with the other customer.

'All right,' he said.

'Hi,' she answered. He looked away, shyly. They stood in silence, waiting, and the man rested his hands on the counter. His sleeves were rolled back to reveal his bare forearms and there was an ugly scab on one of his fingers. She thought about saying something, but he began to drum his fingers on the counter. He was about fifty by her reckoning, weathered looking and a little short, but not unhandsome. His lower lip ended in a purple mark at one side.

'Here you are, Evan,' said a voice, and a second man appeared from the garage and entered behind the counter. He was in his overalls and carrying a white box. 'Got here yesterday,' he said as he put the box down.

'Tidy,' the man said. She waited while he paid the mechanic. 'Ta, Elwyn,' he said and nodded to her before leaving with the box. Elwyn then seemed to notice her for the first time and a puzzled expression came over his face.

'Can I help you,' he said. Hesitantly, she began to explain what had happened, growing more self-conscious as she did so. Elwyn's eyes opened wider with every detail she related, until they looked like they were about to escape his head. When she had finished, he looked overcome, as if he were about to faint behind the counter.

'You walked all that way?' he asked.

'Yes,' she said, embarrassed.

'And you want me to drive to the dam and restart your car?'

'Is that too much?' she said. 'Do you know anyone else that could help?' Elwyn shook his head and walked away, back into the garage. She was about to leave when he re-emerged behind the counter holding a set of keys.

'We'd best get going then,' he said. 'I'll lock up now.'

4

Evan knelt to inspect the carcase. The flesh at the ewe's throat was lacerated. The fleece around it was dyed with blood, spreading outwards from the wound in a stain the colour of spilt wine.

'Yeah, same again,' he said. 'How many more did you say there was Bri?'

'Nine in all,' said Brian. He agitated the plastic plug of his hearing aid. Evan had known him for as long as he could remember. There was something missing in the water at Brian's farm, and the bones in his ear had not developed as they should. He was old now, even for a farmer, and had travelled no further than Powispoole cattle market in all his life.

'Definitely a dog,' Evan said. A buzzard waited above them, its breast pushed forward in a mid-flight belly flop, its wingtips outstretched like splayed fingers.

'It's that John Davies it is,' said Brian. 'He's the one that has the kennels. It's him that breeds them.' He jabbed a finger towards the hillside, the other side of which Evan knew was Davies's farm. 'He's done it before. I know he has. There's others that's seen him letting them loose.' Evan stood up and wiped his hands on his jacket. 'He's no good that John Davies,' Brian went on. 'He's done it on purpose. He's never liked us being here. I fought with his father before him when he was alive.'

'I don't know,' Evan said. 'No one saw anything, I suppose?'

Brian shook his head. 'Who's here to see but me and the ewes?' he said.

'Definitely a dog.' Evan said again. 'Maybe two. Nine dead in one morning.' He shook his head.

'I know it's that John Davies,' Brian said. He began to cry, silently at first, then in long, wheezy breaths, the tears spilling over the grooves of his face. 'I can't go on like this. Thirteen thousand pounds we lost last year.'

Evan patted him on the shoulder. Outward displays of emotion always made him feel uncomfortable, unless they were from Sioned or Ceri. He wished he had brought Sioned with him now.

'I'll ask around,' he said. 'See if anyone knows anything. Maybe have a word with John. Let's go back anyway and see Gwyneira shall we?' Brian nodded. They made their way down the slope to where they had left the Land Rover and drove back to the farmhouse.

Brian's yard was littered with broken plastic tubs and half empty sacks. Old tyres and sheets of corrugated iron were piled against rusting machinery, and the outbuildings were bowed and sunken with age, the shingles on their rooves foaming with green and mustard-coloured mosses. Inside the house, a television was playing loudly. Evan removed his boots by the empty shell of a grandfather clock and went through into the living room. Gwyneira was seated under the dresser as always, her head slumped asleep against the backrest of her chair and her mouth open, revealing her irregular teeth. Light from the vacuum tube television flickered blue across her face. Brian grumbled at the game show that was playing and turned the volume down. Gwyneira woke up and stared at Evan in confusion for a moment before smiling.

'Hiya, Gwyneira,' Evan said. He fetched himself a chair and Brian left the room.

'Hello, Evan bach,' she said.

'Come to see you, I have,' Evan said, patting the back of her hand on the armrest. They spoke for a while, and she asked after Sioned and the other members of his family in turn. He talked about anything he could think of: the farm, jogging, even the biscuits they had bought from the new supermarket in town, growing fearful of the moment when the conversation would wither away into uncomfortable silence. The room smelt of aqueous cream and disinfectant. Brian shouted something from upstairs.

'Eh?' Gwyneira called back. Brian said it again,

something about scissors, then suddenly she was gasping and fumbling for the mask beside her. She grabbed hold of it and pressed it to her face, hurriedly twisting the dial on the cylinder next to her chair. Evan looked away so as not to embarrass her. That can't be how you're supposed to use it, he thought. He could not remember what it was that she had. Sioned knew. Whatever it was, it was terminal. It looked it, at least. He looked over at the smaller, still-working clock on the far wall. It had once been his father's and had hung in the hallway when he was a child; but his dad had given it to Brian in payment for some work a long time ago. Evan said something about needing to go back and Gwyneira nodded behind the mask.

'I'll be back again,' he said. 'You look after yourself and that Brian!' She waved at him with her free hand.

It felt good to be back in the Land Rover. As he pulled away from the farm, he looked in the rear-view mirror and saw Brian standing in the yard, watching him go. Evan blew out his cheeks and sped away down the lane. Brian was close to the edge of something, poor bastard. He had seen it happen before. Brian had had some awful luck, but then so had others. The screw was always tightening on the farms; it never slackened. Whatever happened, you had to push against it.

The sound of Gwyneira struggling for breath stayed with him as he made his way home. He needed to clear his head. There was still enough light left for a run and he decided he would stop by the old railway line. He would have to run in his boots but that could not be helped. Turning off and up the narrow valley, he pulled into a passing place and took off his jacket. He ran down the slope into the trees below. The railway had once run through these mountains, connecting the two major lines of Upper Powys and linking the north of Wales with the south. All that remained were the stone bridges leading nowhere and the tunnels, hung with bats. He jogged along the ghost of the line, between the twin rows of trees. In the river below, the salmon had finished their fight with the falls and had made their way up into the mountains. If he had looked, he might have seen the otter watching him from the far bank before it slipped back into the water and swam noiselessly away. Instead, he kept his eyes on the path ahead and glanced up occasionally at the slopes above. He could see the hedgerow that divided Jenkins' land from Wozencraft's. There was a field near here where Mike Wozencraft could not let his animals graze, as some protected flower grew there that was poisonous. With a sweat forming and with dusk setting in, he turned around and made his way back.

It was nightfall by the time he arrived home. The scattered farms along the valley were lit against the darkness. It was comforting, seeing the others out there. Coming into the yard, he was surprised to see a car he did not recognise parked next to Sioned's Renault. He drew up next to it. There were at least fifty number plates he had memorised and this was not one of them. He took the white box from the passenger seat next to him and went towards the house, glancing back towards the strange car. From the hallway, he could hear Sioned talking with someone whose voice was unfamiliar. At the table in the kitchen, he found Sioned sitting with the same young woman he had seen at Elwyn's earlier that day. They stared at each other, bemused.

'Evan, this is Sarah,' Sioned said. Evan opened his mouth but did not say anything.

'Oh, that's funny,' said Sarah. 'We saw each other at the garage this morning.'

'There we are then,' Sioned said. 'You were meant to find us here.' Evan just stood there, holding the box. 'Evan, Sarah is going to be renting the cottage. I said that you'd help her with some wood.'

'Oh. Right,' he said eventually.

'Will you show her the wood pile then?' Sioned asked. Evan looked again at Sarah. She was young, perhaps a little older than Ceri, with a slim neck and mousy brown hair in a short bob. Her skin was pale but healthy looking and her eyebrows grew thickly in dark, pleasing shapes.

'Right,' he said and went out of the room.

'And if there's anything else you need, please just ask,' he heard Sioned say.

'That's very kind,' Sarah said. 'Thank you so much.'

'Not at all. It'll be lovely to have you here, cariad. Make sure he gets you a barrowful of logs.'

Sarah hurried after him. When they reached the woodshed, he picked up an upturned barrow.

'Wood's here,' he said, picking up one of the logs and throwing it into the barrow loudly. He threw in another and she joined in. The security light was on. It picked out the fine flecks of rain that had started to fall. When the barrow was full, Evan wheeled it wordlessly down to the cottage, with Sarah following. He upturned the wheelbarrow into the lean-to at the side of the cottage.

'They're good logs those,' he said. 'They're from my brother.'

'Thank you,' Sarah said. 'I did offer to pay for them. Your wife said that I could do some jobs around the farm instead.'

'Did she?' he said blankly. It was too dark to see her face properly. He suddenly became conscious of how rude he was sounding. It was not the girl's fault. 'Well, I hope you'll be happy here,' he said. 'It was my nain that lived here last.'

'Thank you,' she said. 'I promise I'll look after it.'

'There's not much to look after,' Evan said. 'She shouldn't be renting it really, with the state it's in.'

'Oh, I don't mind. I can give it a coat of paint if you like?'

'You do whatever you want. Don't worry. I'll probably see you in the morning then?'

'Yes. Thanks again. Good night.'

'Good night,' Evan said and left.

When Evan was gone, Sarah gathered up some of the smaller logs. The rain sounded faintly on the tin roof of the lean-to. She went inside and dumped the logs by the fire. Unbelievably, the cottage was now hers.

She had arrived at Hafod Farm by chance. Earlier

that afternoon she had ridden back to her car with Elwyn in his van. The car started fine but there was something about the way it was running that Elwyn did not like. She followed him back to Hen Gaer for him to have a look at it properly and wandered around the village while she waited. It was there she spotted the yellowing card in the window of the post office. The card was handwritten and gave details of a cottage to rent in the area for a fraction of the price she was paying back home. She called the number provided and a woman answered who gave her directions which she scribbled down on the back of a receipt. When the car was ready, she drove up to the farm to meet with the woman. As soon as she saw the cottage under the pines, she knew she would take it. The lady introduced herself as Sioned and showed her around, apologetic about the condition of the cottage.

There was a short corridor which ended on one side with a living room. On the other side of the corridor was the kitchen, with a small bathroom and a toilet leading off from it. There was no bath or shower, and the only hot water that was readily available was from the wall-mounted electric boiler above the sink. Anything more had to be heated in a pan on the log burner in the living room, or on one of the two gas rings next to the sink. The rings were connected to a red gas bottle and the kitchen and bedroom were heated by a pair of old storage heaters. The whole place was in desperate need of redecoration. The curtains and carpets were decades out of fashion, but it was reasonably clean, and the damp had not yet taken hold. Sarah loved the old chair in the living room, with its wooden arms worn smooth with use.

Sioned was surprised when she agreed to take it there and then. With the cash she had on her person, along with that she had hidden in the car, she had just enough to cover the small deposit required. Once her bags were in the cottage, she was shown up to the farmhouse. It smelt beautiful, of wood smoke and baking, and they talked together over tea and biscuits. She was a kindly lady and asked lots of questions about where Sarah was from. She skipped over the details of Michael and said that she had come into some money recently and wanted to spend a year or so in the country. This last part was a lie which she regretted telling, but she felt she had no other option. Luckily, Sioned seemed satisfied with this and went on to talk about her family and then the farm. She laughed at the questions Sarah asked about the farm, as if they were the first time anyone had thought to ask them. Her husband was much more reticent when he arrived but that was understandable. In her eagerness to please her new landlady, Sarah had offered to help out round the farm and she now worried what work Sioned and Evan might want her to do. The one and only time she had held a sheep had been at a petting zoo on the outskirts of London.

She placed some of the smaller logs neatly inside the wood burner. Sioned has given her some kindling and she laid it out lengthways on top of the logs. It would be the first fire she had lit on her own. She struck a match and picked up one of the kindling sticks and held the match up to one end of it. The end blackened a little but did not catch fire and the match burnt down until it hurt her fingers. She tried again with another match. The stick would not light, so she tried striking matches and dropping them on top of the woodpile she had made. They burnt themselves into black curls, but the wood did not light. After a while she grew sick of not being able to light the fire and went to rummage through her bag in the bedroom. She came back with a half-bottle of nail varnish remover which she sometimes used when she could be bothered to paint her nails, and she tipped the contents out onto the wood. She threw in another match and leapt back as the liquid ignited in a gust of flame. There was an acrid smell of singed hair. She felt a little stupid but was pleased to see that the kindling was aflame and the fire just about burning. Next to the wood burner was a small stand with a little poker and a brush and spade hanging from it. She took down the poker and pushed the burning wood around for a bit before closing the glass-fronted door. This was her fire, her fire in her cottage. The wood ruptured and cracked and spat against the walls that held it. She stood up, looked around the room and laughed.

It was still dark when she woke. She turned over to be close to Michael, but the sheets were empty. Her mind flooded with awareness, and she sat up quickly. There was only silence. She had thought she might hear owls or the wind moving through the trees, but there was nothing. The rain had stopped and there was no boiler noise, nor even the reassuring hum of a refrigerator. She would have to do something about both of those things. The room was freezing. There was a pile of blankets at the bottom of the bed, and she got out to spread them hurriedly in layers over the duvet before jumping back in. The bedsheets were old and fusty. She needed an oil heater, or an electric blanket or something. As for the fridge, that would have to wait for a while.

Once again, she asked herself what she was doing. Yesterday she felt as though the place had been built for her: her own rustic cottage. Homeless and alone, she had not given much thought to practicalities. She was fully awake now and turned the whole thing over in her mind. How far would it be to the nearest launderette? Did they even have launderettes here? She had never had to use one before. The only time she had ever been in one was to get away from the rain and to share a cigarette with Gill. Then there was the question of what she could cook, especially without an oven. There were pans and other utensils left over at least.

Washing was not going to be fun either. Sioned had explained about the septic tank, so tampons and everything else would have to be bagged and binned. She told herself everything would seem better in the morning after her first cup of tea, then cursed herself when she remembered that she had no tea, nor any milk. There was no phone reception there either, not that there was anyone to call anymore. She lay awake, churning everything over, falling asleep only with the first light of dawn.

Someone was shouting. She was awake again. The room was yellow with the light that filtered through the chintz curtains. Those curtains are going for a start, she thought. In the distance she could hear a man's voice barking something furiously, his calls going unanswered. She put her bra back on and threw on a jumper and her jeans from the day before, tying her hair back up in a stubby ponytail. When she was outside, she could finally see what all the noise was about. Away down the slope, Evan was calling to the dogs. They sprinted up and down the field in long wheeling arcs, turning abruptly at each command and racing in a different direction. The sheep moved together in a swell of bodies, the dogs racing to contain any that peeled away from the mass. She watched for a while, then became aware of just how hungry she was. There was no food left. Last night's dinner had consisted of the fruit and crisps she had left over. She came away from the field and walked over to the farmhouse but slipped just as she reached the lower end of the farmyard. She landed on her side, soiling her leg and forearm in the muck that had gathered there. Cursing, she marched over to the farmhouse and knocked at the door. She tried several times but there was no answer. She turned back and headed for the field. She found a gate into the field and pulled the bolt back with a screech. Evan shouted something to the dogs, and they flattened themselves into the grass. He came over to meet her.

'All right?' he asked.

'Yes, thanks,' she said.

He looked at the muck on her but did not say anything.

'Is Sioned in at all?' she asked.

'No. Gone to her mother's.' He turned to bellow at the dogs.

'Where's the nearest place I can buy food?'

'The supermarket's in Marcherton,' he said. 'Are you hungry then?' She nodded, feeling suddenly childish. 'I wouldn't touch anything in the larder, or she'll have my guts for garters. There should be some eggs in the henhouse though. Take as many as you like.'

'Thanks,' she said.

'I've left you some milk now,' he said and went

back to his work. She thanked him again, but he was too preoccupied with the dogs.

She found the henhouse a little way up from the barns. The run was enclosed with chicken wire, and she stooped low to let herself in through a small door at its end. The brightly coloured hens clustered at her ankles as she made her way down the run and into the henhouse. She found a couple of eggs inside and brushed the straw from them. The hens stayed close to her as she left, clucking softly as she slipped carefully out. Back at the cottage, she collected the bottle of milk she had missed earlier and set the kettle to boil. Once she had cleaned herself and changed, she selected a jug and pan, washed the dust from them and whisked together an omelette mixture with the eggs and milk. Omelettes were about the only thing her grandpa had been able to make; she had ended up doing most of the cooking. In the cupboard she found an old salt cellar, its contents hardened into a brittle cake. With a knife she chipped away some of the salt and added it to the mixture. There was some ketchup, but the sauce had congealed into a brown stain at the bottom of the bottle. She rinsed out the teapot that was out on the worktop and found an old tea caddy but there was only a pinch of dusty tea inside, along with a dead spider lying with its legs in the air. When her omelette was ready, she took it through into the bedroom with the milk and hot water she had made in place of tea and had them sitting up in bed, wrapped in the blankets. The tea substitute was undrinkable, but it was good that she was eating, and she felt a little better about herself.

She set off for town a short while later. The farm track led her down into a broad basin surrounded by a ring of hills, broken open in three places where the valleys entered. Blackthorn hedgerows lined the fields, which were small and studded with the ubiquitous sheep. The road led her past Hen Gaer and over the single-track railway to the far side of the basin where the hills closed in and the estates of Marcherton began. The supermarket was on the far side of town. It felt very strange knowing that this was now where she would shop, that this was not a holiday. The signs were all twice the size, being in Welsh too, though she heard not a word of it being spoken. She filled her trolley, choosing onions, garlic, red wine and anything else that might be good for one-pot meals. They had chillies, but Michael didn't like spicy things and she walked straight past them, realising only in the next aisle what she had done. She went back and filled a bag with them. She found a cool-bag that would do until she could afford a fridge. She also took some liquid detergent for hand washing; she could dry her clothes by the fire, perhaps. Finally, as she was paying, she took one of the SIM cards from the end of the aisle. She had left the battery on her phone to go flat. It was time to start afresh.

She headed into town and parked up by a statue of a man in nineteenth century clothing with a child at his feet. Behind him, a man with a thick beard and dark glasses was sitting on a bench, swigging from a can of something. He nodded to her as she walked past. The town was full of shoppers. A group of women with pushchairs were standing outside the bakers', eating pasties from paper bags. She passed them and went into an old wooden-fronted newsagents to look for a paper. Michael usually bought right-wing newspapers which she hated. Neither of them wanted to back down so they usually bought their own. Gill usually bought what Sarah called 'gossip mags' and she teased her for it, though she would find herself flicking through them whenever she was over at Gill's. Again, she was thinking about them both. She bought what she presumed to be the local paper and went out quickly, as if she could walk away from the thought of them.

There was still roughly five and a half thousand in an account she had, left to her by her grandparents. They had never owned their home and were never able to save much thanks to their pair of selfish daughters. It was not a lot, but Sarah refused to touch the money. It was for emergencies only and she was determined that this would not be an emergency. She needed a job, soon. There was a small shopping precinct nearby and she found a bench inside and sat on it to look at the paper. It was called *The Upper Powys Express* and the headline read "Wind Farm Misery" and had a picture next to it of a lorry carrying an enormous white blade. There was a story about a library closing and underneath that, a story about stolen KitKats. She flicked through, turning over pages and pages of photographs of local schoolchildren, until she reached the job page. There were adverts for courses and a vacancy at a local school, but otherwise there was only a single job advertised at the bottom of the page. It was for a kitchen assistant in a hotel somewhere. She folded the paper up and put it in her handbag. There had to be a recruitment consultancy or a Jobcentre somewhere. She asked a man walking past, who directed her to the park. The park was in the middle of town and was dominated by a pillared building belonging to the council. She walked around it and past a tree-sprouted motte until she reached the building that housed the Jobcentre. The automatic doors opened into a large and mostly empty open-plan office. It was quiet but for the tapping of keys coming from the few occupied workstations. There was a small waiting area where a young man was sitting, staring at his trainers. She took a ticket from the machine next to her which told her first in Welsh and then in English to sit in the waiting area. The man flicked his eyes at her and went back to staring at his feet. It dawned on her that there was going to be some sort of interview and she did not feel like answering questions. The whole place made her feel more miserable, and she had a sudden urge to leave. She crumpled up the ticket and threw it in the bin as she went out. Unsure of what to do next, she remembered seeing an old-style phone box by the bridge in town and she went back to it and called the number of the hotel in the paper. The man who answered asked if she wanted to come for a trial and described what her duties would be. She was getting used to the local accent, with its pitch that rose and fell quickly, making each sentence sound urgent and earnest. He gave her a date for a trial in two days' time and she thanked him and said goodbye.

There was nothing else she could think to do. She could buy a magazine and have a coffee somewhere to pass the time, but the thought of doing that made her feel worse. There were steps down to the river and she followed them and stood under the bridge for a while. The high walls behind her were flood-stained and the bridge had been sprayed with graffiti. She watched the weeds moving in the current and the willows on the opposite bank bending over to brush against the surface of the water. The town clock struck one. She had a sudden urge to wade out into the river, just to feel the water around her ankles. Leaving the riverbank, she climbed back up into the town and made her way over to the car.

At the cottage she unloaded the shopping and packed it away, then immediately got back into her bed. She turned over to lie with the wall close to her face and stayed like that, unmoving, for the rest of the afternoon.

Sarah was not, and never would be, a normal person. It had been many years since she had come to this conclusion and she thought she had accepted it. Normal people had normal mothers, who were loving, responsible caregivers, unlike the selfish, drug-addled bitch she had for a mother. Most had fathers too, and they all lived together in a house with siblings and pets and two cars on the drive outside. Growing up, this was how her friends had all lived. They did not have to be kept safe from their own mothers, left to be raised alone by ailing grandparents. Their parents knew what pasta was and could order Indian takeaways and take the family swimming or on holidays abroad; they could give their children all these normal things. Not having these things made Sarah a lesser person. She stood outside of the life that was reserved for most people. Her situation was unnatural, freakish. Unable to embrace this difference she felt from others, she instead internalised it, pretending on the outside to be normal like anyone else. Not even Gill knew how she really felt. It seemed to Sarah that this latest situation was deserved; it was a punishment for trying to pretend to be normal for so long. This was the sort of thing people like her should really expect out of life.

When it was dark, she finally got up to light the fire. She had only half slept, her body seemingly asleep but her mind unrelenting. The food cooked quickly on the gas ring. She had to keep stirring the onion to stop it from sticking. Opening one of the bottles of wine, she poured a quarter of it into the stew, then filled a glass with it. She drank the wine and ate the finished stew by the fire and felt a little better. Her phone was now recharged, and she played some of the music she had stored on it. She started a second bottle of wine and sang along to the music as the fire burnt.

The fire had nearly gone out when she woke. She was slumped in the chair and could not remember having finished the second bottle of wine. Feeling urgently sick, she ran to the toilet and retched into the bowl for a while. She poured herself a glass of water and took it to the bedroom. The feeling was awful; everything was awful. She curled into a ball on the bed, trying to stop the sickness, wishing all of it away.

5

Late the next morning she was sitting in the same chair, this time clutching a mug of tea. She kept getting up to refill the mug, hoping that the tea might somehow purge her of the acid sickness churning in her stomach. There was a knock at the door. She went to answer it and found Evan outside, holding a pair of wellies.

'Morning,' he said.

'Hi.'

'Sioned wondered whether you could help drench the sheep.'

'Oh,' she said.

'She's got Rachel today, see,' he said.

'Yes, yes of course,' she said. 'Give me two minutes.' When she returned, he had gone and had left the wellies on the doorstep. She tried them on. They were too large, and she had to put on another two pairs of socks before they felt comfortable. Outside, the sky had hardened, and a black squall was moving over the hills. It looked certain to rain and she went back inside for her raincoat before setting off after Evan.

The farmyard resounded with the noise of sheep. Evan let out a sharp, high whistle and waved her over. Michael could whistle like that; it always annoyed her that she could not. Her head felt like it had been packed too tightly and the inside was pressing against her skull. Her mouth was still dry, and the ropes of her gut complained as she walked across the yard. Evan had the sheep penned in at the far end of one of the barns.

'Come and stand this side of the race,' Evan said to her. He pointed to the row of railings leading out from the pen. He had on some sort of backpack and was holding what looked like a water pistol in one hand.

'What are we doing here?' she asked him.

'Drenching the ewes,' he said. 'You hold them, I'll do the gun, yeah?'

'Ok,' she said, looking over at the sheep.

'If you don't do the gun right, you can put it right through the back of their throats,' he said.

'That doesn't sound good. What do I need to do?'

'Over here,' he said and raised the gate at the end of the race. He reached over and shoved at one of the sheep. The sheep came forward into the race, then squirmed as he took hold of a fistful of its wool at the neck and clamped it against the railings, holding it in place with his arm. He pushed the nozzle of the gun into the sheep's mouth and squeezed the trigger. He let go and the sheep shook itself a little before trotting forward into the barn.

'That's all it is,' Evan said. 'It's easier with two though.' Sarah nodded. The whole thing looked very rough. She went over to where the sheep were now moving forward into the race and leant over to take hold of the next one. It backed away from her hands. Evan came over and took hold of it with his free hand, holding it still until she had a firm grip either side of its head, grasping the damp, coarse wool between her fingers. The sheep rolled its eyes away, not looking at either of them. Its head was short and broad and seemed ugly to her, looking more like the head of a bull than a sheep. She felt the strong, animal breath on her face as she held up its head and saw the pink tongue moving under the nozzle of the gun. Letting go, she lunged at the next sheep, determined to grab it unaided this time. It pulled away from her, but she wrestled its head upwards for Evan to spray. The next was easier, as was the following and they began to settle into a rhythm, Sarah breathing hard as she manhandled each of them into place and Evan stooping over to administer each dose. It began to rain, the first few droplets thumping against her coat and then the whole world erupted with the shattering of water, and she pulled her hood up over her head. The sheep that had gone through into the barn started to call.

'I don't know what they're complaining about,' she

said to Evan. 'They're in the dry!' He smiled at her. Still a bit shy, she thought. He had a nice smile though. The rain came down hard, chilling her hands, making it harder to grip the sheep and plastering the curls of Evan's hair flat against his head. She was thirsty again and her bladder was uncomfortably full, but she grasped the next sheep and then the next, and Evan stood patiently inserting and removing the nozzle each time, the rain running down the length of his nose.

Her lower half was soaking, and the trousers were clinging unpleasantly to her knees when the last of the sheep went through. Evan removed the backpack and she followed him out of the rain and into the barn.

'That was good that,' he said.

'Good,' she said.

He ran his hand through his hair and flicked the water away.

'So why do we do that?' she asked.

'Stops liver fluke,' he said.

'Liver fluke?'

'They come from snails. When they've finished with the snails, the ewes swallow them with the grass when they're feeding and then they make their eggs inside them. Does some pretty nasty things to them.'

'I bet,' she said. 'It sounds horrible.' The rain was loud against the roof and the barn was filled with the close, musty livestock smell and the sound of the animals shifting amongst the straw.

'You're doing your first shift at the Dolforwyn tomorrow then?' he said.

'How do you know that?'

'Everyone knows everything here.' He looked away from her as he spoke, his eyes moving over the sheep.

'What else do you need me to do?' she asked. She had pulled her hood back and the front of her hair stuck in wet strands to her face.

He shook his head. 'No, no you've done enough for today. Thanks, Sarah. Sioned should have some lunch ready if you want to go and have a look. I'll be up there now in a minute.'

'Okay, thanks,' she said and pushed her way out through the sheep.

'I meant it about doing up the cottage,' he said. 'Just give me the receipts for paint or whatever.'

'Thanks, Evan.' She ran out into the yard. The gravel clicked with the falling rain like the sounding of a thousand insects. She dashed to the farmhouse door and knocked. Sioned answered, holding her granddaughter in her arms.

'Come in, come in,' she said. 'There's no need to knock. This is Rachel. Say hello, Rachel.' Sarah said hello and Rachel buried her head in Sioned's neck. 'I'll let you get your wet things off. The bathroom's upstairs. There should be a towel for your hair.'

When she was ready, Sarah went into the kitchen. Rachel was busy on the floor with her toys. Sioned placed a bowl of hot soup on the table and invited Sarah to eat. She thanked her and sat down, and Sioned buttered some bread and cut a slab of cheese for her. The soup was good. There was tea as well and soon she was feeling much better.

'So how long have you lived here?' she asked.

'Must be getting on for thirty years now,' Sioned said.

'Did you come from a farm?'

'Yes, from my father's place. It's a bit of a way from here. Up by Llanbrynmair. My brother's had it now for years.'

'Did you always want to be a farmer's wife?' Sarah asked. Sioned looked at her puzzled. It took a while for her to respond.

'What a funny question. Why would I want to be anything else? Your farm is your home.'

Rachel made a noise as if she were about to cry and Sioned went over to her. Sarah wiped the bowl clean with the bread.

'So, do your mam and dad still live where you're from then?' Sioned asked. Conversations always went like this. Each time, she had to decide whether to wait for the other person to ask about her parents or whether to just get it out of the way herself at the start.

'No, I was brought up by my grandparents. They've both passed away now.'

'I'm sorry to hear that, cariad.' She said it simply, without any awkwardness. Not everyone reacted like that. 'I know I'm a lucky one to still have my mother,' she went on. 'Do you have anyone else?'

'Not really. No one I like anyway!' They both laughed.

'I know what you mean,' Sioned said.

'So, do you get bad winters up here?' Sarah asked.

'Sometimes. Not as much anymore. They can be bad though, that's for sure.'

'I'd like to see the place all snowy.'

'Don't tell Evan that. It might look nice to you but when you're digging out ewes from the drifts it's not much fun.'

'I don't know where Evan is. He said he was coming.'

'He could be anywhere, doing anything. I wouldn't be surprised if he's off killing himself running, as if he doesn't have enough to do round here. He'll come in when he's hungry enough, you can be sure of that.'

Rachel waddled over to Sarah and handed her a toy tractor.

'Thank you, Rachel. What's in this soup?'

They talked about cooking for a while. Sarah was surprised that Sioned never used any herbs and Sioned was aghast that anyone could enjoy spicy food. She asked if they were friendly with the other families on the farms around and Sioned answered her by naming them and the connections between them, carrying on for what must have covered miles in every direction. Sarah tried to follow her, but it felt like there were a hundred couples and a thousand cousins, and she began to wish she had never asked. The door opened in the hallway behind, and they heard Evan taking off his wellies.

'Still here then,' he said coming in.

'Don't be rude, Evan,' Sioned said.

'No, no, I didn't mean that. She did a good job with

the drenching.'

'She is the cat's mother,' Sioned said.

'Well, I'd better be off,' Sarah said. The two of them protested and asked her to stay. 'No, I'd better go,' she said, putting her chair back under the table. 'Things to do. Thank you for the food.'

'You're welcome cariad,' Sioned said, throwing an arm around her. She pulled her close and their cheeks pressed together for a moment. Sarah stiffened, then blushed with a warm embarrassment. 'You bring up some washing for me to do now,' Sioned said. Save for Rachel, it was quiet in the kitchen as she left the house.

The cottage was cold again and it took some time to rekindle the fire before she could hang out her wet clothes. She could still feel the press of Sioned's cheek against hers, as if the memory had imprinted on her face. Touch was something you took for granted when you had it. There had been her grandparents, then Michael, and now, for the first time, no one. It was as if her skin knew this and hungered for closeness. She wrapped a blanket tightly around her and fell asleep listening to the fire, her eyes closed against the coming twilight.

The Dolforwyn Castle Hotel was set halfway up the hillside, overlooking the canal and the main road below. Behind it was a broad thicket from which branches rose like broken fingers out of the castle remains. As she drove along the track towards the hotel, Sarah glanced up at the grey ruins above. She pulled into what she took to be the staff car park at the side of the building. It looked less like a hotel and more like a glorified inn. The windows were open to what must have been the kitchen and as she got out, she could hear a radio playing and a man singing along to 'Wuthering Heights' in a contrived falsetto. When she reached the main door, she found a man wedging it open with a doorstop.

'We're not open just yet, sorry,' he said. He was wearing a black shirt tucked into black trousers and what little hair he had left on his head had been shorn to a fine stubble.

'I've come for a trial in the kitchen,' she said. The man stopped what he was doing.

'Sorry, course you have. Sarah isn't it?' He shook her hand. 'I'm Malcolm. Come in, come in.' He led her inside. As he walked, his bald head bobbed up and down and his red tie swung from side to side. She followed him through the lounge and into a bar dominated by a broad fireplace. The grate held the ghost of a fire in its ashes and the smell of wood smoke mingled with the odour of spilt beer. 'Look at these,' he said, pointing to the beams. Some were very worn and looked extremely old, others looked more recent and most of them had visible sockets and circular cavities. 'They took these beams from old ships they broke up at the end of the age of sail. Better than wasting the wood. Just imagine, these were probably sailing round the world a few centuries ago.'

She tried to take in what he was saying but found herself watching the odd way he walked instead. He took her into the kitchen. It was noisy with the fans going and the blare of the radio. Every surface was of the same stainless steel. In a corner underneath the window, a man in an apron and chequered trousers was inspecting the contents of a large chest freezer.

'John, this is Sarah,' Malcom said to the man.

'Hello,' John called, not taking his head out of the freezer.

'She's come to help you out here in the kitchen.' Malcolm turned to Sarah. 'I'll leave you in John's capable hands,' he said and walked his Jurassic walk out through the far door. John closed the lid on the freezer.

'Hello, I'm John. I'm the chef as you can see,' he said, pointing to his swollen stomach. They shook hands. He had a short beard that began as pure white near his temples and moved through every shade of brown until it was practically ginger around his mouth.

'Well then, young Sarah. Do you think you could start by making up some garnishes for me?' He showed her where everything was, and she put together a garnish of lollo rosso and curly lettuce with some sliced cucumber and tomato. 'Nice,' John said. 'If you could stack them up over there ready for me.' He sang as he worked his way around the kitchen, unloading the different fridges and fiddling with the dials on the gas oven. 'You're doing a good job there, Sarah. We need an icebreaker, don't we?' he said. 'Do you know any good icebreakers?'

'Not really,' she said.

'Okay, I'll start then. What's your favourite tropical disease?'

'My what?'

'Come on,' John said. 'What's your favourite tropical disease?' Sarah laughed.

'Um, cholera?' she said.

'Nice, nice.' John nodded. 'Very Victorian. A good old-fashioned colonial disease.'

'What about you then?' she asked.

'Oh, it's got to be Ebola, hasn't it? I mean, you've got it all there. You've got the grand slam when you've got Ebola.'

The garnished plates stacked up as they talked and eventually the first order came through on a screen on the far wall.

'Chuck us one of those baguettes, young Sarah,' John said. 'I tell you what, you'll have blisters on your blisters after today with all that chopping.' When the first order was ready, a young woman dressed in a black uniform came to the hatch to collect it. She picked up the plates and Sarah saw her bare forearms marked with silvery lines of scar tissue. Sarah smiled at her. She did not smile back. 'Emma,' John said when she was gone. 'One of those hippies.' The screen rang out with another order and then another and soon Sarah broke into a sweat trying to keep up with them. The afternoon went on and John talked and sang, and the fryers bubbled, and the plates came back in dirty stacks which she loaded into the face-steaming dishwasher. She gave up trying to elicit a smile from Emma and made her mind up not to like her.

She was glad when the lunch shift was over, but it

had gone all right and John had been great fun. He let her choose her own lunch from the menu before they cleaned down the kitchen. She chose fish which he cooked for her with lime and salt. He thanked her afterwards and she gave Malcolm her bank details and arranged a few more shifts with him. The pay was desperately low, and she drove away tired and stinking of oil. It felt good though, being around other people, and though the blisters were already coming up, as John had said they would, in no way did she miss sitting for hours at a desk with a screen in front of her.

When she arrived home, there were two more cars parked in the farmyard. She changed her clothes and went through the cupboards until she found a large stock pot which she filled with water and placed on top of the wood burner. She was going to start heating the water she needed for washing on top of the fire. Her hair was greasy again and smelt of the fryers, and a pan full of hot water and a jug now felt like a treat. Before she lit the fire she remembered about the chickens. Sioned had asked her that morning if she could mind the chickens from now on and had shown her the bin where they kept the feed. She went back outside and collected some feed in a bucket and carried it up to the henhouse. The hens came noisily down the run and fussed at the wire, waiting for her. She undid the latch of the entrance and stooped over to get inside the enclosure. The birds gathered at her feet and pecked furiously as she scooped out the feed and shook it out over the bird-combed ground. She felt good amongst the hens, watching their tails bobbing and their beaks darting down for the grain. The feed was almost gone when she heard someone making their way up to the henhouse. She turned awkwardly in the run and peered over her shoulder to see who was there. A young man was approaching. He stopped by the entrance to the run.

'Hiya,' he said. He was tall and quite thin, and his hair was thick and dark above his half-moon ears.

'Hi,' she answered and began to make her way out.

'You must be Sarah,' the man said.

'Yes.'

'I'm Richard. Rachel's dad.'

'Oh right, yes. I've met her. She's very cute.' She was still stooped over and had to reverse out from the run so that she could pull the door closed. He watched her as she backed out and she sensed his gaze lingering on her thighs and rear.

'You're staying in the cottage then,' he said when she was out.

'Yes.'

'How's it going? You warm enough in there?'

'Oh, it's not so bad when the wood burner's going.'

'Could do with doing up a bit,' he said. He stood very close to her.

'Yes, I might do something about that,' she said, stepping back a little.

'Well, let me know if you need a hand like.' He winked at her.

'Okay. Thank you.'

'Always willing to help.'

Someone called his name from the farmyard below. They both turned to see Evan standing there. He waved at Richard to come down.

'See you around, Sarah,' Richard said, turning to her again. He walked down to where Evan was standing, and she saw the two of them speak for a moment before Richard left. Evan came up to her.

'All right?' he asked. She nodded.

'We were wondering whether you wanted to come and have some tea with us, with all of us; most of the family's here.'

'That's very kind,' she said.

He cut her off before she could go on. 'There's plenty to go round, you can be sure of that.'

'Right.'

'We'd really like you to come.'

'Okay,' she said.

'Thanks,' he said. 'Thanks, Sarah.'

6

A cold sun scraped along the castle walls, bringing its short day into the valley. That morning the jackdaw colours of night had lifted to reveal a rime growing in milky feathers on the twigs of the trees. The ice was now gone, dissolving with the coming of the light. It was Christmas day, and the Dolforwyn Castle Hotel was shut. In the valley below, pike sheltered among the weeds of the old canal that cut its way upwards from the river. Just short of Marcherton, the canal ran dry, but the river continued upstream, and the festive lights of the town were mirrored in its water. The town clock, lit up in red and green, looked down upon the wreathed lampposts and the illuminations strung up between the houses. From behind the shop windows, saints and snowmen, swaddled in tinsel and fairy lights, looked out through snow-sprayed glass. In Broad Street, a giant Christmas tree had been set up, decorated and switched on with much ceremony several weeks before. Further up the river in Hen Gaer, a roadside fan blew a tubular Father Christmas up into the air, and he waved and prostrated before passers-by as the current blew through him. Beyond the clustered lights of Hen Gaer, the hills were studded with the glow from the farms, each with its own window and its own Christmas tree.

Lambing time was coming, and the sheep had all been marked and separated. Fields of green leaves were now brown where ewes had been left to fatten, and the turned earth stripped of the beets that lay upon it like nodules of flint. The land was sodden, and moisture languished between the grasses of the valleys or ran noiselessly between them on the slopes. The cattle were wintering on silage in the sheds, having poached the ground into a smooth mousse. On the moors above, water came down between the sedges or lay heavy on the stars of the sphagnum moss. Miles of spruce plantation erupted from the moors, the trees aligned in ordered rows, standing dark and still as always. The floor between them was a bed of needles, old and untrodden, but in the branches above, crossbills levered open the cones and eased out the kernels with their tongues.

Away from the plantations, the uplands had been clear for centuries, save for the steepest and narrowest of the gills, on whose banks sessile oaks still sheltered from the axemen. Under these leafless trees, overlooking the chapel at Tan-y-Ffridd, were several figures, distinct against the landscape in the reds and blues of their outdoor clothing. A woman stood still and watched her own breath smoking in the branches. Deeper into the wood, a man pressed his face into the gnarled bark of an oak, first one side and then the other. In the centre of the cleft of forest, another man squatted amongst the roots, listening to the water sounding in the hollow. After a wordless walk up the hillside, the three of them had parted and wandered on silently through the trees.

Across the mountains in Hafod farmhouse, it was close to dinner. In the living room, Richard played with Rachel on the rug. He had pulled up her Christmas jumper and was blowing raspberries on her exposed belly. She squealed with delight, waking the old woman who had been asleep in the chair by the tree. Her dull eyes took in the scene, watched her great-granddaughter squirming for a moment and then closed again, her chin resting once more on her chest. In the kitchen, Evan's brother, Rhys, was sitting in his usual chair by the door, sipping from a pint glass. He was shorter still than Evan, and broader, with thick, muscular thighs and hands like an animal's paws, the palms wide and the fingers short and stubby. He was not yet forty and Evan had seen him nurse the bulk of his gut over the passing years with the many pints at The Drovers Arms. Evan stood across the table from him and drank his beer next to the scalding range. Sioned was busy preparing the dinner and wore a new apron, a tea towel draped over one shoulder. Ceri's paper decorations had been strung up between the beams and the far wall was plastered with Christmas cards. A choir sang carols from an old analogue radio that lived on top of the bread bin.

'Where does she come from, anyway?' said Rhys.

'England somewhere,' Evan said, swilling the beer round in his glass.

'I know that.'

'It was Hertfordshire, or Bedfordshire, or somewhere like that, I think she said.' Sioned drained another set of vegetables as she spoke.

'She's planning on staying then?' Rhys asked.

'I don't know what she's planning on doing,' Sioned said. 'She's been doing all right at the Dolforwyn.'

'Well, it's a posh place isn't it,' Evan said. He did not drink often, and the beer was making him heady.

'Funny thinking of her living in the cottage,' Rhys said.

'Don't know what Nain would've thought,' Evan said. 'Having some girl from off living there.'

'She's not a girl, Evan,' Sioned said.

Rhys took another swig of beer. 'Nain would've liked it, probably,' he said. 'There was no telling Nain. She'd have been the same as her if she weren't brought up on the farm.'

Evan nodded. 'There's nothing soft about her, or nesh,' he said. 'You ask her to do something, and she does it. Never complains. And she helps Sioned out here no end.'

'Yes, she's a good girl,' Sioned said.

'You just said she wasn't a girl.'

Sioned flapped the tea towel at him. 'Come away from the oven, you.'

Ceri had been listening from the hallway and came into the kitchen carrying a box of crackers. 'What's she doing though, living on her own in there?' she asked. No one replied. 'Come on, it's a bit weird though, isn't it like?'

It was Sioned that answered. 'She's done a good job with that cottage, chwarae teg. I was on at your dad for ages about that.'

'Yeah, but Mam, what would you think if I went off and did what she did?' Just then Rachel toddled into the room. She had a trickle of brown saliva coming from the corner of her mouth, which was spread in a wide grin.

'Ych a fi!' Ceri shouted into the living room. 'Stop giving her chocolate, she hasn't had her dinner!' She pulled a crumpled tissue from under her sleeve and wiped her daughter's mouth. 'I just think it's weird. She needs to have a boyfriend or something at least.'

'Maybe she doesn't like boys,' Rhys said. 'Maybe she's one that's like that.'

'Bloody hell,' Evan said. The alcohol had warmed him, and he moved away from the range.

'No swearing, you,' Sioned said. 'It's Christmas. Anyway you all leave her alone; she's only young and she's got no mam or dad or anything.'

'What happened to them?' Evan asked.

'I don't know. Maybe you should talk to her more. You can start now. Dinner's nearly ready, why don't you go and fetch her?'

'Let me finish this first.'

In the cottage across the farmyard, Sarah was packing presents into a bag. She had finished each of them by fastening ribbon around the wrapped gift, tying the ends into a bow, then scraping the scissors along the remaining lengths until they coiled into neat little curls.

The cottage was much changed. She had abandoned finding the caravan park for the time being and had poured all her energy into her new home. The yellow wallpaper had been stripped and each wall given a coat of ivory white paint. She had cleaned the windows, bleached the mildew from the kitchen and had found rugs to cover almost all the floor space. There was new bedding and curtains, and a small low-energy fridge which she found online now rested on the end of the work surface. There were fresh lampshades from a lighting shop in the Marches, along with a new standard lamp, and in the markets of Marcherton and Powispoole she found two mirrors and a series of small watercolours by a local artist. She had the pictures mounted, and they now hung on the walls of her bedroom and living room. She was pleased with the place. It made the time pass, watching the strokes of the brush clearing the old away. It was something like a hobby, one that was soothing and rewarding but somehow never fun. Fun needed someone else.

It was different at the hotel. There was life and noise, staff drinks after shifts, crowds of red-faced customers. There were the stupid pranks John would play, such as battering and deep frying Malcolm's keys, and the chorus of songs when Wales were playing. And there was Bobby the burner, always at the bar every day, with his temples scarred from his habit of placing his cigarettes behind his ears, sometimes too drunk to know that they were already lit. At the farm too, she was rarely alone. She had never known a pair of people work so hard. There seemed to be no break from scanning or spraying, marking or moving. The pens were being made ready for the lambs, and when she said she was looking forward to them coming, Sioned laughed and said 'Oh, bless' and patted her shoulder, as if she were a child that did not know what she was saying. She spent a lot of time with Sioned, who – as well as working on the farm – worked three days a week in an office for the council, ran the farmhouse singlehandedly and undertook all the farm administration. Though she could not match her husband in muscle, she more than made up for it with stamina, and if she was not outside then she would be indoors cooking or cleaning or at the kitchen table with VAT receipts and invoices spread out in front of her. Though she pleaded with Sarah to sit down, and told her she had done enough, there was always something to be done, and even if it was something Sarah hated, like ironing, it seemed fine if they could do it together.

She listened to the radio a lot, sometimes leaving it on with the volume low when she lay in bed and could no longer stand the silence. There was no internet and no signal on her phone unless she walked up to the hawthorn on the hill. She would not relent and buy a television. She was proud of all the things she had done without one, and could picture herself wasting hours sitting in front of programmes she neither liked nor needed if she finally gave in.

Christmas brought a perspective she had never imagined. She missed Gill terribly and that was that. It was a blow to her pride, but the long hours had taken her from self-righteousness to forgiveness, to understanding and then finally to guilt. She could no longer convince herself that she had been right, but there seemed no way back in. There was no way that Gill could find her; she had made sure of that. Whatever there was to be done, it would have to be done by her. She prayed that Gill would reach out to her, that she would find a way across the distance to her. That was the worst part: being desperate for someone to pull down the walls, all the while knowing that she had built those same walls herself and made them fast with her silence and the many miles between them. She tried not to think about it and would get up some nights to walk the lane, as if she could somehow close the cottage door on the knowledge.

The cottage door sounded now with the knock of Evan's knuckles.

'Happy Christmas!' he said as she opened it.

'Merry Christmas, Evan. I'll be two seconds.'

They walked together up to the farmhouse. Evan chatted all the way, his tongue loosened by drink. Sioned kissed her and welcomed her into the hot, busy kitchen where the dripping windows had been flung open, and the room was filled with chatter and carols and the sound of chairs being scraped across the tiles. They chorused a greeting, which she returned, and Rhys showed her to her place. The table was crowded with serving dishes stuffed with vegetables and meats, along with sauces, plates, cutlery, bottles, glasses, napkins and crackers, with the guests packed tightly around the whole spread so that they had to hold in their elbows as they began to eat. It was hard to relax in front of so many people and she felt her appetite wither with anxiety as they piled more and more food onto her plate. She drank deeply from her wine glass as the others talked, until the tightness inside her began to unknit. The food was good, and as they pulled the crackers and read the awful jokes – and Rhys's paper crown split as he tried to force it around the formidable circumference of his head – she laughed with them. For a moment it felt as if the past was gone and there was only the farm and the family here, sharing this table. She felt the stalking approach of emotion, as if the moment had betrayed her to the tears that hunted her, but she would not break. She told herself that she had been drinking, and however nice this was, it was not home.

'Presents!' Sioned said, as the pudding dishes were cleared away. She handed Sarah a small, wrapped box. 'This is from me and Evan.'

'Oh, thank you very much!' The others were silent as they watched her unwrap it. She felt her throat going pink and blotchy as it did whenever wine was joined by self-consciousness. Inside was a necklace and a pair of earrings made from delicately twisted silver. 'Wow, they're gorgeous, thank you!'

'There's one from Rhys as well.' Rhys handed her a misshapen package. Inside was a wooden carving of a hare, sitting up and gazing skyward. It was beautifully done, easily superior to any of the carvings she had seen at the market in Penbury. The head was extraordinarily detailed. It was not as if the wood had been made lifelike in form, but rather as if it had once breathed and run with the other hares and had now been made still.

'Thank you. That's really, really nice.'

'Good bit of kindling that,' Evan said. Rhys rolled his eyes.

'Carved it last week,' he said.

'What, you made it?' The others laughed at her surprise. It was difficult to ascribe something so fine as being the work of his thick fingers. 'It really is lovely. Thank you.' Rhys raised his glass to her, then drank from it. They began to clear away the table.

'Oh, I forgot!' She went over to the bag she had brought and handed out the presents, then watched anxiously as they were unwrapped. She prided herself on choosing good presents, but it was hard when you had not known someone for long.

'It's lovely. Thank you,' Sioned said when her scarf was unwrapped. She kissed her again.

'Ah, that's the stuff, that is,' Evan said, clutching his newly opened bottle of single malt whisky. Ceri and Richard said thank you for the chocolates and for the collection of soft animal toys she'd bought for Rachel, clearly embarrassed that they had bought her nothing in return. Sioned's mother was still feeding Rachel spoonfuls of pudding with her trembling hand and appeared to have missed the whole ceremony. Evan went off to find some glasses as the others began to clear up. Rhys helped Sioned's mother back into the living room and though Sarah tried, Sioned flatly refused to let her help with the washing up. Evan came back and called her across to the hallway instead.

'Here we are then Sarah, let's have us a taste of this.' He poured two fingers of scotch into a pair of tumblers and handed her one. They clinked glasses. 'So, how's it going at the Dolforwyn then?' They talked standing up in the hallway whilst the others busied themselves. The whisky had softened Evan's eyes so that they drooped blissfully at the corners. It was strong on top of the wine, and she found her attention drifting away from what he was saying to watch the purple mark on his lip moving instead.

'So where was it that you worked before?' he asked.

'I worked for a consultancy. But I'm not a consultant. I was just support.'

'What sort of consultancy?'

'Well, when businesses found themselves in trouble financially, they would call us in and we would consult on how they could cut costs, improve income, make savings etc.'

'We could do with that round here!'

'I don't think so. You certainly know what you're doing here.'

'I wish we could cut some costs though.'

'Well, I wouldn't know, she said. 'Sadly, it's cutting staff members that often helps. That's why Malcom hasn't opened today; it's not worth it for the wage costs. You don't have that here though. Sioned said you bring men in to do the silage though don't you?'

'We can't do without them. I can't do everything,' Evan said into his glass. They drank in silence for a moment. Rachel's wailing joined the sound of the television coming from the living room. 'Sioned's thinking of going full time at the council,' Evan said.

'Oh. Right.' Sioned had no time to spare for this and they both knew it. Sarah felt she needed something positive to say. 'Ah, I was going to tell you – Malcolm says I can sell the eggs at the pub and John will cook with them.' Evan nodded. His cheerfulness seemed to have ended. 'Really, you should charge your tenants more,' she said.

'You're joking. I've only got one tenant. Charging more for that place? And with you doing it up yourself? And with everything you do on the farm as well?'

'I don't do that much,' she said.

'No way. I should be paying you. We'd be worse off if you hadn't have come here.' He looked away, embarrassed. 'Anyway, what am I doing talking about all this, it's Christmas, let me fill us up.' He poured out another generous whisky for each of them. 'Iechyd da,' he said and clinked his glass against hers.

They went through into the living room and sat with the others and soon she felt her head nodding with the heaviness of sleep. She woke a while later and looked around at the scene, momentarily confused until her full consciousness returned. They were all facing the television, watching a sitcom Christmas special. Next to her, Sioned's mother was asleep again, the tired folds of her chin resting on the front of her floral dress. Both Ceri and Richard were looking at their phones. Rachel must have been put to bed.

'Phew. Excuse me. I think it's time for me to head back,' she said, standing up. She had the beginnings of a headache.

'No, stay,' Sioned said. 'We'll do some games in a minute. And there's cheese and biscuits yet.'

'No, no. It's time to go.' It went on in this manner as Sioned and Evan and Rhys all tried to convince her to stay, but she politely and repeatedly refused and made herself ready to leave. She thanked Sioned profusely in the hallway and they parted after a long and firm embrace.

It was dark outside, and she narrowed her eyes under the harsh lights of the farmyard. She took another armful of wood from the lean-to and carried it into the cottage with her. With the burner re-stoked, she tried on the earrings in the mirror. She looked different here from how she did back home. Her skin was dewy with the soft water, and she had decided to grow out her bob. Looking in the mirror made her feel queasy and she was afraid she would fall asleep again if she sat down. She went back outside and walked over to the lane instead. It was a clear evening, and the sky was already heavy with the weight of a billion stars. She had seen more stars from this lane than she could ever remember seeing before. Her head throbbed painfully as she looked up at the night sky. It seemed so beautiful and yet so terrible at the same time. Then there was a cough behind the hedge next to her, and even though she knew it must have been a sheep, she found herself dashing back through the darkness to the safety of the cottage fire.

7

Sarah knew from Evan's face that the lamb they had just pulled was not going to respond. They crouched over it together, the ewe next to them licking at its lifeless body. Around them, sheep rustled in the dry stalks that covered the barn floor. A row of them were trapped in the headbangers like criminals in the stocks and would stay there, pinned by the neck until they allowed their adoptees to suckle freely.

'This one's had it,' Evan said. He stood up and stretched, then rubbed his swollen eyes against the crook of his arm. His bare forearms were moist and stained from the birthing. Holding the ewe away, he picked up the limp body by the forelegs and held it out for Sarah to take.

'Can you ask Sioned to skin that one? She'll do a lot better job. Bring it straight back when you can.'

They had told her about skinning but she had not seen it done. The ewe began to call for her lamb. Sarah carried it outside, glad at least to have the cool evening air in her nostrils. She went as fast as she could across the yard to the house, holding the lamb away from her as she carried it. An old table had been set out under the farmhouse window. It was dirtied with ancient smears of brown and black. She dumped the lamb on the table and opened the door.

'Sioned!' she called. 'I've brought a lamb for you to skin.'

'Hang on. I'll be there now,' she answered. She came to the door carrying a tea towel which she then unravelled to reveal a small and bright blade. 'How's he doing?' she asked.

Sarah shrugged. 'Still going.' She stood next to the table and watched as Sioned turned the lamb over and placed the tip of the blade below the bloody cord that sprouted from its belly. She slashed quickly along the skin towards each hind leg and took hold of the tip of the triangle she had made. Pressing the lamb into the table at the neck, she pulled back the skin with her other hand, tearing it away and exposing the raw, purple flesh beneath.

'Evan said you do this best,' said Sarah.

'This maybe,' she replied. 'There'll probably be a machine they'll come out with that'll do this for you soon'.

Taking one leg at a time, she held each of the tiny hooves in her fingers and scored around them with the knife. Her slim arms swelled as her muscles laboured, the tendons bulging from them in ridges as she worked. She put down the knife and reaching through the opening at the belly, pulled each of the hind legs through the hide until the bony limbs were bare. She stepped back from the table. With one hand gripping both hind legs, she tugged at the loose skin with the other, peeling the lamb slowly naked until the coat gathered around its neck and obscured its head, like a child removing a jumper. Taking the knife once more she cut the coat free of the lamb and placed both back down on the table.

'There we are then,' she said.

Sarah stared at the dead lamb, lying just away from its missing coat. 'So the mother's love is skin deep?' she said.

'You what?' Sioned said, wrapping the knife away in the tea towel.

'Nothing. What do I do now?'

'Are you all right to take this to the dead hole?' Sioned asked. Sarah nodded.

The dead hole was exactly that: a dark place where the lifeless were forgotten. Evan had shown it to her the previous day. They were now illegal, but he said he was damned if he was going to pay twelve pounds fifty for every dead lamb to be taken away, so most of them ended up there.

She picked up the lamb. It was smooth and clammy where the skin had been stripped from it. She trudged away from the farm and up the tractor-carved track, following the twilight that had gathered in its twin hollows. Dusk had driven the colour from the grass and the hillside was flecked with pale candles of glowing fungi. It was dark in the valley below save for the glow-worm lights of the farmhouses. As she turned off towards the dead hole, she took a deep breath and held it. Steering her way through the burgeoning nettles, she knelt next to a rusted sheet of corrugated iron, lifted it up and pushed the lamb into the dark hole beneath, trying to shut her ears to any sound that might come from within. Unable to hold her breath any longer, she dashed back to the track, inhaling a lungful of putrid air as she ran. On her way back to the barn, she picked up the lambskin from the outside table. It was limp and damp and felt like rolled dough in her fingers. She carried it down to the barn and made her way inside. The ewe was still calling for her lamb. She could just make out the figure of Evan, moving amongst the animal shadows deep inside the barn. She called to him, and he stepped out into the light.

'Great. Bring it here then,' he said. He went over to one of the pens, reached into it and plucked out a live, bleating lamb. The two of them crouched together in the straw once more. 'Spread the coat out for me will you Sarah,' Evan said, holding the lamb away. She laid the skin out on his lap. The lamb struggled and continued to bleat as the two of them pressed its back into the new coat. Evan held the legs still and Sarah helped slip the wriggling hooves through the leg holes until the coat was on. 'Now then,' he said, and she followed him across the barn. 'Let's see now.' He set the lamb down near the still bleating ewe. The coat was a neat fit and left the iodine-stained umbilical cord dangling beneath it. The ewe stepped cautiously over to the lamb and reached her head around it to sniff at its tail. The lamb trembled on its narrow legs but stopped bleating and instead reached up to the ewe and pushed its head underneath her and began to stab hungrily at her teat. The ewe continued to sniff at its tail. 'Looks all right enough to me,' Evan said, winking at Sarah. Relieved, she placed a hand on his shoulder.

'Will you come for some tea?'

Lambing season had come with snow on the mountains, away to the north where the far blue peaks moved in and out of existence. The hills were awake with the movement of beasts as they pawed at the ground in their millions, their udders swollen with a liquid love, knowing the life inside them, ready to emerge. In the floodlit barns, roles had reversed, and the farmers were now servile, the men treading sleeplessly through the straw like ghosts, moving from one mother to the next and kneeling in service to each of their wombs. Restless, and with wet hindquarters, the ewes lay down with their contractions, and the farmers helped free them of their young, patiently and devotedly clearing away the stiff mucus and releasing them from the swaddling membranes of their births.

Evan kept a near permanent vigil, with Sioned and Sarah, and sometimes Richard and Ceri, taking turns to help. Sarah felt her skin would never be clear of the scent of lanolin and silage. The work was exhausting, and Evan could not have done more than catnap in the last three days. He was asleep now, prostrate on the sofa, his legs dangling over the arm and his feet twitching in their sodden socks. Sioned and Sarah were sitting together in the kitchen.

'It's just thinking about him hiding it from me that gets me,' Sarah said. She had made no conscious decision to tell Sioned about Michael. She was tired and it just sort of came out there and then. They had been talking about it for some time.

'The way the danger of it all must have been exciting for him. I mean, don't get me wrong, if he'd confronted me about it then I'd still have been so hurt. It's like a rejection of everything you are. Like he's taken a long look at everything about you, got to know you intimately, inside out, and then thought "I don't like that".'

'It's not like that,' Sioned said. 'Don't think of it like that.'

Sarah shook her head slowly. 'All of it behind my back.'

'Oh, I wouldn't think much of that. A friend of mine, Jenny Morris, married Ian Hughes, Dai the butcher's son. This was years and years ago. He used to have all sorts of women round. I mean it was no secret with him, he used to bring them home to the house when she was there. Girls from off, usually. And he used to hit her as well. Anyway, I went round there one day to see her, and she was crying, saying he had a woman upstairs again. Said she'd like to kill him. So we made him a cup of tea and we got together everything we could find: every painkiller, every tablet in the house, just as long as he wouldn't be able to taste it. Then we mixed them all into his tea with a load of sugar. I can remember laughing. It was sort of funny. It was her idea. She had to hold her hand over the top of the mug to stop the fizz brimming over. The amount that was in there! Must've been enough to kill a bear.'

'Oh my God, what happened?'

'She gave it him, lay next to him that night listening to his breathing getting deeper, then he just got up the next day and went to work.'

'Jesus Christ!'

'She did get away from him in the end,' Sioned said, moving over to the sink. Evan was snoring in the living room.

'We talked about having children, you know,' Sarah said. It was strange saying it out loud. It felt as if she had transgressed something within herself, as if she had uncaged something she was supposed to be guarding.

'You're young, cariad,' Sioned said. 'There's plenty of time for that.'

'I'm not sure I do want them now.'

Sioned came back to the table to sit with her. 'It doesn't feel like something you've decided when they come,' she said. 'It always feels like it's just things happening to you. That's what it felt like to me. And when they go . . .' She looked away, without finishing.

'Was it hard when Ceri left the farm?' Sarah asked.

'It was. Hard for Evan the most, I think. Not having a son to stay here. Going back to just us. These things are hard for him, I know. His mam died when he was very young. When his dad died, that was the worst. He was the apple of his eye.'

'Would you have liked a son?'

'I had a son.' Sarah stiffened but Sioned continued. 'He died when he was very small, then no more came after that.' She agitated her mug on the table as she spoke. 'I knew something was wrong and I took him down to the surgery and carried him in in my carthen. The receptionist there, she said the surgery was closing, told me to come back tomorrow. I said that something was wrong with him. She just told me she couldn't help me. He died that night. Do you know, that woman's never looked me in the eye since. She goes into some back room when I go to the surgery now, lets someone else speak to me.'

For a while there was only the sound of Evan snoring. Sarah thought about saying she was sorry, then changed her mind. What did that even mean anyway? The time when she could have said something passed in silence.

'I wanted to ask you something,' she said eventually. She felt cowardly, changing the subject. 'I met some people in the woods when I had that flat battery, the first day I came here. It was weird. They were just sort of standing around and touching the trees and stuff.'

'Druggies?' Sioned said.

'Maybe. I'm not sure, though. They were kind of all spaced out and none of them would speak with me, they just went on acting strange.'

'It doesn't surprise me. There's all sorts come to live here. Hippies a lot of the time. Sometimes I think people from England just see this place like it's a blank piece of paper. It's just a big empty space to them, for them to come and do with what they like, away from everyone else. Never mind us.'

'I suppose I'm one of those,' Sarah said.

'You're one of the nice ones. And it's not as if people don't leave. Feels like every youngster who's not a farmer leaves. No one stays. Everything shrinks or gets old. You have to travel now to get anything. The kids that are left go miles to school. You can't even be born here anymore; you have to go to England or Upper Powys. Why did you choose to come here anyway? I mean, here rather than anywhere else?'

'It's silly really. My grandpa and grandma took me on holiday somewhere near here a few times when I was a child.

I liked it. We used to stay in a caravan park. Do you know Reedy Bennock?'

'Rhyd-y-Benwch?'

'Is that how you say it?'

'I know the one.'

'Can you show me where it is?'

'Yes, of course. It's a little way from here, though.' She nodded towards the living room. 'I've been chopsing long enough now. I'd better get his lordship up or he'll be cross.'

'I am glad I came here,' Sarah said. 'To the farm I mean.'

'Yes. Yes, I'm glad too.'

8

By the time the lambing had quietened down, Sarah was sick of talk of tups and theaves, Radnors and Texels. She felt restless with the lengthening of the days and had taken to walking the lanes around the valley. Daffodils were growing in the verges and she gathered them and stood them in vases about the cottage, where their six-petalled collars quivered open to reveal trumpets of yellow. Sometimes she came across sheep that had broken free and were busy grazing the verges or feasting on the salt in the grit bins. There were cattle in the fields on the valley floor, and she watched how they sniffed at the grass before eating it and saw the great bull sidling up to his bride for the morning and nuzzling gently at her neck.

The shifts at the pub were hard work but John seemed fond of her and was not afraid to argue with Malcolm if he felt that he was taking advantage of her. Malcolm had found out about the bar work she had done as an older teen and had several times suggested she take over from him, but John always refused him. He waited until John was dealing with the weekly delivery before approaching Sarah. There was something he needed to do, he said, and he simply walked her behind the bar and pointed towards the taps and the fridge and then left. It did not bother Sarah, though she felt bad about leaving John. There were three men already at the bar. She recognised one of them.

'Hiya, Sarah,' the thinnest of them said, winking. It was Richard, Evan's son in law. He watched her as she served the other men. When they left, he rested his forearms on the bar and leant forward to talk to her. He bragged about some business deal he had completed that morning and how much he had made. She had taken a strong disliking to him, but she was effectively cornered and had no choice but to nod and respond appropriately. He told her she looked good, and she felt pressured into smiling politely, which made her angry. Inwardly, she prayed for another patron to serve. The time passed painfully, and she kept glancing over at the clock. Three young women came in and asked for halves of cider and Richard went quiet. He watched them leave the bar and take their seats on the far side of the room, then two men entered, both in flat caps and check shirts. They came over to the bar.

'It's Jimmy Rhubarb!' Richard said to the one nearest him. 'How's it going Jimmy?' The man ignored him and waited for Sarah to serve him. He was a generation older than Richard and breathed through an open mouth, permanently displaying his five remaining teeth. Sarah gave him his change.

'Prick,' the man said to Richard before walking away. Richard winked at him.

'That's Jimmy Rhubarb,' he said to Sarah. 'Friends with John Davies, that wanker with the dogs. Got into a fight once in the market garden. What happens is, he pulls up a stick of rhubarb and starts to hit old Preece with it, the twat. That's why he's Jimmy Rhubarb.' He kept looking over at the three women, who were laughing amongst themselves. John came out from the far door to the kitchen and caught sight of her. He came over to the bar. He smiled at Richard.

'Hello!' he said. 'It's little Richard, Daddy's champ. How you doing, champ?' John threw an arm around Richard and pulled him close. 'I know his dad,' he said to Sarah. 'Went to school with him. This is his champ. That's what he calls him. Doesn't he, champ?' John was squeezing Richard tight. Richard looked furious and was trying to wriggle away from John's grip, but John had him pinned, effortlessly clamped against the bulk of his body by a single arm. Sarah suppressed a giggle. Rhubarb and his companion were looking over and laughing. 'How's Daddy's little champ?' John kept saying. Richard went red with embarrassment but could not free himself from the arm that held him vice-like against John's dirty kitchen apron. The far door opened again, and Malcolm wandered absently back into the room.

'Right,' John said, pointing at Sarah with his free

arm. 'That's enough women's liberation for you, get back in that kitchen!'

Sarah had a free afternoon the day after. It was bright and sunny, and she decided that today was the day she would drive to the caravan park.

Rhyd-y-Benwch straddled the Severn close to its source, on the eastern slopes of the five-peaked mountain that stood at the very centre of Wales. The river cut a narrow trench through the steep-sided valley, whose slopes funnelled sharply down to meet it. The ground levelled out at the site of an old ford where the caravans huddled along the riverbank and spread outwards from it in rows of gleaming plastic.

For Sarah, arriving at the caravan park would be a homecoming. Her memories were of bright skies, the charcoal smell of barbecues and the sound of water falling on rock. She remembered the pony at the fence and her grandma tearing up a fistful of the long grass and handing it to her so that she could feed it. It was here she remembered feeling at her very happiest. She had clapped as her grandpa took hold of her grandma and waltzed the two of them around and around the caravan. For once, it had felt like there was no love missing in the world. It was how she imagined life must be for normal people.

As she drove in through the main entrance, she was surprised to find that she recognised neither the sign welcoming her nor the office building, nor the timber cabins under the trees. The caravans were all skirted and a different shape from how she remembered. She parked in the visitor car park and walked over to a concrete bridge. The peaty water was the colour of black coffee. She thought she remembered it that way but could not be certain. The nearby pony field was empty. She walked along the road that led through the rows of caravans, following it round until it looped back and she was at the bridge again. Whatever she had been expecting, it was a shock to find she felt nothing at all. None of it was how she remembered, though it must be the same place. She had hoped it would stir something within her, that some deep-seated attachment would speak its name, or at least carry her backwards on a wave of memory. Instead, it felt empty. A television was playing in the nearest caravan, and she became conscious of herself suddenly, a visitor with no one to visit but the dark water. She came away from the bridge, embarrassed. Then she remembered the waterfall. If she could see that again, that might be something. She headed back to the bridge and found a path shadowing the route of the water, heading upstream. It led away from the park and opened out into a broad basin that was rimmed with trees and veined with several criss-crossing paths, the largest of which were route-marked with colour-coded posts. She counted four separate streams, any of which could have led to the waterfall. She chose the steepest and followed its sharp rise through a belt of strong-scented spruces. Next to her, the water fell at noisy intervals like stairs, showing white for a moment between the rocks. She was soon out of breath and stopped beside a break in the woods where the trees had collapsed and formed a spilliken mess of decaying trunks, all of them lank with green moss. The path then narrowed until it became a route worn through the grass, barely more than a sheep track. The stream shrank as it went on, until she could no longer convince herself that this was the way to the waterfall.

It had all been a failure. She squatted down for a moment to rest and to try and think, but she found listening to the water was far better than trying to make sense of it all. Whatever coming here had failed to achieve, the walking was good, she told herself. If she could just carry on, she might outrun her own despair, or at least be too tired to feel it when it came. The trees had ended and she decided she would climb the slope above her and look out from its summit. Her legs burnt from the exertion, and she ascended on all fours, pulling herself up by grabbing handfuls of sedge and glancing over her shoulder to look out over the tops of the trees. When the slope began to ease, she threw herself down on her back and gazed up at the sky, panting. She looked out over the land she had conquered, taking in the hillside scored jagged with water, the trees like growths of mountain hair, and in the distance, the tiny boxes of the caravans. This was not the summit, and she pushed on, moving upwards into the grassy mountains.

The afternoon wore on. What had begun as a spontaneous walk became an interminable trudge across a featureless mountainside. At first, she tried to aim for the summit but gave up when it became clear that no real peak was going to emerge from the blunt swellings that rose in the distance. She was now following a contour across the mountainside, hoping to descend in a broad loop back to the caravan park when the slope eased off. There had been little, if any wind down in the valley, but there was a strong breeze here and she was glad of her walking coat. Looking out, the hills rolled away from her at an even height, showing the sunken valleys between them, their ridges picked out by towers of white turbines whose blades turned silently in the distance. She passed close to a flock of sheep and the nearest stopped and lifted their heads to watch her before returning to the bitten-down grass. A way on from them, she came across the site where one of their number must have met its end. The strewn bones were as clean and polished as an exhibit.

She had brought neither food nor water and when she came to a boundary fence, she made her escape by following it down the mountainside, accompanied by the song of the breeze through the wires. She reached the end of the fence and clambered awkwardly over it at the corner post, her coat snagging on the barbed wire. The whole afternoon had passed without her seeing another soul. She cursed herself for not bringing a map and for leaving her phone in her handbag in the car. Twilight was coming and she was thankful when she spotted a track ahead. She joined it, increasing her pace, stopping at the first culvert she came across and cupping her hand to drink from the cold, trout-tasting water. The track went on for another mile or so. The one building she passed turned out to be a ruined farmhouse with the words *Cymru Rhydd* painted on it, along with a symbol she did not recognise. A light became visible further along the track. This time the farmhouse was occupied, but as she peeled off from the track to approach it, the farmyard erupted with the baying of dogs and a trio of them tore out from the gloom towards her. Alarmed and exhausted, her mind forgot everything she knew about dogs, and she pelted away down the track, not slowing until the snapping around her calves ceased, the dogs stopping at an invisible boundary. Fighting to get her breath back, she heard a distant voice admonishing the dogs in Welsh.

The sun drowned itself in the hills and the valley quickly darkened. She was desperate to get off the mountainside. What if she had to spend the night out here? What if she fell somewhere and could not get out? No one was expecting her, nor did anyone know where she had gone. Every ditch or boulder hid a crouching figure, intent on harming her. A killer stalked the fields, just waiting for a woman alone to walk through them in the dark. Compared to this, the valley floor seemed like sanctuary. She had to descend quickly and find a road. Scaling the fence beside her, she left the track and plunged down the nearest bank, heading downhill as steeply as she could, her toes hammering at the front of her boots. She crossed the next fence and then the next, until the land fell steeply into a dense thicket. What little light was left barely followed her into the woods and she had to pick her way carefully down between the trees, steadying herself against them and stepping over their raised roots. She glanced around her after every few steps to check that nothing else was moving in the dimness, all the while reproaching herself for getting into such a stupid situation. After some time the gradient eased, but the boles of the trees were still thick around her. She started as she flushed a pheasant from the undergrowth, and it clattered upwards through the branches, sending its glottal alarm call reverberating through the woods. As it fell quiet again, she stood still, listening out for traffic noise or anything that might mean civilisation, but there was nothing. Carrying on, the slope began to level out and she thought she could make out what might have been a pathway between the trees. She stooped over, looking around to find its course, then jumped back, as one of the tree trunks moved in front of her. Then she saw that it was not a trunk, saw the furry limbs and tail, dead and dangling from a rope, the snout and long ears, head pointing downwards. Then she was running, crashing through the trees, branches striking at her head, charging down, down, running anywhere to get away. As the trees moved past her, it came to her: fox. Then her foot snagged against something, and she was suddenly falling, turning over and over, knees and elbows smacking against the ground, finally coming to rest, prone on the woodland floor, her mouth filled with dank earth. Her ears rang and she lay still for a moment, fearful of moving, then she wiped her mouth and spat. Slowly she began to pick herself up.

'Are you . . .' The voice spoke close to her, and she heard her own body erupt in a terrible scream. The man who had just spoken screamed also, then clutched at his chest as she backed away.

'God, you frightened the life out of me!' the man said.

'You frightened me!' Sarah screeched back at him. Fear came out as indignant rage.

'Who are you?' the man said.

She couldn't answer him. He stepped forward and she froze as he took something from his pocket. It was a small torch, which he switched on and shone at her. She screwed up her eyes and held her hand up in front of her face.

'What are you doing here?' he asked.

'I was just walking,' she said.

'Walking?'

'Yes.'

'Why here, in these woods?'

'I was trying to find a way back to the caravan park.' She answered him automatically, too afraid to do anything else.

'So you're lost?' he said. She nodded. 'And you're on

your own?' The man shone his torch over her body. 'That was a fair fall,' he said eventually. She said nothing. He pointed to her left hand. 'Shall we have a look at that?' Again, she could not answer. 'It seems we frightened each other. Your hand?' He spoke with a clipped English accent. From what she could see of his face, she made out a long jaw and a heavy brow over high cheekbones. Unable to think any longer, she held her hand out in front of her and he shone the torch over it. It was mud-stained and two of the knuckles had opened, the wounds glistening red as berries. He was tall and had to stoop down to inspect her trembling hand. He held her wrist in his long fingers and asked her to try moving it. She winced, 'Just superficial damage I think, but I'm not an expert.' He switched off the torch. 'The caravan park you say?'

'Yes.'

'Rhyd-y-Benwch?'

'Yes.'

'That's quite a walk away.' She said nothing. 'If you are lost then I'd better take you there.' He turned around and began walking away through the trees, then stopped when she did not follow. 'Come on. This way,' he said.

9

The sun had crested the rim of the hill and shone down between the trees where the heads of the sorrel opened and turned their purple veins to the coming light. In the clearing below, bugles had broken the earth with their blue spears, spreading in formation across the exposed ground. On the slope, Evan began to ready himself, taking hold of the long handle of the winch with both hands and digging his heels into the woodland floor. The hill rose sharply, so that the roots of the upper trees grew high above the tips of their cousins below. As he dug in, he crushed the fat blades of the ramsons into the soil, releasing more of their pungent sweetness into the air. Across from him, Rhys bent over the chainsaw and yanked at the starter rope. The engine fired but did not start, and a pair of wood pigeons blustered away through the branches. He tugged again, and the woods throbbed with the violent rasping of the saw. He bent low next to the tree and began the first sink cut into the trunk. The blade bit into the flesh of the tree and the bright, white innards sprayed out in a heavy mist across the ramsons. Evan began to work the winch, feeling the rumble of the saw through the handle as he moved it back and forth. It was still cold and the streaks of sunlight through the trees shone on his steaming breath. Rhys moved to the rear of the tree and began the felling cut. Evan could see the trunk beginning to lean as he shortened the cable with the winch, directing the path of its fall away from the other trees. Rhys stepped away from the tree and called. Evan let go of the winch as the cable grew slack and moved quickly behind the anchor-tree next to him. The birch gave a bow then flung itself at the ground, fracturing branches and skidding a short way down the slope before coming to rest. With the chainsaw still running, Rhys came away from the raw stump that remained and made his way down to begin butchering the tree.

Evan watched him as he worked. His face was hidden behind the visor of his forestry helmet, but the delight was clear in his movements as he trimmed the branches away. Rhys loved his work and despite his stocky frame, skipped nimbly over the slashed and silvery trunk, methodically dismembering the boughs from the narrow body. Evan reached down and unhooked the strop from the anchor tree. He was about to fold it together when something made him look away and up the wooded slope. High above them, someone was moving amongst the trees. The figure vanished, then re-appeared, the outline dark against the sun for a moment before disappearing again. Whoever it was, they were making their way across the hill. Evan dropped the strop and started moving briskly up the slope, cutting a steep path through the woods. He looked upwards, trying to track the movement through the trees. The holly grew thick between the trunks and twice forced him off-course, so that when he felt he had drawn level with the stranger, there was no sight of them ahead. He stopped to listen but could hear nothing above the noise of the saw working below. There was only stillness. Alone amongst the trees, he leant against one of the slender columns to catch his breath, feeling the crisp body of the lichen beneath his glove. The woods came to an end a short way ahead and rather than pursue the stranger any further, he turned instead in the direction from which they had come. He traced what he thought must have been their path. When he reached the boundary of the woods, he examined the stock fence and found it bowed at the corner post. The staples were loose, and the wire deformed.

By the time he made his way back, the sawing had stopped. Rhys removed his helmet, held up a gloved hand and sniffed one of the logs he had cut.

'Having a moment, were you? Smell that,' he said and thrust the log under Evan's nose. 'You can't beat that smell. Lovely. This one's good for carving as well. Look at that. Beautiful.'

'There was someone up there you know,' Evan said. 'I saw them.'

Rhys shrugged. 'What are you going to do about it?' he said.

'Who do you think it was?'

'I don't know, do I,' Rhys said, picking up another log. 'Could be ramblers, kids, Scouts, anyone. Are you going to help me with this wood or not?' Evan joined in, the two of them sorting through the wood and grading it into different piles. He kept glancing back up the hill.

'Why are you so bothered anyway?' Rhys asked.

'Whoever it is, they're wrecking the fence.'

'I can let Gwilym know if it makes you feel better.'

'What's it to do with him?'

'They're his woods.'

'These were Dad's woods,' Evan said, putting down the wood he was carrying. 'I thought they were yours now?'

'No, no. Dad sold these before he went. They're Gwilym's now. He lets me take a tree when one needs taking out. Like this one here.'

'He didn't tell me he'd sold them. I thought all the woods went to you?'

'All the woods? There's the pines at home and you've got them. No, the woods are long gone. Suppose he didn't want to hurt your feelings. Besides,' he said, lifting the saw onto his shoulder, 'you'd only have cut them all down if you'd thought it meant more grazing for your sheep.' He carried the winch away towards the waiting trailer.

Evan had found their father dead in the bottom field, lying on his back, as if asleep. A waxcap was growing close to his ear and the sheep were still grazing indifferently about him. He had felt the dampness of the dew in his dad's hair as he held him and waved the flies away from his lips. He wondered now what else the man had kept from him before his mouth closed forever that morning and the fingers of grass stole his warmth away.

'We loading up then?' Rhys said as he came over. 'It's not that good for burning. Leave it to season at least six months. Don't try burning it before then. It'll go quickly as well.'

Evan adjusted his gloves and picked up the coiled cable, slinging it across his shoulder. Before he turned to head back to the trailer, he looked away again and up into the woods above.

He drove them back to Rhys's place and they carried the saw and other equipment back inside. Rhys rented his flat and the workshop below it from Geraint Ty Gwyn. Evan waited in the workshop whilst Rhys went upstairs to change. There were several workbenches and a giant lathe, along with various tools and carvings distributed around the room. His nose caught the familiar tang of linseed oil and varnish, and the resinous, faintly singed smell of wood shavings. He picked up the nearest of the carvings. It was of a doe and her fawn. He ran his finger over its smooth surface, feeling the shape of the doe's back before touching her at the ears and hooves with his fingertip. How Rhys could do what he did always puzzled him. His brother had never held an interest for the farm and used to stay indoors to play when they were children, while Evan went out to work with their dad. Unlike Evan, he had wept and wet the bed for months after the cancer had taken their mother. Evan loved him and respected him, but he never understood him. They had fought only once, when he was twelve, an episode he could recall as lucidly as the day it happened. That winter, snow had turned the hills smooth and white, covering the fingers of the wasted trees and capping the hedges in a thick layer, like the peaks on their father's brush before shaving. Though he could not recall why they had argued, he remembered with a stomach-stirring guilt, the bloody nose he had given Rhys and the hot liquid falling on the fine crystals of snow. He had held handfuls of the snow to his brother's face, who cried as it turned into a red slush that poured through his fingers. When it finally stopped, Evan walked the two of them back with his arm around his brother, the snow creaking beneath their feet like the grinding of teeth.

He had promised Rhys and Richard a drink in The Drovers Arms. His brother's drinking was another thing he did not understand but he had never challenged him about it, despite Sioned insisting he should, and he was not going to start now. They collected Richard on the way and parked a short distance from the pub at the old cattle market.

The Drovers Arms was Rhys's pub of choice. The building was a tasteless mix of pebble dash and old beams and was, as Evan often pointed out, in urgent need of redecoration. The sign outside was so badly weathered that the drovers were now featureless and appeared to be driving their sheep into an abyss. Tourists mostly passed over it in favour of the more attractive and more expensive Red Lion further up the road. Inside were a few tables and a pair of dark and cigarette-burnt booths. Copper kettles and agricultural paraphernalia clung to the walls or dangled from the ceiling. With better care, the bar could have had rustic appeal, but glowing plastic tap handles had been affixed to the ancient wood and the prices were scrawled in chalk on blackboards displayed behind it. The smell inside was tolerable but the toilets were not spoken about, and the patrons re-emerged from them as quickly as they could.

The moment he saw Rhys, Will the landlord began pouring him his usual lager. Gwyn the Waun was drinking at one of the tables, holding his pint in two hands, his arthritic thumbs sticking out like stubby antennae. At the bar was John Davies and next to him, Jimmy Rhubarb. Davies was a large man with a distended gut and a fleshy neck that flapped about under his chin. His eyes were close-set, and his thick lips were partially hidden by the stiff, three-coloured quills of his moustache.

'All right,' Evan said. Davies nodded in return. Richard scowled at the pair of them. Evan's dad had hated Davies; he knew that much, but Evan liked to think he treated others fairly and would not let that colour his judgement. When Will poured the last drink, Evan paid him and carried his pint over to stand with Davies and Jimmy.

'All right. How's it going?' he asked.

'Not so bad. You?' Davies said.

'Yeah, numbers are good this year. How are your Devonshires doing?'

'Well. I've only got a few, but they've nearly all of them lambed three times in these last two years.'

'Bloody hell,' Evan said, putting down his beer.

'Yep. Only got to look a tup and they're pregnant.' They carried on, Jimmy sipping quietly at his pint and Richard coming over to listen. Richard had a history with Jimmy's eldest and had ended up in the back of a police van after they had fought one carnival night. He stood close by, scowling at Davies and Jimmy.

'I was going to ask you, actually,' Evan said. 'Brian lost a few sheep a while back. Reckoned it was dogs. I came to see, and it looked that way to me. Have you had anything similar?'

'No.'

'Oh. Just wondering with those kennels you've got.'

Davies interrupted him before he could continue. 'There's nothing wrong with my kennels,' he said.

'No, no. I'm not saying there is.'

'I keep my dogs well.' He had straightened himself up and stood directly in front of Evan, his bristly moustache level with Evan's eyes.

Evan held up his palms. 'I know. I was just wondering if one of them might have–'

'That Brian needs to keep his mouth shut,' Davies interrupted again. 'Everything that goes wrong with his farm he points the finger at me. It's his own fault he can't look after his ewes.' He shook his head, sending the folds of his neck flapping. 'Dogs tearing out throats! I've got ewes of my own. Why would I keep a dog that would do that?'

'I wasn't saying–'

'You'd best mind your business, Bowen.'

'Yeah, piss off Bowen.' Jimmy had come away from the bar and was standing next to Davies. He rocked slightly on his heels, clearly feeling the drink more now that he was standing up.

'Fuck off, Jimmy,' Richard said, drawing level with Evan.

'What, you going to make me are you, you scrawny

little shit.'

'Hey, stop that now,' Will said from behind the bar.

Davies had fixed Evan with a stare and would not look away. Evan met his eyes with his own.

'Got your fucking rhubarb with you, have you?' Richard shouted.

Rhys came over to stand between Jimmy and Richard. 'Hey, we'll have less of the lip you two,' he said, pointing at each of them.

'Outside then, is it?' Jimmy said.

'No. We're off, now,' Rhys said, reaching an arm out across Richard and Evan and drawing them back.

'Good,' Davies said. He and Evan were still staring at each other.

'Come on!' Rhys said. They left their drinks where they were. Gwyn the Waun had not moved throughout.

Outside, it was bright and fresh.

'For fuck's sake boys. I drink in there. What do you think you're doing?' Rhys said.

Richard was still looking back at the pub. 'Tell you what we do,' he said. 'We get a load of his sheep into the trailer, and we drive them—'

'No, leave it,' Evan said.

'Come on,' Rhys said. 'I've seen enough to be honest. Nice quiet drink it is with you two like. Bloody hell.'

Later, Evan and Richard unloaded the wood into the old barn at Hafod Farm. Richard said he would go and see if Sarah needed a hand with any logs and Evan stayed to split some kindling. Sioned was in the lambing shed across the farmyard. He could hear the high, whinnying call she made to get the sheep away from the troughs so that she could fill them. Picking up an empty disinfectant tub, he filled it with nuts from the feed bin and went inside to join her. Together they attended to all the pens, wordlessly dividing them between each other. The sheep jostled one another and butted at their knees to get at the hard, brown pellets they spilt along the length of each trough. Evan spotted a few with the beginnings of foot rot and went out to fetch the treatment. When he came back, Sioned was attending to a late pair of lambs that were just being born. He cleaned out one of the nursing pens ready for them, forking the rancid straw into a barrow and replacing it from a new bale. When both were out, they each carried a yolk-stained lamb to the newly prepared pen, holding them by the forelegs and feeling the pulse beating hot and high against the grip of their hands. As they walked, Sioned bleated gently to the new mother, making sure she was following. Evan left her to see to the rest of the pens. Holding the syringe between his teeth, he caught those sheep that needed treating by the back legs with his crook, then pinned them against the side of the pen to inject them. Sparrows wheeled around him, flying above the sheep and settling to pick amongst the straw before darting back out into the daylight. He looked over at Sioned occasionally. Two nights ago, he had woken her up by sleepwalking to the corner of the bedroom and holding onto her grandmother's old dresser, saying 'she's got her head up, she's sick to lamb'. They had laughed about if for much of the next day, but it had worn off now. Things were back as they were, with the two of them saying very little to each other. Well, she could take it or leave it, he thought. How could you fix something when you did not know how it was broken in the first place?

That evening the wind carried away the heat from his back as he ran. He felt stronger, as if the last of winter had been shaken from his bones. The fronds of the bracken had not yet returned but the flowers of the gorse were a bright, wagtail yellow. The grass was raised in mounds where the moles had been feeding. The fields were plagued with these claggy eruptions, breaking out in rows like shingles. He would have to get the traps out again. When Ceri was a girl, he had given the dead moles for her to hold and to stroke and had even popped the occasional one into Sioned's pockets for a laugh.

He passed the hawthorn and looked over his shoulder at the farm below. Hafod was too small for a commercial hill farm, especially with the price of lamb these days, something he found hard to understand, as it seemed expensive enough at the supermarket. Before, farming had been mixed, but few could afford to do that now; it was cattle in the valleys and sheep on the hills. If he had been born in the drier east, he might have ended up as one of those posh English farmers with their rich agribusinesses. As it was, he had to work at least one day a week for someone else, just to make ends meet. It was a hard fight to get anything from the land. His dad put the sheds in, but he could never expand the farm and nor could Evan. Sometimes he spoke to his dad in his mind, and he did so now, telling him not to worry. However hard it was, whatever sacrifices he had made, the farm was safe.

10

'Are you hungry?' the man asked, closing the gate behind her. He walked very quickly, tackling every gradient at the same pace, however steep. Sarah was breathing hard and trying not to let it show.

'No,' she lied.

'We're out of the woods, literally and figuratively.' She could see him a little better now. He must have been somewhere in his mid-thirties. He was wearing a dark fleece and hat and camouflage trousers and carried a small rucksack with him. They had covered a fair distance together already, following an indistinct path through the trees to a low stone wall which eventually ended at a stream. They had been hugging its banks for the last half hour. 'Have some water, at least,' he said, taking a metal bottle from his sack and unscrewing the lid. When she did not take it, he drank some himself then passed it to her. She rinsed out her mouth, then gulped at the copper-tasting water and thanked him. 'I'm Rob by the way.' When she gave no reaction, he took the bottle from her and packed it away. 'And you are?'

'Sarah.'

'Well, nice to meet you, Sarah.' His teeth showed in a smile. 'Even if it is a rather odd way to meet.' He looked around, checking for something. 'Ready to move on?'

They crossed over several long and mercifully empty fields; the last thing she wanted to do was to have to bypass a herd of cows in the darkness. Rob asked about her as they walked, wanting to know where she worked and how she had ended up in Mid Wales. She was too tired to do much, other than answer his questions as simply as she could. He said that he was a conservation officer on a wildlife reserve, the name of which she had seen on some tourist leaflets at the pub. She was only half listening to him when the cry of an animal came to them across the fields, a pained squawk which jarred her already frayed nerves.

'What was that?' she said.

'Tawny owl,' Rob answered and continued with his monologue about the reserve.

'I thought they went "twit-twoo",' she interrupted.

'They make lots of noises.'

He led them out from the fields, over a stile and down what looked like a farm track. The owl had started something, and Rob spoke all the way, telling her about owl behaviour and how their wings are serrated so they can fly silently, and how one famous wildlife photographer in Mid Wales lost an eye peering into one of their nests. He was midway through another owl anecdote when the track ended next to a bungalow and met with a tarmacked road. They stopped as a security light came on and they saw each other clearly for the first time.

'This leads up to the road to Rhyd-y-Benwch,' Rob said.

'Okay. I'll take it from here. Thanks for showing me the way.'

'I'm happy to walk the rest of the way with you.'

'No, that's fine.'

'Are you sure?' he asked.

'Yes. But thank you.'

'You need to go left when you reach the other road.'

'Okay.' She waited for him to say goodbye. He put a hand up to the back of his neck and rubbed it.

'Look, I'm sorry if I was curt with you when I first found you. You can never be sure who you'll come across, or what they're doing.'

'No, it's fine. Don't worry. Goodnight and thanks again.'

'You might need to take that hand to minor injuries. I could go with you, if you have trouble driving.'

'No, that's all right.'

'How will I know you've got back safely?'

'I will.'

'Okay,' he said. 'Well, goodnight, Sarah.'

'Goodnight.'

She remembered little of the rest of the walk back, only the rhythm of her legs and the smooth surface of the seemingly endless road. At Rhyd-y-Benwch all was dark, save for the squat, toadstool-shaped lanterns that lit the driveway running through it. Her car was where she left it and she said an inward prayer to someone, to anyone, when the engine fired into life. She met only two vehicles on the drive home and when she was back inside the cottage with the door locked behind her, sleep felt like the only god worth praying to.

The next day she was too exhausted to do much, other than to walk up the hill to call Malcolm so that she could arrange to have her shift at the pub moved to the day after. It felt like she had worn all the cartilage away in her knees, and her legs were so stiff that she yelped whenever she went to sit down. When she set out to work the following day, she was glad she had changed her shift, as Richard had come over to help Evan in the yard. Despite being married, he was one of those irritating men whose inflated opinion of themselves leads them to assume that every female wants nothing more than to have their manly affections directed towards them. He was always coming to help her when she did not need it, ignoring her protests. Anything he had to say seemed to be directed at her chest and there was usually a comment about her appearance. Most of all, she was sick of his deliberately-accidental way of touching her, making sure their bodies met when they were working or brushing up close to her if he passed her in the corridor.

It was a Friday, and the pub was busier than normal. Malcolm ended up taking her place in the kitchen so that she could help Emma serving. Emma was not as bad as Sarah had first thought and she had warmed to her when she told her about her background, especially her useless mother. They talked quite a lot together and one night when they were cleaning down the kitchen, Emma confided she had been addicted to cocaine as a teenager and had taken money from her family and friends, insinuating that that taken from the male members of her friendship group had come at a price. She was part of some movement called the New Wilderness League who had converted the old chapel at Tan-y-Fridd to use as their centre, and she was always trying to encourage Sarah to go along to one of their meetings.

The two of them had to squeeze past crowds of noisy drinkers to deposit the food at packed tables. Poor John was working as fast as he could, having little help from Malcolm, who was too busy ranting to be of much use. Sarah waited at the hatch for him to carry across the next meal.

'Bloody Cardiff,' he was saying. 'Why should we have to listen to them? We've got nationalists in the north, socialists in the south, and here's us stuck in the bloody middle! Do you know what they want me to do now? They want me to print all my menus in Welsh as well. When's it going to end? I bet that's a nice cushy little translation job for someone. The whole thing's ludicrous.' When he finally brought the meal over, she carried it over the heads of the drinkers to a lone man seated in the corner.

'Here you go,' she said, placing the meal in front of him. She was about to ask if he wanted any sauces but stopped when she realised: it was the same man from the other night.

'Hi,' Rob said.

'Oh. Hi.' She stood still, trying to reconcile his presence with the surroundings of the pub.

'Sorry. I didn't mean to startle you a second time.' He looked quite different in the daylight. She could see now that beneath the heavy brow, his eyes were a Baltic blue, despite his dark hair. His jumper was rolled back at the sleeves and his broad and bare forearms rested on the table. 'You got back all right then?'

'Yes. Yes, thanks.'

'Good.' Neither spoke for a moment. 'Is this nice then?' he said, pointing to the jacket potato she had set down.

'I don't know, I've never had it.'

'That's a great advert. Come to the Dolforwyn Castle

Hotel – we've never tried the food.'

'The cheese is award-winning,' she said, softening. 'You can have a refund if it kills you.'

'That's very generous. Well, I can see you're very busy here, Sarah. I'll leave you to get on. I just wanted to make sure you were okay.'

'Thank you,' she said.

'What time do you finish, if you don't mind me asking?'

'Four-thirty,' she said. 'It's busy today.' Rob looked disappointed.

'Are you working tomorrow?' he asked, putting his hand up to his neck and rubbing it.

'No,' she said, suddenly conscious of the hairnet and dirty apron she had on.

'There's a talk on at the reserve: 'Bringing Back the Beaver'. Didn't know if you would fancy it. Do you like beavers?' He didn't wait for an answer. 'Doesn't matter. You won't see one anyway.'

'Okay. What time?' she asked.

'Two o'clock.'

'I'll see you there then.'

'Really?'

'Yes.'

'Okay. Great. See you then.'

They both said goodbye and she left for the kitchen, smiling to herself, this time passing by the front door and pocketing one of the leaflets for Afon Twymyn Nature Reserve.

Sarah had passed the turnoff for the reserve before but had never driven up the Twymyn Valley. She was joined in the car park by half a dozen other cars. Murmuring couples filed down the path towards the entrance to the reserve. She questioned whether this was really a good idea. Ahead of her, she could see the white scratch of the Twymyn falls like a seam of quartz through the mountainside.

She felt self-conscious arriving alone and stood

reading the interpretation boards at the entrance before following the others. As well as the main building, there were several others marked, along with some cabins in the woods. The woods were veined with walking routes marked in red, green and yellow, and the reserve ended in twin pools close to the river. The trail from the car park led her to the main building, a large and elegant construction of timber called 'The Ark'. Inside, people were helping themselves to hot drinks and some were already seated in rows in front of a projector screen. She took a glass of water and sat on one of the back rows.

Shortly afterwards, a man stood in front of the projector screen and clapped his hands. The room went quiet. He was a red-faced man with a quiff of white hair which stood stubbornly upright. He began the talk by playing a short video. She looked over at the few people who remained standing and saw Rob amongst them. He was scanning the crowd and smiled when his eyes eventually met with hers. She returned the small wave he gave her.

The talk was better than she imagined it would be. She had loved anything to do with woodland creatures as a girl but had seen little wildlife beyond the country parks of the southeast. The man explained how beavers had been hunted to extinction for their luxurious fur, and for their scent glands whose musk made fixatives for perfumes. Without beavers, he said, we have had to coppice woodlands ourselves and rivers are more unpredictable and prone to flooding without their dams. The audience emitted a collective groan when the man listed the groups that objected to their reintroduction.

'It's the usual suspects, I'm afraid,' he said. 'Farmers, landowners, gamekeepers and so on. People who don't seem to understand that beavers will actually help them with their respective industries. I attended one community meeting run by the Wessex Beaver Project and one man stood up and said "That's all very well but I won't have them taking my fish!"' The other attendees laughed but Sarah had to wait to find out beavers were vegetarians. After audience questions and a round of applause, the talk was over, and the room began to fill with voices once again. She went over to where Rob was waiting for her.

'Hi.'

'Hi. Thanks for coming. Did you find it interesting?'

'I did, actually.'

'Good. We're already scoping some sites in Wales. Hopefully we can have our first beavers here in the next few years, if we can get enough people on board, politically speaking. Anyway, as you're here, may I show you around?'

'Yes. Sounds good.'

Rob led her along the trail through the reserve, showing her each of the different areas and speaking excitedly throughout. The residential cabins they passed had grass rooves and tin chimney stacks. Close to the ponds was a bark-covered 'Bug Area'.

'We have school groups come here quite often,' Rob said. 'The kids love this area. We take them pond dipping as well. Look.' He lifted a loose and rotted stump. Half a dozen startled woodlice scuttled away from the light, legs moving at speed under plates of grey armour. Rob looked disappointed. 'Just woodlice today,' he said, replacing the stump. 'You know they're crustaceans, like crabs and lobsters. In Welsh they're called wood-pigs.'

'I like that: wood-pigs. You know, I'd have loved this when I was a kid,' Sarah said. 'Especially pond dipping.' He looked pleased.

'This way,' he said. 'The bluebells are just beginning to flower.' He led her along one of the waymarked trails and into the woods. It took a moment for her eyes to adjust as they slipped under the trees.

'Oh my God!' she cried out. 'They're beautiful!' For as far as she could see, the ground shimmered with ethereal violet, the heads of the flowers spreading out over a green world, in a swell of silent electricity.

'That's not even all of them,' Rob said. 'There's plenty more coming to join them.'

'It's so lovely.'

'They're very old these woods. Atlantic oakwoods

like this are very rare now. Once, most of the country would've been covered with trees of some sort, from one end to the other.' They moved deeper into the woods, following a narrow path amongst the bluebells.

'Listen,' Rob said, raising his index finger. From a distance she could hear short bursts of sound like the crackle of fireworks, only deeper.

'A woodpecker!'

'Yes, I've seen him. A very handsome Great Spotted.'

They talked together, following the long trail through the woods. This time Sarah directed questions at Rob, asking about the centre and his role there. He was a Cambridge graduate and had been a working resident of four different reserves across England and Scotland. He had his research published in several well-respected journals and a number of his articles had been featured in a famous wildlife magazine. He said he had twice been consulted on camera for BBC documentaries. It was clear he was deeply passionate about the natural world, to the extent that he was once arrested for obstructing the building of a bypass. He was now entering his third year at Afon Twymyn he said. As they neared the end of the trail, he stopped.

'I've got one more thing to show you: some early arrivals.' He led her over to a nesting box on one of the trees, taking care to tread between the bluebells. He lifted the lid of the box for her. Inside was a tangled heap of translucent skin which she stared at for a moment before realising she was looking at a brood of recently hatched chicks. Their eyes were closed beneath large, dark lids and their frail bodies sprouted puny tufts of what must have been the beginnings of feathers. 'Pied flycatchers,' Rob said.

'That's amazing. How many of them are there?'

'I don't know. Let's count them.' He pursed his lips and made a sucking sound. In a second, seven tiny mouths were in the air, open and ready for food. The two of them smiled at each other.

Rob's cabin had the woody smell of a warm shed and the

same sockets of gossamer spun into every corner, where the spiders nested undisturbed. There were various maps and charts pinned to the walls, marked with coloured stickers and pins. Above the bed was a large print of an osprey, taking a fish from the Dyfi as Rob explained, his friend having taken the photograph. Rob sat cross-legged on the bed. Sarah continued to look around the room as they talked.

'So, are the rest of your family into conservation and the environment like you?' she asked.

'God, no. No, I'm definitely the black sheep of the family. A terrible disappointment to them, I'm sure.'

'Oh, come on,' Sarah said. 'You're an Oxbridge graduate.'

'Yes, but that's par for the course. It's expected in the circles in which my family moves. Perhaps if I'd read PPE or set my sights on the City, then they would be a bit more understanding. We've had some pretty heated debates, shall we say, in the past.' He shook his head. 'You wouldn't believe it, having to sit at breakfast with my father checking the FT. Do you have any siblings?'

'No.'

'Well, my brother's high up in some consultancy firm, making him the favoured son.'

'Which consultancy firm?'

'Talbot & Russell.'

'Ha! That's funny. I used to work for them.'

'Really?' He described his brother for her. She had not met him, though she thought she may have seen him visiting the office. She sat down on the bed.

'Isn't it funny,' she said. 'All the connections it turns out we have?' 'Take any two people and I bet you'd find a connection. There must be so many millions there that people never discover. You could live your whole life and not find them out.'

'I suppose that's the nature of chance,' he said.

'Not fate then?'

'I don't believe in fate, only coincidence.'

Sarah said she was not so sure, having the habit of

reading omens into things she found significant. She was about to give the example of them meeting together in the woods but thought better of it. The conversation ended in a mildly embarrassed silence. Just to break it, she pointed at a framed photograph that stood on his desk, from which a formidable looking woman looked out at them, smoking a large cigar.

'Who's that?'

'That's Grandma Sinclair, my mother's mother.'

'She looks great.'

'She was,' Rob said. 'She kept a menagerie of animals in her garden. It was called a garden, but it was more like an estate. She had so many plants and used to teach me the names of all of them. She didn't really do that with anyone else but me. There was no one else like her. I must have been about thirteen when she died. Once, we had a family party on a yacht in Poole Harbour. It finished all too quickly for Grandma Sinclair's liking and she rowed a dinghy to the mainland in her high heels, with her Martini glass, hoping to carry the party on somewhere else!'

'So it was her you got your love of wildlife and nature from?'

'I hadn't thought of it like that. Yes, I suppose it was. It's not only love though, it's a very real duty and responsibility that all of us share.' He pointed a finger in the air as he made his point. 'We're the ones that are suffering for not taking care of our planet. Anyway, before I start lecturing, shall we go and get a drink and say hello to some of the others?'

They left the cabin for the kitchen at the rear of the Ark, meeting a man emerging from the compost toilets on the way. The man looked at Sarah and raised an eyebrow at Rob. Rob introduced the man as Sean and Sarah shook hands with him, making a mental note to wash her hands once she reached the kitchen. He had a worn face, with gums shrinking back from long teeth, though when he spoke his mouth issued with the soothing, voice of a therapist. Rob explained afterwards that Sean was manager at the reserve, although he did not live on site as his wife did not like the damp. She was a yoga teacher and she said it muddied her chakras or something similar. Before they entered the kitchen, they greeted a very tall women called Sally who was carrying a corrugated iron sheet to attract reptiles. Sarah admired her loose, waist-length grey hair as she walked past. In the kitchen were the remaining staff members, who fell silent when they saw Sarah enter with Rob. Rob introduced her to Julian, Lucy and Pete and set about making tea.

'So, what brings you to the reserve?' Julian asked. He had been introduced by Rob as Sean's son. He was wearing combat trousers spattered with a green, messy substance Sarah could not make out. She explained that she had been asked there by Rob. Julian and Lucy exchanged a smirk.

'Rob doesn't normally bring friends back here,' Lucy said, loud enough for Rob to hear. He ignored the remark, or else pretended not to hear it above the noise of the kettle boiling. Lucy and Pete had been introduced as a couple. Lucy was fair and looked younger still than Sarah. She was sun-freckled along her bare shoulders, showing either side of the straps of her top. Her boyfriend Pete had his dreadlocks tied up out of the way and held his mug in both hands. As Rob's guest, Sarah felt like a curiosity, and Julian and Lucy wasted no time in questioning her as to where she was from and where she worked. The round of questioning was stopped by Rob who came over with the tea.

'You don't have to answer these reprobates,' he said.
'We're just interested in your new friend,' Julian said.
'Exactly,' Lucy added.

'Well, I make it a rule never to answer questions from botanists, and neither should you, Sarah. Anyway, you were all talking about something before we both arrived. What was that?'

'The government's just confirmed they're planning to expand fracking into national parks,' Lucy said, suddenly serious. The news clearly disgusted everyone in the room.

'It's just insane,' Julian said. 'They think anything to do with the environment is just wishy-washy, left-wing bullshit. As if caring that the countryside you live in isn't a lifeless shithole is for weak, airy-fairy hippie-types. It's all about money. Trash the landscape, rip it all up. As long as it makes a dollar it's good. I'm sick of it.'

'I know,' Lucy said. 'These people talk about 'responsibility' and 'making difficult decisions' but they're ultimately the most irresponsible of them all. This country is obsessed with wealth, power, arrogance, winning, greed. It's all about beating the next guy. "I'm better than him. I've made more money. I'm more powerful". These people don't need all these billions. It's just about ego. They hated losing as children and now we're all going to suffer for it. They say they love this country; they don't, they love a myth. Our real country is being destroyed by them, because it's not the land they love, it's the money they can make out of it.' Pete said very little, but nodded in approval as Lucy spoke, still holding onto his mug.

'But it's more than that,' Rob said. 'It's already happened. We go around warning what will happen, what might happen, and that makes it easy for these people to stick their fingers in their ears and their heads in the sand because it doesn't fit with their money-making ideology. We've already ruined the planet. We've deforested it, polluted it, overheated it, emptied the oceans, driven whole species to extinction. You name it, we've done it. Yet still we warn what 'might' happen. The whole planet has been trashed already. Sometimes I think making these wildlife documentaries does more harm than good. They painstakingly film what little is left, and people think "isn't the world wonderful" and feel happy to continue to sit on their arses doing nothing.'

The conversation continued in this way for some time, before becoming bogged down in the geological details of fracking. Rob turned to Sarah and asked if she wanted to go back outside. She said that it was probably time for her to head back anyway and said goodbye to the others. Julian made Rob promise in front of all of them that he would invite Sarah again. She knew that once she left, they would all be talking about her. Outside, the sky had dulled with the ageing of the afternoon, though the path back was still bright with the celandines that had crept out of the woods to meet it.

'You did enjoy yourself?' Rob asked.

'Yes. Definitely. I really did,' she said.

'And you'll come again?'

'Of course.'

She gave him her mobile number when he asked and left him with a promise that she would visit again. As she drove away, she looked back at him through the rear-view mirror and watched him, watching her drive away.

11

"I know you better than you know yourself, Sarah Acton," her grandma had said. As a young teen she had thought this ridiculous. It was surprising then to find herself acting in a manner she did not recognise as her own. She was used to this sort of attention from men, but it was different now she felt free, plus Rob was something new. Yes, he was good-looking, but more attractive than that was the intensity he had, the passion sharpened by intelligence. He messaged her in the evening following her visit. She walked out to stand in the lee of the farmhouse until she had signal and there it was. This began an earnest exchange between them, a rally of messages which went on day and night. She had a signal at work and the sudden explosion in texts did not go unnoticed, with John teasing her for 'sexting' during work hours. At times she felt stupid for acting like a teenager. Other times she told herself she deserved the excitement of it all after everything that had happened. Sioned encouraged her when she told her about it, saying she was young, and it was right that men were chasing after her.

On her second visit to the reserve, she helped Rob crome the ponds, standing waist-deep in waders that glued themselves to her body with the pressure of the water. Together they scooped out forkfuls of tangled pondweed with the four-pronged cromes leaving it in piles by the side of the water so that everything living could crawl back to safety. He took her to see the waterfalls and they saw a grey wagtail splashing beneath the falling water, its tail waving at them from the rocks. Later, Rob was called away by Sean, as a television crew had arrived and were filming for a rural affairs magazine. He kept apologising to her as they walked back to the car park. She stood close to him and waited for him to move towards her, but he only rubbed at his neck with his hand and said goodbye. When she arrived home, the messages continued just the same.

> *There is something else I wanted to show you*, he wrote that evening. *It is a secret though, really.*
>
> *Ok. Is it a nice secret? x*
>
> *Yes. Have you ever slept outside, under the stars?*
>
> *No. Only camping.*
>
> *Would you like to go further into the hills with me and spend the night there?*
>
> *Sounds fun. Would it be scary though?*
>
> *It's not scary. Can you get here Weds afternoon? Bring lots of warm clothes, bivvy bag, sleeping bag etc.*
>
> *Ok. Will see you then. x*
>
> *Looking forward to it. x*

Desperate to talk about it with someone, she sat up in bed that night and wrote a long and sincere apology to Gill.

On the Wednesday afternoon she found Rob in his cabin, still packing. He was stuffing a large expedition rucksack with cans of lager. A bottle of economy vodka disappeared inside with the cans.

'Jesus,' she said. 'Is that all booze in there? Are we having a party?'

'It's not all booze. Anyway, this stuff's not for us. I have wine, olives, cheese etc. for us.'

'Classy.'

'That's me.'

'Who's all that for?'

'You'll see.'

'You're keeping me in suspense, are you?'

'Something like that.'

They set off together through the woods, Rob checking with her that she had brought everything she needed. She had had to look up what a bivvy bag was but had found one in the army surplus store in Penbury. He walked alongside her, at her pace, his binoculars at the ready, moving like a pendulum against his chest. She said she did not like surprises, which was a lie, but he would only tell her that they would be passing by a stone circle on the way to their destination. The fragrance of the bluebells ended with the woods, and they followed a footpath upwards until they met with a farmer's track that pushed its way up and into the hills. The afternoon was hot and cloudless as they left behind the lustre of the valley. Beside her, the hedgerow frothed with blossom, sheltering the swaying heads of the cow parsley and the stitchwort that grew beneath them. St Mark's flies blighted the air, coming too close to her with their dangling, unpleasant legs, so that she had to bat them away from her face. They left the hedgerow for another footpath and soon the tines of the mountains appeared on the horizon and Rob pointed out each of the peaks and named them for her. She liked how excited he was to show her everything, yet he seemed unable to relax. She could sense how conscious he was, how he looked over at her when he thought she could not see. He spoke a lot as they walked, telling her how humans are evolved to live amongst trees and around fires, not in the lifeless concrete of cities. Silence agitated him, it seemed; he was too aware of her. It was only when he spotted a flying shape in the distance that his attention was torn away. He raised the binoculars to his face and mumbled something, then was gone, a giant rucksack on legs disappearing down the slope towards whatever it was. She stopped and waited for a while, but they had almost reached the stone circle, which she was impatient to see, and she went on a little further alone. There were a half dozen standing stones when she got there, protruding from the grass in what could only vaguely be described as a circle. The stones were stubby and reclined as if with a sickness, and their skins were disfigured with a vomit-coloured lichen. There was an interpretation board nearby, but it had been weathered unreadable, the laminate rising up in broad blisters and the writing bleached to a memory by the sun. She felt sad thinking how much it must have meant to people once, only for it now to be forgotten in a field, visited mostly by the indifferent sheep. The rucksack re-emerged and jogged up the path towards her. Rob apologised; the goshawk he was hoping for was just another sparrowhawk.

All things shone softly in the sun with the passing of the afternoon, and they walked for miles along the landscape of ridges that divided the uplands from the valleys below. Skylarks sang on the breeze above their invisible nests, and in the distance the white titans of the turbines harvested the same air. Sarah liked seeing them turning, but Rob told her that – amongst other things – they ruptured the lungs of any bats unfortunate enough to come near them. He asked a lot about her, and she ended up talking about Gill for some time, which felt good, though she changed the subject when it got round to Michael. The hillside became more rugged as the evening drew in, and with the first of the trees, any semblance of a path evaporated, and they had to pick their way amongst the jagged crags that now sundered the land apart. Soon they were weaving through a mixed woodland and the deepening sky was lost in the spread of the many branches. Sarah was about to say that she could smell wood smoke when Rob spoke out into the trees ahead.

'Noswaith dda Rhodri!' he called. They were coming to a small clearing where an outcrop broke apart the canopy above and from which a man's face now emerged in reply.

'Noswaith dda, y Sais digywilydd!' the man shouted back. 'Iaith y nefoedd, ti'n trio siarad? Ble ti wedi bod? Mae syched arna i!' He clambered up onto the rocks and watched them approach. 'Mawredd Mawr! Ti di dod â hogan ddel i ddweud helo! Bobol bach!' They rounded the rock face to where his bivouac was now visible. A fire smouldered gently in the clearing, surrounded by a ring of stones and a single camping chair. Behind the fire, the rock opened in a shallow cleft where the man's possessions were stowed on a tarpaulin sheet. A short way away, another tarpaulin was strung up between two trees and pegged taught to the ground, the tips of a hammock protruding either side.

'Welcome one and welcome all,' the man said, throwing his arms wide. He sat cross-legged on the rock and looked down on them like some sort of Cambrian yogi. He wore a jumper that looked as old and as green as the hills. The mound of his belly swelled beneath it, which, combined with the scattered beer cans, destroyed any air of asceticism he might have had. His skin was dry, and his eyes were dark. 'Sorry, I was having a little snooze when you turned up,' he said.

'You could clean up round here you troglodyte,' Rob said. The man dangled his booted feet over the ledge on which he was sitting and jumped to the ground. Rob introduced the man as Rhodri. He took Sarah's hand and kissed it with a theatrical flourish.

Rhodri had dragged a log out of the woods and Sarah now sat on it, by the fire, listening to him sing. He was sitting in his camping chair and had taken his boots off. They sat next to him like a loyal dog, greasy with dubbin, whilst he steamed his feet over the fire. He was singing 'Wichita Lineman' with surprising beauty. Rob had been gone a while now; he had work to do, he said. They had eaten earlier, at twilight, and Sarah now finished the last of the wine, pouring it out into the mug from Rob's flask. When she looked back from the fire into the blackness of the woods, her eyes still burnt with its light and she could see almost nothing. Rhodri sang into the fire, then up at the space above them. The cup-holder in his chair held his fourth can of export strength lager. When he finished singing, there was only the crackle of the wood as it burnt and the faint scream of boiling sap.

'You have a lovely voice,' Sarah said. The giddy pleasure of the wine had spread to her legs.

'It was my mam that taught me to sing,' he said. 'Beautiful voice, she had. Best in the choir, always.'

'What sort of stuff did she sing?'

'Oh, all sorts. Chapel stuff mostly.' He pointed at her. 'You can't be full, you know. All that wine and olive stuff. Let me make you something.' He had a way of leaning in conspiratorially as he spoke.

'No, I'm fine, thank you.'

'Come on,' he said, getting up very cautiously from his chair. He looked like he was over-compensating, moving with the deliberateness of someone trying not to appear tipsy. 'I'll do you some bacon and egg.' He carried over a large stone and set it down by the fire. Its surface was dipped in the centre, forming a shallow well. He brought over a handful of small sticks and a larger one, the end of which he rested amongst the embers. 'She was wonderful, my mam,' he said. 'It felt like it was just me and her against the world, growing up.' When the stick was burning, he moved it onto the stone and began a small fire on top of it. 'People pick on you, you know, when it's just you and your mam. The kids at school, they see how the other grown-ups are towards her, so they go for you. It's like they can smell weakness.'

'Did you get into fights?' Sarah asked. Her own experience of school had been one of invisibility. She had managed to avoid trouble mostly by working hard not to stand out.

'Yeah,' Rhodri said. 'Lots. Got kicked out of a lot of schools. I supposed that's why everyone wanted me to join the army. Discipline or whatever. Once, I ran away from school and caught the bus all the way to the coast on my own. Wanted to see the sea, see.'

'I bet your mum was proud though, when you did join,' she said. He had already told her several stories from his army days.

'I don't know, really.' The fire on the stone was going strong now and he added a couple more sticks to it. 'She went into hospital when I was still young, as her jaw was all locked up. They said it was malnutrition. She gave all her money to the chapel see, and she fed me well, but she didn't leave anything for herself. They ended up breaking her tooth before they got the feeding tube in. After that, they put me in different people's houses, and I didn't see her for a long time.' He went over to his chair and took a couple of large swigs from his can, and the two of them watched the fire quietly for a while. Rob could be heard, moving somewhere in the woods. Rhodri fetched an egg and some bacon and selected another stick. He swept away the fire on the stone in a spray of sparks and dropped the rashers onto it. They seared loudly and with a powerful smell, and he knelt down to crack the egg over them.

'How did you end up here then, after the army?' Sarah asked.

'There was a lot that went on between the army and here, and I was in the army a long time,' Rhodri said. The egg and bacon were already done, he gathered them in some bread and handed it to her. The bread soaked up the salty, wood-smoked yolk. She was certain it was the best thing she had ever tasted. 'I ended up here because old lanky legs over there found me face down drunk in the Twymyn. Another minute or so and I'd have been dead. He asked me to move camp up here. Keep an eye on his rodents for him.'

'They're mustelids.' Rob's disembodied voice came out of the darkness of the woods. 'And you're spoiling the surprise.'

'Well, maybe I'll catch one and have it on the fire,' Rhodri shouted into empty space. 'Then I'll tell you whether it's mustard or pine they taste of.'

By the time Rob returned to sit with them, Sarah was wearing her sleeping bag and bivvy bag over her legs to keep warm. Rhodri poured a vodka for each of them and covered himself with a blanket.

'Well, I might as well tell you now,' Rob said. 'I wanted you to see the pine martens, if we can.'

'Pine martens?' She had heard of them but had no idea what they looked like.

Rob nodded. 'There's a project to bring them back. The recovery team reintroduced a small population from Scotland here. Few people knew what, if any, population remained here and so they contacted me, thinking it still might be a case of reinforcement, rather than reintroduction of the species.'

'Rewilding,' Rhodri said, looking a degree drunker now. 'He loves it.'

'I was one of the only people who knew whether a native population remained in the Cambrian Mountains.'

'And do they?' Sarah asked.

'Only just.' He told her all about the project, how

they captured martens in Scotland and brought them to Wales and started them off in release pens. The translocated martens were all fitted with radio collars and monitored by members of the project. He said his role was mostly advisory, describing himself as an ambassador for the last of the native martens. 'It might sound silly, but secrecy is important for custodians of wildlife. There are few people that know about this and now you're one of them.' She moved along the log to sit closer to him.

'To the last of the marticans and the return of the natives!' Rhodri said, raising his mug of vodka. The talk went on about the martens, Rob saying how they were good for the red squirrel population, then he moved onto the beaver project, and they started discussing what else could be brought back. Sarah said she would like to see the wild horses return, but Rob said there was not much hope of that. He had pocketed a pinch of spruce needles and every now and then he popped one into his mouth to chew out the spicy flavour.

'He'll have wolves living up here with me next,' Rhodri said.

'And why not?' Rob said. 'They're a keystone species. If people only knew what benefits they would bring. We're happy to devastate even more of the land, just for the sake of our pet dogs, and don't even get me started on cats. But wolves, why they're bloodthirsty killers aren't they, not the shy, unassuming creatures zoologists make them out to be. It's like they embody all of civilisation's fears about the wild and people just want rid of them. They think turning everything into a giant garden will make it paradise but they're wrong; they need the sublime, or else it's not paradise. What is paradise without the wolves?'

They talked on until Sarah could no longer stay awake and she lay down and fell asleep, looking over at Rob, with Rhodri still tending the fire.

She woke in the night to find her face cold and wet, pressed as it was against the trampled earth. The rest of her body was cocooned in the soft swaddling of her sleeping bag, itself protected by a plastic shell. Rob was asleep close by but Rhodri was still awake. The fire had burnt low, and he sang softly in Welsh as he watched the dying embers. His song was sad and strange and tender, and she tried to fix it in her memory whilst the dew gathered steadily about them. As she listened to him sing, her mind moved in and out of consciousness and in that liminal world of near sleep, the unknown syllables became somehow familiar, as if she knew the words herself, and it seemed then like she was remembering, as if she had spoken it all herself, a long, long time ago.

Rob woke her at dawn, whispering her name and shaking her lightly at the shoulder. Rhodri was asleep in his chair, his head back and his mouth open as if collecting rainwater. The fire was out. Though still weak, daylight had entered the glade, pushing strongest through the trees where it showed in bands of glowing haze. Now was the best time, Rob said, and he asked her to come quickly. She pulled her boots back on and excused herself whilst Rob waited for her a short way into the woods. Squatting down amongst the mosses and the dripping ferns, she heard the life of the morning throbbing in the throats of the birds and felt the dew that soused the green earth, damp against her naked thighs. Rob led them deeper into the thickening trees which threatened to strangle out the dawn, then they broke into a clearing and had to climb a steep slope, steadying themselves by grasping fistfuls of scrub.

Already exhausted, Sarah rested her hands on her knees, and Rob signalled for her to be quiet, placing one finger against his lips before moving stealthily onwards, into the woods. He knelt in a patch of undergrowth and motioned for her to do the same. She waited as he scoured the woodland with his binoculars, before he pointed ahead excitedly and handed them to her. At first, she could make out nothing, then a flicker of movement made her train the binoculars on a fallen log in the distance. A long, furry body was making its way across it. The creature stopped, looked around – she thought at her – and then sniffed at something on the log.

'Wow! Amazing!' she whispered to Rob. She watched as it buried its head somewhere in the bark. It looked to her like a stoat or a weasel, but with a long, bushy tail like a fox. Suddenly the marten sat up, then scurried away along the log, out of sight.

'It's gone,' she said to Rob. He frowned and took the binoculars back from her.

'I baited that log earlier,' he said. He kept watching. A minute or so later, he pointed again.

'That's why. It's Scratcher, look!' He thrust the binoculars at her again. She looked and saw another marten, bigger this time, moving assuredly onto the log. 'That's Scratcher,' Rob said again. She watched him whilst Rob whispered to her about Scratcher and the kits he had sired. He was clearly Rob's champion.

They stayed on after Scratcher left, pressed uncomfortably against the undergrowth, neither of them caring, only happy to be there together, watching the woodland stir itself awake.

She arrived home by midday and ate ravenously, then slept for much of the afternoon before going to the farmhouse to bathe and scrub and to shave her armpits and legs. Rob had offered to come over to the cottage with some wine that evening, and she wanted to be absolutely ready. She washed, conditioned and blow-dried her hair and used a body butter for the first time in months. She plucked her eyebrows, then cleansed, toned and moisturised her face. For her eyes, she used her standard curlers and mascara but with eyeliner added and a little eye shadow. She dabbed scent behind her ears and brushed her lips with a subtle gloss she had forgotten she owned. All her underwear seemed a little shabby, but she chose the best of them and wore a new top she had bought in Penbury, along with the tightest of her jeans.

At the cottage, she riddled the wood burner, then opened the valve and built a small pyramid out of crumpled paper and kindling, followed by some thicker sticks. The pile was ablaze with a single match, and she added a few of the smaller logs, placing them strategically about the flames, ready for the big logs to follow. She spread some blankets out in front of the fire as the room began to warm. Sean had a four by four at the reserve, which Rob sometimes drove, and she listened out for the sound of it coming up the lane. She heard Evan coming in on the tractor instead and went to make a snack to distract herself. The knock at the door startled her when it came. Rob had to stoop low to enter the cottage. He handed her two bottles of wine and explained he had been dropped off and had walked the last part. She gave him a tour of the cottage and fetched some glasses and they both sat down in front of the fire. They talked for the next two hours about where Sarah was from and Rob's family, the projects he had worked on, the places they had both visited. They talked about the animals Rob had seen, how ants farmed aphids and how fox hunting might return, and they told each other stories, like the time she had made a little classroom out of shells on the beach when she was a small girl. Eventually the wine was gone, and the evening was dark, and he had still made no move to even kiss her. She grew more and more impatient and in the end announced she was getting ready for bed. Rob said nothing he just rubbed the back of his neck with his hand as she went to fetch her wash things. She pulled off her top and scooped out some of the water that had warmed on the wood burner into a basin. Facing away from him in her bra and jeans, she wetted a flannel in the warm water to wash.

'Are you not getting ready?' she asked. He opened his mouth to answer but did not speak. 'There's enough water here for the two of us.' Still he said nothing. 'Suit yourself. I'll just have to get undressed by myself.'

She turned and brought the flannel to her neck, then stopped, as she finally heard him coming towards her. She felt his body press against hers and his face in her hair, and she reached round to meet his mouth with her own as he placed his hands upon her. He held her gently at the shoulder as they kissed, his other hand brushing tenderly over her waist and down across the silvery lines at her hip. Her skin, starved of the feel of another, delighted at his touch. They pulled at each other's clothes, their mouths always returning to meet, until the last were gone, and they moved quickly together towards the bedroom. He ran back for his wallet, and she saw his trembling hands tearing open a wrapper, and as she waited, she stroked his back, running her fingers gently over the knots of his spine. She lay back and he moved over her, gathering her breasts in his hands and mouth, then they kissed as she guided him into her. Everything was new and different: the shape of his body in her hands, the feel of him. Her mouth opened in excitement as he moved against her, and with small noises she drank in the foreign scent of his neck close to her face. He lay on her afterwards and she felt the spent weight of him, holding him by the hips, unwilling to let him go. They did not speak. Shyly, he rolled away, then they held each other, naked and slippery, the two of them giggling like children.

12

The sap had broken through the scales of the countless buds, and the trees were now in full leaf. Sheep stretched up to the branches, plucking away everything they could reach. The bracken was good and green along the hills where the year's new fronds had unfurled. At the front of the cottage, the honeysuckle climbed ever onwards, feeling its way with restless tendrils, and the same bullfinch fought itself each day in the kitchen window, until Sarah ceased to notice the glassy tapping in the background.

Sarah and Rob now saw each other as often as they could and were texting each other continually whenever they could not. If they were not making love then they were walking the land together, and Sarah had learnt the names of medlar trees and crack willow and could spot red campion, nuthatches, cardinal beetles, orange-tip butterflies and more. Rob was due to come over that afternoon but right now Sarah was waiting for someone else.

'No, don't turn up that one, wait until you see the grit bin. Hello? Hello?' The phone had gone silent again. She was standing in her usual spot below the farmhouse, trying to get a signal. The wind was strong and carried the sound of a vehicle climbing the lane. Between the gaps in the hedgerows, she saw a red-roofed car appear, then disappear. 'That's it. You're here!' she shouted into the phone. She ran down into the farmyard as the car shook the rungs of the cattle grid and came to a stop above the cottage. Then came the bizarre sight of Gill treading tentatively away from her car in her trainers, the wind buffeting her loose, long hair.

'Hello gorgeous!' she shouted. Sarah ran to her and the two of them squealed, throwing their arms around each other and swaying together in their embrace. 'I've missed you, hun,' Gill said.

'I've missed you too. I can't believe you're here. This

is the farm,' Sarah said, stepping back from her. Gill nodded and pulled the hair from her eyes. 'Come and see the cottage.' She held Gill's hand as they came down from the farmyard, unable to let go of her just yet.

'I'm so glad I got through to you eventually,' Gill said. 'I didn't know where I was. This is the middle of nowhere. How do you ever find the place again?'

They stopped next to the cottage. 'This is it,' Sarah said.

'Oh, wow. This is lovely. Look at the little windows. So sweet.'

'Come inside.' She showed her around the rooms and talked her through the colours she had chosen and why.

'So there's no shower?'

'No.'

'You just strip wash?'

'Yeah, you get used to it. Don't you like it?'

'Of course I like it,' Gill said. 'It's cute.' They sat down to have coffee. 'So, first things first. Rob,' she said smiling. 'Tell me *everything.*'

Sarah was glad to. She told her the story of how they met, where he was living and the work he did. She showed Gill a picture of Rob on her phone and Gill nodded approvingly.

'Yeah, he's hot all right. He went to Cambridge then?'

'Yeah, you can see some of his research online.'

'Wow. Why does he live in a shed though?'

'It's not a shed, it's a cabin.'

Gill said that her and Tony had been thinking about marriage and they talked about possible venues. It was then that Gill mentioned Michael. She said he had finished with the woman from work and had gone to live with his mother.

'You're sure it's over between you and him?' she asked.

'Yes, I'm sure.'

'I mean it was eight, nine years?'

'I know how long it was.'

'I haven't spoken with him,' Gill began. Sarah could tell that all had not quite been forgiven between the two of them. 'But if he wanted to get back at you, he would've done something about you trashing the house. Called the police or something. I bet you any money he would want to get back with you now. What do you think?'

'I think I never, ever want to see him again.' She said it louder than she had intended.

Gill looked at the coffee in her hands. 'I'm glad you're happy,' she said. Sarah said nothing. 'You know you can always come and stay with me and Tony whenever you like. Actually, that was something I wanted to tell you. They're looking for people at Tony's work. If you wanted, you could say you had a career break or something. Only if you want to. But, if you're happy here?'

'I am,' Sarah said.

'It's only that I miss you.'

'I know. I miss you.'

'Do you know what you're going to do when you've finished working at the hotel?'

'I'll think of something.'

They both tried to change the subject. Sarah wanted to talk about Rob, but Gill wanted to go over everything Sarah had left behind. In the end, Sarah suggested that she show Gill around the farm. She showed her everything from the henhouse to the hawthorn on the hill but had to suppress her frustration, as she could not get Gill to be excited about anything. Gill's mind seemed to be elsewhere, the view even failed to impress her, and by the time they arrived at the farmhouse, Sarah was silent with annoyance. Sioned welcomed them in and sat them down in the especially tidy kitchen to have tea. She fussed over them, bringing them bara brith and butter on the best crockery.

'Now, there's no spices in that,' she said. 'Only tea, as it should be.' Gill thanked her. She sat opposite Sarah, her back straight and her elbows tucked in. She answered Sioned's questions politely. 'You've driven all this way and you're driving all that way back again on the same day? Why don't you stay? We could have you here in the farmhouse if there's no room in the cottage.'

'No, I'm fine, thank you. It took less than four hours to get here,' Gill said, looking at Sarah.

Sioned talked about the hens and said Sarah must give Gill some eggs to take away with her. Gill said very little. She was not rude, but she mostly just sipped her tea through her plump lips. Sarah had always been jealous of Gill's lips. Evan came into the kitchen, gave a short greeting, then left without whatever it was he had wanted. Sarah grew more and more frustrated, and when Sioned looked over at her appealingly, she suggested that they go back. She was embarrassed and moved quickly away from the farmhouse when they said goodbye.

Rob had taught Sarah how to fold firelighters out of newspaper and she said she would show Gill how. The two of them sat on the living room floor of the cottage and quietly turned the paper in their hands, folding the sheets into concertina shapes.

'Tell me what you're thinking,' Sarah said.

'I'm not thinking anything.'

'Yes, you are.'

'Well . . . It's just–'

'What?'

'You seem very friendly with the people here.'

'They're nice people.'

'I know. They seem like very nice people. You get on with them well?'

'Yes, of course I do.'

'It's just funny, seeing you happy here.'

'Maybe it is funny. I am happy here, though. In a way, it's like I'm closer to what is "me" now, here. I can't explain it. It's like waking up for the first time.' Her own words surprised her.

'You'd rather be with them here than back home with me?'

'No, no, it's not that.'

'Really?'

'Of course not. You know how much I care about you; you're my best friend and you always will be.'

'It's just that I miss you, a lot.'

'I know. I miss you too.'

'I wish I had you back.'

There was a knock at the cottage door. Sarah had forgotten that Rob was due to arrive. She apologised to Gill and went to open the door.

'Hi!' Rob held a cotton bag and was beaming. He leant down to kiss her. She took him through and introduced him to Gill. They shook hands.

'Very nice to meet you, Gill. Sarah's told me all about you.'

'And she's told me all about you.' Gill said.

'Look what I've got!' He opened the cotton bag and displayed its mucky contents. 'Pignuts! Freshly foraged on my way here.' He went off to the kitchen to rinse and salt the pignuts. The two of them went back to folding their firelighters.

'Here,' Rob said, coming back through with a plate carrying the newly cleaned pignuts. 'Try one.' Sarah took one of the chestnut-sized roots and bit into it. She felt she had to say something nice for Rob's sake. She tried not to laugh at Gill's reaction to her pignut. 'Sort of a nutty, celery flavour,' Rob said.

Gill swallowed hers before it was properly chewed. 'You don't like celery,' she said to Sarah.

'Oh. Really. Don't you?' Rob asked.

'Not really,' Sarah said apologetically.

'Sarah told me you live on a nature reserve. I've never met anyone from a nature reserve before,' Gill said.

'There are more of us than you might think,' Rob answered. 'But yes, I've lived in quite a few places actually. As long as it's away from the city. I can't stand being away from the country for long.'

'That's what's good about living in a garden city, like us,' Gill said. 'It's like being in the country, only you're so close to London. Do you keep animals on the reserve?'

Rob looked confused. 'Not quite,' he said. 'We like to think of ourselves as guardians, caretakers, if you will.' He started talking about environmental stewardship. Sarah went to make more coffee.

'What do you do if you want a night out?' Gill asked when she came back in. Rob looked confused again.

'There are pubs, I suppose,' he said.

'I expect you have to book a taxi?'

'Or walk.'

'Walk?'

'Yes, it's probably about eight miles back from the nearest pub.'

'You can't walk that!' Gill said, laughing.

'Why not? Anyway, one tends to make one's own entertainment.'

'And you do that without wi-fi?'

'There was life before wi-fi.'

'I know, but I couldn't live without it. Do you think the two of you will come down to visit us soon?'

Sarah and Rob looked at each other. 'We haven't talked about it yet,' Sarah said.

Gill said that it was time for her to head home much earlier than Sarah had expected. The three of them went out to the farmyard to say goodbye and Gill and Sarah embraced once more.

'You better let me know straight away if you do get engaged,' Sarah said.

'Oh, I will. Dress shopping. Bridesmaids. Yes!' Gill hugged her again, then said goodbye to Rob. Sarah felt something like sadness as she climbed into the car. There was an awkwardness now that had never been there before, a distance between them that Gill's visit had not shortened.

'You'll drive safely, won't you?' Sarah shouted through the open window. 'Of course, hun.' Gill said. 'Speak to you later. Love you!' They waved to her as the car went over the cattle grid and disappeared into the hedgerows.

'Do you feel good having seen her?' Rob asked.

'I don't know.'

'You must do. I've been wanting to tell you – I have

another surprise back at the Twymyn.'

'I'm exhausted, Rob. I don't think I'm in the mood for surprises. Can we just go to the cabin?'

'No, this is a relaxing surprise. Honest. Have you a swimming costume?'

'God, I'm not going wild swimming today. I said I wanted to try it and I do, but just not today. It's not even a hot day.'

'We're not going wild swimming. You just wait and see.'

There was a bikini top and a pair of bottoms that Sarah had scooped up when she had emptied her underwear drawer before leaving for Wales. They were not matching but they were all she had, and she followed Rob in them now, wrapped in a large bath towel, walking barefoot beside the path between the cabins and feeling the wet lick of the still damp grass against her feet. They heard a screech, followed by a woman's laughter up ahead. Rob looked back at her and grinned. She followed him around the back of the residential cabins to what she had assumed was a large, wood-panelled water tank, but when they rounded the corner, she found the tank open and filled with faintly steaming water. Lucy and Pete were in the water, Pete with his dreadlocks tied up and with Lucy's arms folded around his neck. They both cheered as Rob and Sarah approached, and Lucy ordered them to jump in.

'Wow! I didn't know this was a hot tub,' Sarah said. Rob pointed at the long roof of the residential cabin.

'A solar-powered hot tub, no less.' They shed their towels and clambered in excitedly. The water was blissfully warm and she sank her shoulders into it, away from the cool air. Lucy leant over the side and brought her hand back holding a glass.

'Prosecco?' she asked. 'There's raspberries as well.'

They drank and talked and watched the light of the evening change. Lucy and Pete left before them, then Rob and Sarah were kissing and holding each other, until Rob said they had to get back to his cabin urgently. As she dried herself in the cabin, Rob sat on his bed and looked through his phone for something. He set the phone down, as the first few bars of Marvin Gaye's 'Let's Get it On' began to play. Sarah stopped drying herself.

'You are joking,' she said. Rob laughed and pulled her close.

Later, they lay naked on his bed, Sarah with her head resting on his shoulder and her arm across his chest.

'I am going to that conference, by the way,' Rob said.

'The one in Scotland?'

'Yeah, Stirling.'

'How long is it?'

'Monday to Friday.'

'That's a long time.'

'I'm sorry.'

'No, it's okay. I said I would look after Rachel at some point.'

'Who is she?'

'Rachel. Ceri's daughter. You remember?'

'I thought Sioned was her mother?'

'That's Ceri's mother, Rachel's grandmother. I have explained this to you.'

'Oh. I've not met them though, have I?'

'You haven't met any of them. I'd like you to meet them. We've been invited to dinner anytime.'

'Hmm.'

'Terrified of children, are you?' She poked him in the ribs as she said it.

'No,' he said indignantly. 'I led a school group round here just the other week if you recall. I get on very well with children. That doesn't mean I think there should be any more of them though.'

'You're just saying that.'

'I am not. The best, most responsible thing one could do is to not have any children. There are seven thousand million people now on this planet. Think about that. It's insane. We need to do something radical about overpopulation, not add to it.'

'But you not having any children isn't going to stop other people from doing it.'

'No, but I don't want to be a hypocrite.'

'So what happens if all the people like you don't have children? Then the world keeps filling up with all the people who don't care. Is that what you want? Wouldn't it be better to breed more "custodians" as you call them?'

'No, I think there should be some sort of blanket ban.' He sat up. 'There's nothing inherently valuable about human life. Humans are parasites. I don't care if that makes me a "species traitor", or whatever. All we've done is drive extinction, reduce biodiversity, poisoned this, plundered that. And you can't even blame that on systems of power. You can't say it's capitalism or some evil, controlling elite. It's in our nature. Before we even had the first agricultural societies, we killed off most of the great megafauna. Drove magnificent species extinct. And that was just as hunter-gatherers, with clubs and spears.' He mimed throwing a spear.

'Ssshhh!' Sarah said. 'So loud. They'll hear us in the other cabin.'

'Do you think anyone heard us earlier?' he said, grinning. She slapped his bare chest.

'What's the conference about anyway?'

'Preserving the capercaillie.'

'What's that?'

'A big and very vulnerable bird. I'll have to take you to Scotland sometime. It's so beautiful. Not as beautiful as you, though.' He reached down to kiss her.

Rob went straight to sleep that night, but Sarah lay awake in the darkness for a long time, thinking over everything Gill had said.

13

Talking to Rob had made her late. It was the first time they had been apart for more than two days and he was unable to call her as much as she would like.

Earlier in the week, Sioned had driven her mother to a hospital appointment in England and Sarah had looked after Rachel for the afternoon, taking her to the reserve to show her the mini-beasts. She was counting down the days until Rob returned from Scotland. Emma from work kept on trying to persuade her to attend one of her group's meetings, and Sarah finally agreed, if only to make the last few days pass faster. She followed the signs to the lead mines as instructed and turned off for Tan-y-Fridd, where a sign welcomed her to the Derwen Centre. Emma was waiting for her outside the old village chapel.

'Sorry!' she said, winding down the window.

'There's visitor parking over there,' Emma said. 'I'll wait here for you.' Her seriousness still irritated Sarah, who was not sorry and would rather have spent longer on the phone to Rob.

The village was unusual. There were farm buildings as standard and a row of terraced houses, all finished in slate, but all of them were painted in the same colour scheme of forest green and white, and as she walked back through the village towards the chapel, she passed signs naming each of the buildings or directing her to different parts of the centre complex, each of them neatly produced and finished with the same logo of an oak tree with the letters 'NWL' underneath. The chapel itself looked magnificently done out, with its tall windows hand-painted with murals depicting mountains and forests.

'I got a bit lost,' she lied to Emma.

'The hedgerow sermon is nearly finished,' she said. 'It's Tamsin speaking today.' Sarah resented Emma's attitude

131

but she went after her, following her through a gate and along a path beside a stone wall towards a field. There were at least thirty people in the field, nearly all of them sitting cross-legged in the grass. At the front was a woman standing and speaking. Emma sat down amongst the audience and gestured to Sarah to do the same. The grass was still a little damp but this seemed to bother no one. Next to them, the congregation sat in enraptured silence. The woman before them had a powerful, yet soothing voice. She was short and plump, with a round face and a network of creases at the corners of her eyes, and had long, mostly silver hair which hung loose and brushed at the small of her back. Strangely, her feet were bare, as were those of many of the congregation, and she wore a simple burgundy fleece and baggy trousers as did the others.

'You see, in the past,' the woman said, 'people huddled together in their towns and cities and were afraid of the forests. We're all used to stories like Little Red Riding Hood. They saw the woods as dark and dangerous, home to fell beasts and black magic, full of wild, painted peoples who worshipped strange gods. Civilisation as a word, comes literally from the city dwellers. Cities, with all their noise and all their traffic and all their smells, were seen as mankind's glorious triumph over nature. Nature was wild and irrational in comparison. So, in terror of the woods, men cut them back, as they do so today, bringing what they see as light into darkness. As crazy as this now sounds to us, nature was an evil to be fought. But as many of you will know, the city takes over the life of man and woman. If you don't believe me, join the commuters on the Tube in London for a day. You'll see a million faces absorbed in the worries of the city. And so, to ease the nagging of their souls, city dwellers built buildings and huddled into them to worship. But it was no good. Over the centuries, as nature was destroyed and the wild places rolled back, people suffered on the very streets they had created, despite the churches they had built. Cut off from their own nature, inwardly they atrophied, and so it went on, so many of us continuing to subject our souls to continued misery. Yes, "civilisation" brought many benefits, but those benefits conceived in the cities came at a terrible price: the withering of our very Selves.'

Sarah was reminded of the few times she had been to church in her life. She had never taken any interest in religion but this was different at least, and what the woman was saying was more interesting.

'Blinded by the distractions of the city, by the lights and screens, the sugar and fat that we cram into our faces, the billboards everywhere, distracting us with half-naked women, we forget who we are. We are no different from the land and the animals. We are *inseparable* from them. We are not in control, despite what the government and corporations will tell you. They would like you to think we are the masters of the birds and the beasts and the fowls of the air, but we all know from the unfolding environmental disaster that this is simply not true. And if we are to return to what we used to understand, before cities and "civilisation", then we need firstly to engage in regular communings but also, we need to apply the knowledge we derive from them to our daily lives. It's not good enough to have an experience which transcends the false dichotomy between man and nature during a communing and then just forget about it afterwards. The experience must transform us. We need to carry our newfound understanding with us, to meditate upon it, to go back to it. Only through sustained practice can we arrive at true, lasting, experiential understanding.'

The woman went on for some time and Sarah lost the sense of what she was saying. She was distracted for a while when she found an orb weaver spider making its way through the grass in front of her. A ripple of movement passed through the assembled crowd. They seemed to be preparing for something.

'In the Indian subcontinent,' the woman went on, 'they had the sense, traditionally, to associate trees with knowledge and wisdom. I hope that in today's communings you discover your own wisdom, and if you are able to put this into words, that you will share it with us afterwards. For now, though, perhaps we can say together why we are here and recite our creed, leaving a minute's silence afterwards to reflect.'

Then everyone present bowed their heads and began to chant together.

'I am the sun's fire in the coming of the dawn
I am the splendour of the sky's dominion
I am the unyielding mountain, cleaving open the ancient earth
I am the unending river, the forest's steam, the brightness of the dew
I am the flower that opens to the love of its creatures

We are the light of stars in the fullness of the heavens
We are breath and stillness and the currents of the air
We are the skin of the land and its blood-hardened rock
We are salt in the waters of the conquering sea
We are the young grass, the knotted wood, the wisdom of trees

In everything is me and I in everything
We are forged of the same stars and all of us undone in this earthly crucible
I will cease to be sundered from the land, to be detached from its knowledge
I pledge myself to go back to the earth, even as I live
To be inseparable from its life, to be bound to its essence
To feel its ineffable power, in the joy of this union
To know the supreme principle, manifest in my Self.'

The field became quiet and the congregation still. Heads were bowed and eyes closed. It was as if the words were settling into the ground. The blissful expresseions on some of the faces made Sarah want to laugh, but she respected the reverence they had for the natural world. She wondered what Rob would think of them.

Heads lifted and eyes opened, and she wondered whether she should clap. She was glad she didn't, as they started to get up and talk amongst themselves.

'What did you think?' Emma asked her.

'Yeah, it was interesting. I liked what she had to say.'

'That's Tamsin. She's the founder of the NWL. You're very lucky to hear her speak today. She doesn't really give hedgerow sermons anymore, but hers are the best.'

'What is NWL again?'

'The New Wilderness League. Come, I'll show you around.'

Emma led her through the village, pointing out the various buildings. There were members of the congregation already hard at work, a group of them plastering an outside wall and another busy in the market garden. The whole village of Tan-y-Fridd had been colonised by the community. Those that were not working stopped to speak with them, all of them very friendly and all of them seeming especially pleased that Sarah had come along for the day. Emma showed her around the chapel with its high and magnificent ceiling, ancient wooden pews and painted windows, now brilliantly illuminated by the sun. At the back of the chapel was the Derwen Centre shop, which sold books and artworks alongside a variety of whole foods. The room smelt strongly of incense and patchouli oil. On the wall was a rota marked with names and setting out shopkeeping duties for the months ahead. Sarah read the titles of the books on display. In pride of place were three works by Tamsin Montgomery entitled *Nature: Our Nature*, *The Path through the Woods* and *Songs for a New Wilderness*. A man entered the shop carrying a cardboard box. He was slender and middle-aged with thick-framed glasses. He apologised for his absence and introduced himself as Simon. He had a very firm handshake.

'How do you like the Derwen Centre so far?' he asked.

'It's very impressive,' she said. 'It looks like you've put a lot of hard work into it.'

'We have indeed. So where are you from, Sarah?' She told him but said how much she now liked Mid Wales. Emma waited at the shop entrance as they talked. Sarah explained that she was here with Emma and had already attended the morning session. Simon was very glad and said, that she was lucky to hear Tamsin speak.

'I would highly recommend you read one of her books. They're life-changing. Did you enjoy this morning's sermon?'

'I liked the poem everyone recited at the end,' Sarah said.

'That's our creed. You might find it a little cheesy, along with some of the things we do here, but it was written by all of us, as a group effort. We do things communally here; there are no dictators. And as you can see, we have no dress code, no robes; we wear what we like.'

As they were leaving he pushed a copy of *Nature: Our Nature* into Sarah's hands and told her that she should only pay for it if she enjoyed it. She thanked him and left with Emma.

'Simon used to be a marketing manager,' Emma said outside. 'But he quit his job as soon as he met Tamsin.' She pointed at the book in Sarah's hand. 'And he helped pay to publish that, the first of her books. Are you hungry?' She led Sarah into what must have once been a barn. It was now set out like a canteen with strip lights and rows of wooden benches, and the whole space was filled with the savoury smell of an organic café. A young man with a ponytail and wearing an apron whispered a greeting to them and seated them at one of the tables. The others present spoke to each other in subdued voices, as if it were a library, not a canteen. The woman nearest her finished what seemed to be a private prayer, opened her eyes and began to eat. The man with the ponytail brought them a light green soup in hand-carved wooden bowls. Emma closed her eyes, savouring the first spoonful. Sarah tried it. It was perfectly seasoned and felt nourishing. An old man waved at them from one of the other tables and they waved back.

'So how did you end up here?' Sarah whispered.

'I'm from Penbury originally,' Emma replied. 'I've been here nearly three years now.' It was clear she felt uncomfortable talking about the past, so Sarah asked her what she liked about the centre.

'My life didn't have any meaning before I came. I was unhappy, but everyone made me feel really welcome here. It's like having a really big family, only every single one of them cares for you. And the teachings make you feel . . . I can't describe it. People talk about being "at one" with nature but they don't really know what that means. When you truly begin to understand and see yourself for what you really are in the world, all your problems seem like nothing. You finally have a purpose and a way to get rid of them all. But you should find out for yourself. There's a beginners communing every week. You should go to it.'

'What is it?'

'You'll find out. It'll open your eyes. Trust me.'

It was better now that Rob was back. She had found it a torment to be left alone. As she watched him half-naked, sitting stooped over his desk and staring at his laptop, she worried. What was she to him? How had he been with other women, and what had ended it between them in the past? Would she be enough for him? Maybe he found her dull or disappointing, if not now, then in the future? Could she be sure of her own feelings for him?

'Robert Clare,' she said, reaching a leg out from under the bedsheets and poking his ribs with her toe.

'Yes, lovely Sarah Acton,' he said, without taking his eyes from the screen.

'What are you doing?'

'I'm studying the latest tracking data. Seeing what Scratcher's new chums are up to.'

'Oh.' She ran her foot over his bare skin. He had a dint in his nose that was just visible from this angle. She had asked him about it, but he avoided telling her how it came about. 'Did Jenny used to go with you when you were studying animals?' She had managed to get the name of his ex-girlfriend out of him a few weeks ago. They had been together for seven years. Sarah was desperate to know what she looked like and had tried hard to track her down online. He had let slip that Jenny had done some modelling work, which made Sarah moody and snappish towards him for the rest of the day.

'Do we have to talk about this?' he answered. 'We went bird watching, as she liked birds. Okay? Come on.' He shut the laptop. 'Get your boots on and let's go.'

Rob led her in a completely new direction this time, not leaving through the woods or via the track but crossing the valley floor and following a steep path that led into open moorland, where the heather was just coming into colour. There the path turned away, but they followed the breaks in the heather instead, treading between the yellow claws of bird's-foot-trefoil that grew amongst the rocks. The air around them throbbed as if with some great, invisible engine, as insects fed amongst the purple flowers or perished in the sundew's glistening tentacles. They rested in the lee of a jumble of rocks. Sarah told him all about her visit to the New Wilderness League, about the hedgerow sermon and the old chapel and the book she was given to read.

'I've heard of them,' he said. 'I knew they had the chapel at Tan-y-Fridd. I didn't know they had quite so many people living there already.' He stood up and strapped on his rucksack again. 'It sounds harmless enough. I'm not sure what standing around looking at trees is supposed to achieve though, or whatever it is they do. A fat lot of good that is, buying up land just to stare at it. Look.' He pointed out to where a wake of kites was circling.

'There's loads of them,' Sarah said.

'We're lucky we don't have grouse shooting on these moors. That lot wouldn't last long with the gamekeepers.'

They went on, leaving the moor and dropping down until the wiry clumps of heather dissolved and the ground underfoot became open grass once again. Rob was still talking about the kites.

'You know they sent the Gurkhas to guard the last kite nests here in Mid Wales from egg collectors. These were the last native British kites and . . . oh bloody hell!' He stopped walking. Ahead of them was a line of freshly laid fencing. He mumbled something under his breath and marched over to the fence. Squatting down next to it, he removed his rucksack and pulled out a pair of compact bolt cutters, then began deftly to snip through the wire.

'What are you doing?' Sarah said.

'This is a public footpath. Bloody landowners.'

'You can't do that, it's someone's property!'

'It might be their property but it's our right of way. He knew that, whoever it was that did this.'

'That's not the point, Rob. You can't just go round damaging things that don't belong to you.'

'What am I supposed to do then? They're the ones acting illegally.'

'Stop it, Rob!' He took no notice.

'Look, this will never come down. They just hope that over time our legal right of way will become forgotten about. I can show you this one on the map, along with hundreds of other rights of way that are now completely inaccessible thanks to people who do this.'

'I don't care Rob. It's wrong to do what you're doing! You should lodge a complaint or something.'

'Well, it's done now.'

'Yes, it is, isn't it?' She rattled the loose wire. 'Look at the state of it!' He shrugged.

'I can contact rights of way next time if you prefer but I'm highly sceptical they'll do anything.'

She followed him silently and at a distance afterwards. He gave up trying to start a conversation, as she would not respond. Eventually, he apologised to her, but she told him to apologise to the farmer instead. She was still angry, and there was silence nearly an hour later when they had to descend sharply down a scrubby hillside, lowering themselves on hands and rear. For a while after the slope, she thought she could feel something odd, and tried to twist herself around so that she could inspect her lower back, where her top sometimes rode up from her walking trousers, leaving a bare patch of skin.

'What is . . .? There's something . . .' Rob walked over to her.

'You've got a tick, look,' he said.

'What!'

'It's latched on and feeding.'

'Get it off me! Now!' she shouted. Rob laughed. 'Don't laugh, get it off me now!'

'I can't get it off you now. I haven't packed the tick tweezers.'

'Tick tweezers?'

'Yes, I didn't bring them, sorry. I'll get it off when we get back.' He couldn't help laughing.

'Can't you just pull it off now?'

'No, it might leave the head in and that could get infected. You'll have to wait. Come on.'

'I can feel it moving!' Sarah screamed. Rob nearly doubled over with laughter.

'No, you can't.'

'I can!'

When they were back at the cabin, Rob pinched the tick close to her skin and carefully pulled it out with the tweezers.

'There he is,' he said, holding it up for Sarah to see. 'They're arachnids, look.' Trapped by the head, she saw four pairs of legs waving feebly from a flat body.

'That is absolutely disgusting. Are you sure you've got it all out?'

'I think so. You shouldn't burn them like they used to, as they can regurgitate back into you in response. I'm surprised you were aware of it. You're lucky it didn't make its way up to your armpit.'

'Have you got anything to drink?'

'Yes, I have actually. You're lucky you spotted it. Leave it to feed for a few days and you could end up with Lyme disease.'

'What does that do?'

'Tick fever? It can kill you, if you're unlucky and don't get medical attention.'

'That's nice to know. Thanks.'

He laughed and opened some wine for her, then

dabbed her tick bite with antiseptic cream. He rested his head in her lap. They sat together in happy silence, Sarah drinking the wine and running her fingers through his hair, stroking his scalp in tender circles.

In the upland country of Mid Wales, sheep were always and everywhere grazing, from the fertile valleys to the remotest and most inaccessible of the hillsides. They had no need to fear the barrels of the farmers, which were forever aimed towards the foxes and the crows with whom they shared the green landscape. In this way they were kept safe from vulpine jaws and the corvid's beak, but they were also connected to an agricultural network that ran in lorries along roads, from field to market to slaughterhouse, a network which, through the giant ports, transcended the boundaries of the island itself.

At one of these ports, a contaminated shipment had arrived undetected, and in one of the vast pig-fattening units in the north of England, the beasts devoured it, taking the particles of virus into their very cells which were forced to replicate it until they burst. As the pigs sickened with a high fever, their breath became viral plumes, spreading the pathogen to the neighbouring sheep, whose owner, in ignorance of the infection, loaded them into a lorry destined for the market at Carlisle. Before any alarm had been raised, the network was spreading the virus across the country, with live-transit lorry loads moving between the major livestock hubs and at least one infected consignment destined for the cattle market at Powispoole. In this way the damage was done, and a plague came to the hills of central Wales.

14

Rob's dismissal of the New Wilderness League persuaded Sarah to return to the Derwen Centre as Emma had suggested. She was growing frustrated at always feeling inferior in knowledge and needed to do something away from him. Besides, it was not only about Emma's persistence; Sarah had come round to liking her and agreed to attend the next beginners communing session.

She made sure she was early this time and met Emma outside the old chapel, where a group was gathering in readiness for the session. The woman leading the group shook her hand and introduced herself as Ruth. She had a long nose and chin, and her hair was cut close to her head and tapered sharply into short stubble at her neckline. Though she was dressed in outdoor clothes like the rest, hers were meticulously clean and she had an overall neatness, as if she were attending an interview or inspection, rather than an outdoor gathering. She kept a stern expression on her face, of the kind Sarah imagined a Victorian schoolmistress might wear. At precisely two o'clock, she addressed Sarah, Emma and the five others assembled.

'Welcome all. It's lovely to have so many of you here on this beginners session. I recognise a number of you but can see one or two new faces, so we'll start with the very basics, try a little session indoors first and then we'll go out into the woods, before coming back for a final indoor session and discussion. Is that okay with everyone? We're not going far today, as it's a beginners session. There are several wild spaces we've secured across the mountain but we're best to keep the initial walk short to start off with. Now, does anyone have any medical conditions I should know of?'

Ruth led the group inside the chapel and invited them to sit in the pews as she made sure the doors were closed and pulled the curtains shut across the small windows.

She stood in front of them, below the pulpit and underneath the illuminated windows.

'So what is communing?' she said. 'For the benefit of those of you who are new, have you ever looked out across an ocean and felt a deep sense of peace? Have you ever been bowled over by the beauty of a mountain range? Has the sound of a river moving made you feel supremely calm? Have you ever lost yourself in a wood until you're overwhelmed with awe at the majesty of the trees that surround you? Once, I rode a camel with an adventure group into the desert and we were all rendered speechless when the scenery around us finally flattened, and there was nothing but sand in every direction. No one could talk, it was just too powerful an experience.'

The chapel reverberated with this new sermon. Motes of dust smoked around her in the coloured light. 'What we are not told is that these are experiences that can be cultivated. And we don't need great mountain ranges or endless forests. We can create them right here, in our very own wildernesses.

So why would we want to do this? Throughout history, ascetics, hermits, yogis, have all gone to the wilderness to seek wisdom and experience. Only by being close to the natural world and experiencing its power does revelation come. Only by being able to still and calm our busy minds can we truly experience peace and develop any sort of understanding. And that is what we are going to do today. We are going to shut off the noise of our minds and concentrate our awareness. We are going to ignore all else, until we are aware only of ourselves and the nature around us. Once we can effectively still our minds, we can become open to the truest understanding that comes from experience. Sure we can read books and watch programmes about how nature is connected, or what the world can teach us about ourselves, but this is nothing compared to the real, life-changing, transformative awareness that comes from *experiential* understanding, not intellectual understanding. Perhaps this all sounds a bit wordy, so the best thing now is for us to begin.

By trying for yourselves, you might better understand what I'm talking about. So . . .'

She went over to the window and took hold of a long pole that was resting against the wall. Taking the weight of the pole at her shoulder, she dragged across an enormous, heavy curtain that had been affixed above the windows, until the last of the light was extinguished. In a measured and markedly softer voice, she spoke to them through the darkness, directing them to sit with back straight, hands on knees, head slightly lowered, eyes loosely closed and tongue resting behind the teeth.

'We're going to start by concentrating only on our breathing. Whenever our awareness wanders, we're going to bring our awareness back to our breathing and we'll do the same outside.'

She asked them to think first about the space outside the chapel, then inside, then starting with the crown of their heads, asked them all to run down the length of their bodies with their minds, relaxing each area in turn, releasing any tension.

'Now, just place your awareness at the edge of your nostrils. Watch the breath going in and out. Just concentrate on that sensation. Don't try and control your breathing, just observe it. You're going to start thinking of things in the past and things in the future. You'll find your mind just doesn't want to keep still. All sorts of thoughts will try to interrupt your concentration. Don't get cross when you find your concentration wandering, just bring your awareness back to your breathing. Every time you find yourself thinking about something else, calmly go back to your breathing.'

She repeated something similar every few minutes. At first it seemed easy, and Sarah wondered what could possibly be the point of it all. Then she realised her mind was playing a tune over and over that had been on the kitchen radio at work the previous day. She went back to her breathing but found herself wondering what Rob was doing, then planning her meal for that evening, then remembering something funny John had said a couple of weeks ago. Each time she did as Ruth said, but even when she became aware that she was successfully sustaining her concentration, the thought of that small sense of achievement interrupted it. She tried to stop remonstrating with herself for letting her thoughts wander and then she found herself fighting sleep. After a while though, her mind became more still. Arbitrary images entered her consciousness unannounced: a corridor of the office in which she used to work, the inside of Michael's car, the dandelions from her childhood, a hotel room in which she had stayed many years ago. Eventually, even these subsided and an intoxicating heaviness settled upon her as the last ripples of her thoughts became still, and there was only the slow, deep, in and out of her breath. Other unwelcome thoughts still intruded, but it became easier to let go of them and to go back to her breathing. Time seemed to dissolve and there was only stillness. Without knowing how long it had been, in the depths of her concentration, Sarah became aware of a voice and the drawing back of the curtain. She was enjoying her tranquil state and did not want to be stirred from it. Ruth said that she did not want to disturb their minds any more than necessary at this point, only to lead them out of the chapel and into the woods together. They were to form a chain and try their best not to let their minds be distracted on the way. If they wanted to, they could change their object of concentration to their feet.

The group left the chapel in a line, and for most of the time Sarah looked at the ground as they climbed the hill towards the nearby woods. It seemed astonishingly bright, and the air was scented and cool against her face. As directed, each of them had a hand on the shoulder of the person in front. Emma was behind her. It reminded Sarah of the pictures she had seen of soldiers that had been gassed in the First World War, but that was thinking about something else, so instead she switched her awareness to the steady rhythm of her walking. Like the in-out of her breath, she watched her feet as she had not done since she was a child, moving back and forth, one and two, over and over. They reached a clearing in the woods where Ruth arranged them in a circle.

She told them to close their eyes and they went back to their breathing, as it had been in the chapel.

'In a moment we're going to open our eyes and separate,' she said. 'Try to keep your minds free of all distracting thoughts. It is time to encounter the landscape. Allow your now heightened awareness to explore your surroundings. Look, touch, smell, listen, taste if you like, but keep your focus. Direct yourselves. See what understanding comes. If you find your awareness diminishing, close your eyes and go back to your breathing for a while. Go now, each of you. She held up a small whistle. I will call you when it is time to go back.'

Sarah peeled away from the swiftly dissolving circle and moved under the nearest of the trees until her nose almost touched its trunk. The bark was raised in vertical ridges and the grey skin was dusted with green and encrusted with sage-coloured frills of lichen. Its surface was cracked, like mud baked dry by the sun, and she reached out to brush against its course texture with her hand. The trilling of a bird sounded in the distance. Wood warbler, she thought, then realised this was not concentrating. She went back to examining the tree, closing her eyes and drawing in the odour of the bark which carried a damp sweetness that was unlike the cut wood she had become used to. Sunlight pushed its fingers between the limbs above and broke upon the outspread leaves, leaving a mottled brightness that played about her. There was a captivating keenness to her own senses. Her mind was both playful and utterly absorbed, as if she were a child again, watching raindrops running down the car window next to her. It came to her then that the group of people she had happened upon on her very first morning in Mid Wales must have been NWL members communing in the woods. Strange that she should find herself amongst them now. As the thoughts came, she found herself losing focus and so closed her eyes, bringing her mind back from its wandering and drawing in the breath of the woodland once again.

On the following Sunday, Sarah closed the door to the cottage and straightened out Rob's collar for him.

'This is a nice shirt,' she said.

'Are you sure I shouldn't have brought some wine or something?'

'No. It's only lunch. Come on.'

She had finally got him to come for lunch at the farmhouse with her, having refused any further walks together until he agreed upon a date. She ushered him in through the farmhouse door and into the narrow hallway where the air was fragrant with roasting fat. Sioned and Evan were waiting for them in the kitchen and rose from the table to greet them.

'This is Rob. Rob, this is Sioned and Evan.' Rob went to shake Evan's hand but banged his head on one of the low beams of the kitchen ceiling before he could get to him. Sioned winced.

'Mind your head,' Evan said, smiling. He shook his hand.

'Lovely to meet you both. I'm sorry I haven't brought anything.'

'No, don't be silly.' Sioned said. 'We don't need anything. Sit down, sit down.'

'Now that's a proper table,' Rob said, knocking at the table top as they sat down. 'Something smells good.' He thanked Sioned as she served him first, placing a hot plate of roasted lamb and potatoes and boiled vegetables in front of him, all of it soused in a steaming, nut-brown gravy. Evan was first to start once they were all seated and served. Sarah glanced up from her food as she ate. She wanted Sioned to like Rob and was looking out for her approval.

'Mmm, lovely,' Rob said. 'This is the first meat I've had since that squirrel.' Sioned and Evan stared at him.

'Yes, Rob's new hobby is eating roadkill,' Sarah said.

'Really?' Sioned asked. Sarah smiled and nodded. 'Well, I never! Eating squirrel, Evan. Have you ever heard?'

'Squirrel!' Evan said, laughing, then the four of them were laughing together.

'You should try it,' Rob said. 'It's free, it's an invader, what's not to like?' He gestured towards the window. 'You have a lovely view from here, by the way'. Evan nodded, his mouth full of food.

'Yes, you can see out to the clock tower at Hen Gaer from the top of the bryn,' Sioned said. 'There's some more gravy here, Sarah, if you want it.'

'Thanks,' Sarah said. 'Where did you go early this morning in the Renault?'

'It was my turn to visit Brian and Gwyneira, poor things. Gwyneira's at death's door. Brian's still deaf as a post.'

'No change there,' Evan said. 'Where is it you've come from today then?' he said to Rob. Rob described the location of the reserve, talking them through the exits along the main road until they recognised the one that led there.

'Oh, it's down by Pendinas, Evan. Have you met Bron then?' Sioned asked.

Sarah did not know the woman, but Rob clearly did, though he looked surprised that Sioned should know her.

'You know Bron? Yes, she keeps us on our toes. I wouldn't like to cross her, that's for sure!'

Evan pointed his knife at Rob as he chewed, nodding in fierce agreement. He finished his mouthful. 'What is it then, pasture or woodland?' he asked.

Rob answered by describing the layout of the centre, not giving any acreage but listing its areas by habitat. He went on, talking about the conference facilities at the Ark and listing the famous names that had spoken there. Sarah tried to explain who some of them were, but it seemed that neither Evan nor Sioned recognised any of them. Rob was still going even as Evan was close to clearing his plate. She wondered whether she should change the subject.

'Do they give you funding for that then?' Evan asked.

'Yes and no. We're a charitable trust, so we try to raise most of the money to cover costs ourselves.'

'The eggs are selling faster than the hens can lay them,' Sarah said to Sioned, but she was too preoccupied with the men's lunches.

'That's great,' she said with her back to her, readying more of the lamb.

'Yes, very nice they are too,' Rob said before turning back to Evan. 'Are all these fields yours then?' Evan described the borders of the farm, though he left out the woods his father had sold.

'Oh, talking about funding,' Rob said when he had finished, 'they're debating bringing in a new scheme as part of the greening of subsidies.' He laid his knife and fork down together on his empty plate. Sioned looked pleased. He explained the proposed arrangements which involved altering payment of subsidies to encourage farmers to leave land aside, untouched. Evan was sceptical.

'Sounds all topsy-turvy to me. Why should they pay farmers to do nothing with the land? That's like paying us not to farm.'

'It sounds like a win-win situation to me,' Rob said, sitting straighter in his chair. 'Farmers are still in business, and we have a healthier landscape, greater biodiversity and so on.'

'Doesn't sound like my cup of tea,' Evan said dismissively.

'Well, with all due respect, it might have to become your cup of tea. I don't think we'll be paying the farmers over the odds to keep sheep forever.'

Sioned stood up and began to collect the plates.

'I'd like to see what everyone'll eat when there's no farmers,' Evan said. 'People like sheep anyway. Don't you? They're wildlife, aren't they?'

'Not really. They're originally from Iraq. Hence why they've radically transformed our native landscape.' Sarah scowled at him, but he took no notice. Sioned was readying the pudding.

'They're Welsh now though aren't they?' Evan said, forcing a smile. 'There's nothing more Welsh than sheep!' He was clearly finding this difficult. Sarah was already preparing what she would say to Rob later.

'But is it right they should be a symbol of Wales when they strip her hillsides, leaving everything bare and barren?'

Sarah aimed a kick at his ankle under the table, but her foot jarred against his chair leg instead. This was not what she had expected. Even with her back to her, she could sense Sioned's unease and tried to change the subject. 'They're saying it's going to be a really hot summer,' she said.

Evan ignored her. 'Farmers make a living off these hillsides,' he said. 'Having a load of trees and birds isn't going to pay the bills.'

'But this is the problem.' Rob was becoming more animated. He gesticulated as he spoke. 'People see it as all about money. How much money can we make from the land? What can we do to it to extract more money?'

'Do we look rich to you?' Evan countered, hotter now. 'Where's all this money?'

Sioned poured custard on the last of the puddings and set a bowl before each of them. She kept her eyes on the table when she sat down.

'This is precisely the point. The irony is that most of you farmers are losing money. We pay you good money to keep these hillsides lifeless. And then when we try and find a solution so we can pay farmers the same not to abuse the landscape, you don't want to know, do you.'

Sarah found her mark under the table this time, but Rob did not look away from Evan.

'Rob!' she said.

'Farmers work hard for their money,' Evan said. 'Do you understand that? No one's going to pay us to go tramping all over the countryside, all over people's private property, just to look at some birds!' His scalp had grown red under the thin curls of his hair.

'Evan! That's enough,' Sioned said, but Rob was in full flow now.

'It doesn't matter how many furrows you've scranleted, or whatever. What matters is the sheep chewing the hills to nothing and the rain washing straight off them and the banks bursting further downriver and flooding half of England.'

'Rob, shut up!' Sarah shouted at him.

'And the countryside is for everyone, not just for landowners,' he added, ignoring Sarah.

Evan stood up sharply, sending his chair skidding across the tiles where it came to rest against the range behind him. 'Do you think we have it easy? Do you think we don't care about our farms and our land? You want us to all leave our homes to make way for people like you?'

'Evan, sit down!' Sioned shouted at him. The puddings were untouched.

'No, I don't think you care, if your idea of looking after the land is "keeping the place tidy", ripping up shrubs and trees, killing the moles, putting down pesticides that decimate everything. What about sheep dips? They were a great idea, weren't they? And don't tell me it doesn't still go on illegally.'

Sarah jumped up from the table and barged her way past him. Unable to bear the embarrassment any longer, she stormed away from the kitchen, stabbing her feet back into her boots and marching out into the farmyard beyond, her untied shoelaces whipping bursts of powder from the dry earth. She stood by the cattle grid, too ashamed to even bring herself to look behind her at the farmhouse. Soon, she heard the slow approach of Rob's footsteps and whirled round.

'What the fuck was that?' she screamed at him.

'I'm sorry.'

'You're sorry?'

'Well, it pisses me off.'

She cut him off before he could go on. 'It doesn't matter,' she said. 'You don't do that. You don't say those sorts of things to people! You're their guest. Why can't you just keep it to yourself? I can't believe you've just embarrassed me like that!'

'Sorry. It's just . . . people don't understand. It's so frustrating this attitude. These hills should be full of goshawks, not crows.'

'Stop. Just stop. What do you think gives you the right to behave like that? What is this enormous fucking privilege you have that means you can treat people however you like? Are they just ignorant peasants to you?'

'No. Of course not.' He looked away. He went to

speak but at that moment a fighter jet tore down the valley, banking as it passed and revealing its triangular underside before disappearing. The scream of the jet split the air so savagely, his words were lost in its thunder. He waited for the noise to subside.

'I'm just always trying hard to do what's right,' he said.

'What's right? And what is right, Rob? Is it feeling so justified, you . . .' This time Sarah was silenced by a second fighter jet which followed the path of its sister aircraft, setting the valley trembling again for what felt like minutes.

'You know what?' Sarah said when she was sure she could be heard again. 'It doesn't matter.' She walked away from him towards the cottage, stopping once and turning around. 'Goodbye, Rob,' she said.

15

News of the discovery of the infection broke the following day. On television, in newspapers, online, the virus occupied every headline. Nationwide movement of stock was halted immediately, but the disease had already been spread about the country, and the number of reported cases increased by the hour. The news showed graphics of the progress of the disease. Multiple yellow skull and crossbones appeared, clustering in Mid Wales and other areas. Footage was shown of farm animals crowded into barns, interspersed with scenes of men emerging from vehicles, dressed head to toe in white coveralls. Infected animals were rendered useless as livestock, and in harbouring the contagion, represented a severe risk to neighbouring farms. Interviews moved from nervous farmers to furious union leaders. Epidemiologists began to speak of an epizootic and MPs were accused of paralysis. Areas identified as infected were sealed off with blue and white police tape and disinfecting stations appeared everywhere, with buckets and scrubbing brushes marking the previously invisible borders between lands. The footpaths were closed and all movement across the countryside other than that deemed essential for landowners was prohibited.

With the world around her in the grip of a fever, Sarah moved between the triangle of work, supermarket and home but otherwise did little else. She ignored Rob's calls and messages; that was easy after Michael. She saw no way ahead, other than to cut him out as well. At first, she thought about leaving for home and staying with Gill as she had asked. Then, emboldened by her last escape, she thought about moving again, only further this time. She had proved to herself that she could do it; it was just a matter of wiping the slate clean once more. The roots she had put down were far shorter this time and would be far easier to pull up. She thought about moving to Ireland, or to France, or buying a boat with her savings, or a one-way ticket to another continent. Life was a well of limitless experience. There were festivals to go to, drugs to try. She could learn a new language, or sleep with another woman, or live in an ashram in India. She might end up a croupier in a casino or a therapist helping others. She pictured herself living in a cave by the Mediterranean somewhere, catching fish for food and cooking them on a fire on the beach. Mostly though, she felt too tired to do anything. The weight of it all had exhausted her and it was as much as she could do to get to work and back. Work was something unspoilt at least and broke up the monotony of being in the cottage, staring at the same ancient walls. It was untrue what people said: there are no soulmates. It was just luck that brought people together, nothing more, and with her luck there was little chance things would ever go right for her. Perhaps she was just not the sort of person who should be in a relationship.

John and Emma both said they were worried about her, and she herself was conscious of how slow she moved and how little she now spoke. Even Malcolm had asked her three times so far if she was all right. She felt distanced from her own body, which seemed to move in spite of her, and her gaze was almost permanently lowered, so she noticed little of what went on around her. In this way she was surprised when, returning from a shift at the pub, she nearly walked into Richard's van, which was parked across her usual route along the farmyard towards the cottage. Both rear doors were open, exposing the jumble of contents inside. She could make out a covered shotgun and some giant lamps, but there was also a confusion of metal, of the kind displayed at the old ironmongers at Penbury. She looked closer and saw devices there she did not recognise, some of them displaying serrated edges, like rows of rusted teeth.

'Having a nosey, are you?'

Sarah started at the voice; she had not heard Richard approach.

'No,' she said.

'Looks like it to me,' Richard said. He grasped the

open doors in each hand, trapping Sarah between him and the van. 'Something I can help you with?'

'No,' Sarah said again.

'You been having some trouble with that man of yours? The lanky English one?'

'No.'

'Cos if you were, I could help out, like. Always happy to help a girl.'

She refused to respond and barged against one of his arms to get past, but he resisted, gripping hard onto the door so that she found herself leaning against him. She stepped back and met his eyes, fixing him with her stare.

'Did you want something?' he said.

'No. You're in my way.'

'You could ask me nicely to move out of the way.'

'I'm not asking you for anything. You're not letting me go.'

He let go of one of the doors and with faux graciousness, gestured towards her way out. As she moved past, he let his arm fall from the door so that his fingers brushed against her. She wanted to run towards the cottage but resisted in case that might gratify him in some way. She could hear him laughing but did not turn around. Energised with rage, she paced up and down the cottage, determined to do something about him. She had tried not to let him get to her in the past but right now, on top of everything that had happened, she was furious with him. An idea came to her, and she tipped over the rubbish bin onto the lino floor by the sink. She rummaged through the putrefying contents until she came to a bundle of tissues near the bottom. When she had what she wanted, she went quietly out of the cottage and waited for Richard to disappear into the old barn before creeping over to his van. Slowly and as quietly as possible, she opened the passenger door. The door pocket was filled with sweet wrappers and other rubbish. She dropped one of the two empty condom packets she had with her into it and covered it with some of the wrappers and pushed the other one down the back of the seat for good measure. There was no way of predicting when they would be discovered but it was the best she could think of for the moment. Pleased with her work, she got back into her car and drove away from the farmyard.

After a sodden winter, the spring had been unusually dry. Now the warmth of summer was setting in, with the dry spell predicted to continue. As the soil hardened, the earthworms retreated deeper underground. Lizards basked above them on the open rocks, readying for the hunt, and the once glistening molehills, now pale and desiccated, crumbled in the heat of the sun. Along the hedgerows that lined the roadside, the bindweed had opened into white bugles, and swallows flitted about Sarah's car, unnoticed by its miserable driver. When she passed the giant dairy farm a little way beyond Hen Gaer, she paid no attention to the police tape strung along its perimeter, or the crowd of vehicles belonging to the valuers and others that now crowded the farmyard. The land around her was changing. The official advice from the government on containing the infection was unclear and many had begun to take matters into their own hands. In desperation, farmers were sealing themselves in, barricading the smaller lanes with bales of disinfected straw. Unable to lose herself in the hills as she wanted to, either by car or on foot, Sarah thought she would visit Emma at the Derwen Centre instead. It was well removed from Afon Twymyn reserve and Hafod Farm, and she had been made to feel welcome there, plus Emma was neutral and a friend, and had offered to talk with her. The more she thought about it as she drove, the better the idea seemed.

Emma lived in one of the converted farm buildings at the Derwen Centre. She had shown Sarah her room the last time she had visited. Sarah left her car in the official visitor parking and was greeted by several NWL members as she tried to remember which entrance they had used last time. She had no way of contacting Emma, as she had told her that mobiles were distracting and were discouraged at the centre, and there was no Wi-Fi available, other than that supplied to the senior members who ran the official office at the old chapel. When she found what she thought was the correct door, she knocked and waited. She knocked again and there was still no response, but as she came away from the doorway, the door opened, and an old man greeted her.

'Hello, my dear,' the man said. 'Can I help you?' He had an estuary accent and wore a threadbare dressing gown over his clothes. His crepe paper skin showed at his neckline and his face was poorly shaved, perhaps due to failing eyesight, as his soft-looking eyes were magnified by a pair of chunky glasses.

'I was looking for Emma,' Sarah said.

'Yes, she's here. Come in. Come in love.'

'Sorry to bother you.' She stepped inside.

'Don't be silly, love. I'll take you through.'

She followed behind the man. He made slow progress, shuffling tentatively down the corridor in a pair of tattered slippers before stopping outside an open door. Inside, several women were seated on sofas around a coffee table. One of them was wiping tears from her face and smiling as another two embraced her. Emma looked up at her from one of the other sofas and came over immediately.

'Hi,' she said.

'I'm so sorry to turn up without any warning,' Sarah said.

'No, it's fine. Here.' She closed the door on the room behind her. 'We've just been on a communing. It's been quite emotional for Julie. You've met Walter then?' The old man was working his way further down the corridor. He turned around slowly and waved.

'Hello, Walter', Sarah said.

'Do you want a tea?' Emma asked. 'Let's go through to the kitchen.' They caught up with Walter and waited for him to enter the kitchen at the end of the corridor. Emma opened one of the cupboards and Walter reversed into a soft chair in the corner of the kitchen. 'What sort of tea would you like?' She listed half a dozen different varieties.

'I'll have rooibos, thank you,' Sarah said.

'Tea, Walter?'

'Usual, thank you, sweetheart,' he answered.

They sat together at a table with their tea.

'So,' Emma said. 'Did you end it, or did he?' The question took Sarah by surprise. She hesitated a moment.

'I did,' she said.

'What happened?'

She told her, reluctantly at first, skipping over the details, before eventually recounting everything that had happened. She told her about Michael, about Gill, about her journey to Wales. She told her about the farm, about how she had barely spoken with Sioned since the day of the argument. Other league members came in and out of the kitchen, making their own drinks, or stopping to talk with one another. Walter snoozed in his chair as another man updated a noticeboard behind him. They drank another tea and then another. Emma told her about her parents splitting up when she was in her early teens, how she had hated her mum's new boyfriend who moved in with them, that his moving-in 'present' to Emma was a box of contraceptives he left on her bed, which he found hilarious, and how she moved out shortly afterwards at sixteen. They talked until the sunlight from the window moved and fell upon the snoozing Walter and across the table before them, lighting up the grain of the wood, their steadily cooling drinks, and the silvery slashes on Emma's arm. Emma excused herself, and another man entered the room and greeted her.

'Sarah! Lovely to see you.' It was Simon, whom she had met in the shop previously. He shook her hand. 'Do you mind if I join you?' He asked how she was, and she pretended that all was fine out of politeness. She asked after the centre, again out of politeness, and Emma returned to find Simon talking about the NWL's latest acquisition of land.

'It's a meadow, not far from here and very beautiful. I can't claim any credit for it. It's all Ruth's doing. She's a financial whizz. Used to be a solicitor in her former life. Have you been to the meadow, Emma?'

'Yes, for the first time today. It's lovely. We had a communing that had a really powerful effect on Julie and in a very good way.'

'Well, they can be very healing and empowering things, communings,' Simon said. Have you been on a communing yet, Sarah?' Sarah said that she had. He asked her to describe the experience. She remembered mostly how peaceful it had felt but was amazed with herself for how clearly she could recall the experience.

'That's great,' Simon said. 'We'd love to have you on another. I found it really helped me to work through all my hang-ups and bugbears. Just being able to talk it through with others afterwards is really cathartic. The Japanese do something similar called 'forest bathing'.' Sarah sat listening as Emma fetched some biscuits, offering one to Walter in his chair. 'But this is what science is telling us,' Simon went on. 'That health and happiness are directly linked with immersion in the natural world. In the city we're suffocated and bombarded by stimuli, and I think our lives suffer accordingly. They've found that in the countryside our attention improves, and our creativity is demonstrably better. There's now a proven increase in energy and vitality, corresponding to the time we spent outdoors. Urbanisation has pretty much led to an epidemic of depression and mental ill health. Anyway, I'm going on again. I'll shut up and leave you two alone now. Hope to see you again, Sarah. See you, Walter.' Walter waved as Simon exited the room.

Half an hour later, Sarah felt that the biscuits had just made her hungry. Her conversation with Emma had not been the same after the interruption, though it was clear that they shared an understanding that had not been there before. Walter groaned as he struggled to get out of his chair.

'Are you going for food, Walter?' Emma asked.

'Starving,' he said.

'Here, we'll come with you. You ready for some food?' she asked Sarah.

They accompanied Walter to the canteen, opening doors for him and supporting him over a rough section of cobbles. The canteen was busier this time and the many subdued voices formed a constant murmur in the background.

They were brought a cheese and pasta bake this time, which Walter devoured in moments. Emma ate hers slowly and mindfully, concentrating intensely upon every mouthful. A woman with a shaved head walked past and sat down alone at a distance from them, further along the table. With his plate clear, Walter spoke to Sarah. He was a little deaf, speaking at a volume far higher than the other members present, although they did not seem to mind him.

'Course, we used to smoke in them days, keep the flies off. Where those fields were is all houses now.' He was telling her about his time working in the fields as a youth. 'We used to eat the celery straight out of the ground. Tasted beautiful. Not like the stuff they have in the supermarkets now.'

'Is that why you ended up here when you retired?' Sarah asked. 'To be away from the city again?'

'I was retired a long time before I came out here.' He paused for a moment, trying and failing to catch the attention of one of the servers. 'Never had a wife or any children and my sister lives in a home in Plymouth. Why live a lonely old life when people look after you here? I'd rather my pension goes to something worthwhile like this place. Course I've always loved the natural world. Used to collect bugs as a nipper. We even used to go nesting, I'm sorry to say. There was one main reason I came here though.' This time his waving was noticed, and his empty plate was exchanged for a bowl of vegan ice cream, which he began as soon as it was set in front of him. The woman with the shaved head began to cry. No one seemed particularly concerned. Walter jerked his thumb in her direction and then tapped his temple.

'What was the reason?' Sarah said eventually.

'What was the reason what? Oh. Death,' he said.

'Death?'

'Death, my love. Comes to us all. Especially old fogies like me,' he said, winking. 'I could never bring myself to believe in God and heaven and all that. Doesn't seem very likely. There was a boy that lived on our street when I was growing up. He got ill and his head swelled up like a balloon. He was dead within weeks. Now why would God go and do a thing like that? Poor little bloke.' He threw down his spoon and patted his stomach. 'What's going to happen when you die? Do you think you'll be a ghost? Where will you be without a body? What age will you be? Will you be well or ill? How long will you be around for? Will you be able to visit places, contact the living? It doesn't make sense. There's more questions than answers. I met Tamsin when she was giving a talk when I was still down in London. I said to her, "I'm terrified of dying, petrified!" She told me that deep within us all, when you strip everything away, there is the bit that's essentially you. Raw consciousness she called it. It's like our very selves. Not like a spirit that can float about without a body or anything daft like that, but like our very essence. And that essence, that's no different from the essence in all life, in all living things, it's just we feel like it's different, and we spend our lives worrying about stupid things. When we die, our bodies will make more life and so will our minds. This raw consciousness will just be part of more life. It's like our souls get recycled the same as our bodies. Isn't that a wonderful thought? So you see, there's no need to be afraid of dying.'

Emma tapped Sarah's arm, as she had not noticed the person waiting to take her plate. She thanked them but when she looked back at Walter, his head was nodding with sleep.

Sarah felt better on the drive home, as if some small distance had been placed between her and what had happened. She would start that book that Simon had given her on her first visit when she got back. Just as she thought this, she passed the great dairy farm on her way back into Hen Gaer. There the cattle, whose mouths and hooves had broken out into angry blisters, were being prepared for slaughter. A colossal pyre had been laid, for the government had rejected mass vaccination and settled on a contiguous cull, and across the countryside the killing had begun on a massive scale.

16

Coming home from work later that week, Sarah was diverted across the river and had to use the back road home, along with all the other traffic. The crisis had escalated to the point where the government had been forced to draft in the armed forces, and the people of Marcherton had stopped to watch as convoys of dark green lorries passed through the town. Roads were closed off so that military engineers could help construct the pyres for the slaughtered animals and prevent smoke from drifting dangerously across the roads. Disinfecting stations were established, manned by squads of uniformed men, and drivers slowed as they passed the curious sight of camouflage on the narrow lanes of the hills. As she came into Hen Gaer, Sarah was flagged down by one of the soldiers. She wound down the window for him to speak.

'Can you tell me where you're headed today?' he asked. She told him. He looked surprisingly young and had a white spot under his chin, crying out to be squeezed. The men behind him held pump washers in place of assault rifles. He seemed satisfied and asked if his men could disinfect the car. She agreed gladly; it was tiresome having to wash it down each day. It seemed a futile gesture compared with the task they faced in trying to prevent the spread of the infection. The Cambrian Mountains stretched almost the entire length of Wales. Sarah had seen how isolated some of the farms were, and they sent animals to graze in gullies that could barely be reached. Whatever the government department had calculated, there was no mathematical model that could predict just how many sheep there were, deep within those mountains.

When she arrived back at the farm, she dunked the scrubbing brush into the bucket of disinfectant that had been left out and scrubbed her shoes down as usual whilst the tractor went past. She started to make her way down to the cottage, but there was a loud shout behind her.

'Oi!' Evan had stopped the tractor and thrown open the cab door. He jumped down, leaving the engine running, and came towards her.

'And the car as well.' He pointed towards it. 'Boots and wheels, every time in, every time out.'

'The car's been done already,' she said. 'Some soldiers cleaned it when I was passing through Hen Gaer.' He looked taken aback for a moment, but his face hardened again.

'So do it again. You could have picked something up on the way back.'

'It's only a few miles Evan. I'm sure I wouldn't have.'

'You can't be sure of anything.'

'Okay. Well, the soldiers know what they're doing,' she said.

'How do we know that?' he said. 'They're not from round here.'

'I'm sure they do. I know what to do and I'm not from round here.'

'No, you're not, are you.' For a moment there was only the diesel grumble from the tractor. 'Do it again,' Evan said and went back over to the tractor. Sarah watched as he drove out of the farmyard, the great wheels battering the cattle grid and throwing out clumps of dried-on sludge behind them. She saw Sioned leaving the farmhouse and waited for her to come over.

'What did he say?' she asked.

'Nothing.' Sarah said. 'How's things?'

Sioned rolled her eyes. 'Ceri's in a foul mood and she's not saying why. Richard's got a mark on his face and he's not saying how. And you know what he's been like.' She nodded towards the tractor making its way down the lane. 'He's doing my head in.'

'What about the animals?' Sarah asked.

'Fine, so far,' Sioned said. 'It's the government that's the problem. They're saying they can't compensate farmers properly for livestock lost. It could be the end for all of us.'

'I'm sure it won't,' Sarah said, disappointed with

herself for how unconvincing it sounded. 'You're all right though, aren't you?'

Sioned gave her a weak smile. 'I'm sorry Sarah. I'm sorry for everything.'

'Don't be,' she said, putting her arms around her. It felt different hugging her, more of a farewell than a reassurance. They said goodbye and she climbed down to the cottage, closing the door on the landscape behind her where, in the far distance, the pyre at the dairy farm was ablaze. The smoke billowed and rose in a column, high into the air, so that all who lived in the three adjoining valleys could see the rise of that bitter pillar that was the colour of death.

Sarah was enjoying *Nature: Our Nature*. Tamsin wrote well, breaking down her more complex, philosophical arguments into easy steps and providing many relevant, everyday examples. There was still some dense theology in there that she was not used to reading, but it was much more engaging than the drier books on landscape management Rob had lent her; he had no time for arguments that were neither objective nor empirical. A good deal of the book seemed to be spent outlining the concept of the Self, which Tamsin described as the fundamental essence of each of us, upon which everything about us as individuals is based. Tamsin likened the Self to what other religions and movements describe as the 'spirit' or 'soul'. She wrote that just like the Self, there exists a similar supreme underlying principle behind nature and the universe; what many might think of as God. Our greatest mistake, she argued, is that we think of ourselves as separate from nature, when in fact we are identical in essence to it. The essence of each of us and of the universe around us are one and the same. Tamsin called this 'Natural Monism'.

It was enough to bring Sarah back to attend a second hedgerow sermon. She found the communings she attended over the following weeks helpful as well. Her mind felt calmer and clearer. She felt more in control, as if she now had some power to direct her thoughts away from the worries and unpleasant memories which followed her. There was no need to dwell on the recent past. She bought up more of the books from the Derwen Centre shop and devoured them when alone in the evenings.

Spending time at the Derwen Centre, Sarah became aware of just how much the New Wilderness League had achieved within a relatively short space of time. The movement was growing fast, and the league held ambitious goals for the future, seeking to quadruple the number of 'wildland' sites it owned for communings and sermons within the next two years, as well as to establish two new centres beginning as satellite annexes to the Derwen Centre. This expansion was possible partly due to the continuing fall in land and property prices locally but mainly through shrewd investment of the donations of its members, who themselves worked there in their free time, cooking, cleaning, coppicing, gardening and so on. Multiple buildings were being renovated at once, with the league counting builders, carpenters, plasterers and an electrician amongst its number, combined with an endless supply of labour. All of this was made possible under the directorship of Tamsin, Ruth and Simon, who ran the centre as a trio, though votes were held regularly to decide upon more mundane issues.

The spread of the virus had affected the league, but three of its wildland sites were at a sufficient distance from livestock to allow legal access, though this did not stop its members from being regularly challenged by farmers and other landowners. Frantic with worry, many farmers were spending days and nights awake patrolling their lands, desperate to keep away anyone or anything that could potentially be carrying the infection. For those whose animals succumbed to the virus, the sentence was bleak. Helpless to prevent the onset of its symptoms, they could only watch as eyes became unresponsive and lameness and dehydration set in, followed by lesions, blisters and a frothing at the mouth. They were asked to help with the slaughter of their own animals and the building of the pyres. Bales of straw were stacked, along with old railway sleepers and even coal, and all of it soaked in red diesel, whilst the men in their white coveralls did their grisly work. Vets stood by as the animals voided themselves in fear, before slaughtermen raised bolt guns to their heads, firing speeding steel into the creatures' brains, then standing back as the legs collapsed to wait for the convulsions to subside, before driving a second rod, stained blue, into each bloody hole. Front loaders scooped up the blue-sprayed carcases, half skewering some of them in the process and loaded them onto the pyres. The larger cattle were carried in chains to the pyres and raised high into the air by diggers, ready to be roasted. As the flames swaddled the stacked carcases, the men stood back from the terrible heat and watched the stiff-legged corpses blacken and burst. Some wept openly at the sight, others held back until the men had left. For all of them, even when the pits had been dug and the remains buried, that smell: the sickly, fatty, acrid, charred and calamitous stench of it all, would stay with them for life.

At work, Malcolm was morbidly obsessed with the unfolding crisis and would follow John and Sarah round the kitchen reading out articles from the local newspaper whilst they tried to work. There was to be a meeting held locally, open to the public, where spokespeople from the various communities could register their interest in speaking. Unable to attend himself, Malcolm asked Sarah to go, saying it was a 'fact-finding' mission but really wanting her to report back with all the gossip. She found the community hall at which the meeting was being held at the foot of yet another castle ruin and had to park by the church and walk up to it, as the car park and street were crowded with vehicles. The doors and windows of the hall were open, revealing the press of people inside. She was early, though clearly not as early as most, as she and the others now arriving had to squeeze their way through the packed bodies to reach a space inside. The rows of plastic chairs were all taken and there were many more people standing behind them. It was uncomfortably hot and smelt of the men's waxed jackets. Despite the heat, a hatch to a small canteen was open on one side of the room, where a pair of elderly women were selling tea and coffee from a giant metal urn. The crowd faced a short stage on which a dozen people were seated in a semicircle. There was a woman wearing a chain of office and a man who was badly sunburnt. She recognised Simon from the Derwen Centre and, with her pulse suddenly racing, Lucy from the Afon Twymyn Reserve. She scanned the faces in the room but was relieved not to find Rob's amongst them. In the centre of the semicircle, a man, clearly the chair, was turning a pen nervously in his fingers and stuttering his way through an introduction. He could only be half heard through the coughing and the audience members talking amongst themselves.

The meeting was to start with a short speech from the woman in the livery collar, introduced as the mayor of Llanfair, which would then be followed by an opportunity for the audience to ask questions, before the person to her left then made their speech and so on. The mayor stood and addressed the audience.

'Prynhawn da pawb. Good afternoon, everyone. Thank you for coming to this meeting. We are here of course to discuss a very sensitive matter. I know how important this is to many of you and I'm sure emotions will be running high. It is my hope that we can answer some of your questions today and that we can agree upon what is best for our whole community. Everyone will have a chance to have their say. Let's be respectful of each other and take the time to listen and to consider the views of others.'

The mayor's speech passed with little controversy and with few questions, as did that of the next two speakers, but when the time came for the sunburnt man to speak, the audience were alive with questions. The man represented the Farmers Union of Wales and the Marches and was forced to face one tirade after the other, as members of the audience stood up to voice their desperation and berate the union for its impotence. This went on for some time, with the chairman ineffectually trying to intervene. To Sarah, the whole thing felt like a waste of time. She would wait until Simon spoke then leave. To the union leader's visible relief, the debate moved on to the next speaker. Only then did Sarah spot the man waving at her from the crowd across the room. It was

Evan's brother, Rhys. She pushed and excused her way over to him.

'Hiya, love,' he said softly. 'You all right?'

'Yes, thanks.' She answered. 'How are you?'

'I'm all right. Things have been better though.' He shook his head. 'This virus – not good.'

'How long do you think it will last?'

'We'll see what they say here. It's how many it gets, and with compensation what it is, it's the end for those that get it. I just heard about John Davies. He lost everything last Monday, waited for them all to leave, then went into the barn with his twelve bore and never came out. Funeral's next week.'

'God, that's horrible,' Sarah said. Rhys told her that he had done some felling work at the reserve. She hoped he would not ask about Rob. The speaker moved on to Lucy, who nervously read out her speech from a piece of paper, but she was shouted down before she had even finished.

'Our challenge is how we are to contain the virus without risking the lives of some of our most precious wildlife, or damaging their habitats,' she went on. 'Containment is possible.'

'That's a load of rubbish!' shouted a man sitting very close to the stage. 'You don't have any control over these animals. They come and go as they please and they take the virus with them.' Lucy looked appealingly at the chair. The mayor spoke instead.

'Please sir, can you keep questions and comments until the end.'

'We understand the concerns of livestock owners and want to work with them to keep their animals safe,' Lucy read on. 'We are working closely with representatives of the ministry to minimise risk wherever possible.'

'Yeah, I bet you are,' came a voice from further back in the audience. 'I bet you're great mates, you and the ministry. I think it's disgusting that you're allowed to carry on whilst we all lose our livelihoods.'

Sarah felt sorry for Lucy. She tried to answer the men,

and made every effort to try and justify the preservation of wildlife under the circumstances, repeatedly listing the various measures the reserve had taken to try and keep farmland safe. Nothing she said, however, could placate the overwhelmingly hostile audience. One man stood up from the row of chairs.

'We've got the worst infection rates in the whole country here!' he spat. 'I don't care if it's got two legs, four legs, a hundred legs; if it comes onto my land, it'll get a dose of lead. It's as simple as that!'

Lucy looked understandably relieved when the chairman moved the discussion on to the next speaker. Simon stood up next. He started by explaining the purpose of the NWL and what they did at the Derwen Centre, then went on to address how they were responding to the virus. He was a good speaker, as Sarah had not doubted, but whereas Lucy's speech was met with hostility, Simon's was met mostly with indifference. Some got up to leave, others talked amongst themselves at full volume. When Simon had finished, the chairman asked for any questions and pointed to a bored-looking man holding his finger in the air.

'Do you paint yourself up in different colours as well? I thought this was about people with a living to make. What use are you lot wandering around in trees like a bunch of savages?'

The chairman said something about his choice of language but there were sniggers from the audience. Simon thanked the chairman but said there was no need for the gentleman to be reprimanded.

'We are proud savages,' he said. 'Savage originally meant people of the woods and that is what we are here. In the past, people like us were disparaged as heathens and savages, but we embrace these terms. This is Powys, land of the pagans, literally the countryside.' Before he could go on, there was a shout from the audience.

'Why don't you fuck off back to England!' There were some cheers and clapping, but most had their backs to the stage by this point. The chairman could hardly be heard.

'Right, I think I've seen enough,' Sarah said to Rhys.

'You take care now, love,' he said. 'And don't go anywhere you shouldn't go. I mean that. It's not safe. You just stick to your business. And keep away from Evan. At least until the virus is gone.' She nodded.

'Thanks, Rhys,' she said, and he held his hand out for her to shake.

Now that he was back on the reserve, Rob allowed himself to relax. The dawn chorus was in full voice and in the distance, he could hear the falls of the Twymyn calling through the trees. He had to be doubly cautious, times being what they were. All movement across the land now had to be in darkness. This he was used to at least, having honed his senses through years of experience navigating in low light. There were the bilberries he picked and ate as well, though it was fanciful to think they improved night vision. He resented the virus as much as any farmer for having rendered his work effectively illegal overnight. He had a duty to continue, regardless of the danger in which it placed him, and had adjusted his routes after much careful watching and waiting in order to avoid the various patrols that had appeared along his way. Here, though, he was safe, and he felt he could descend through the woods with his eyes closed, guided only by the sweet scent of the dog rose that grew along its border.

He was hungry and busy planning his breakfast when he emerged from the trees and stopped dead. He knew at a glance that something was wrong. The space around the cabins ahead was too frequently walked upon for him to make out any tracks, but he could tell that someone had exited the woods without using one of the established routes and had likely returned the same way. Looking ahead, he could see a dark patch had appeared on his cabin. He drew closer, until the dark patch began to take shape, then stopped when he realised what it was. The body hung limp in its impalement, claws still visible, fur still lustrous, the lifeless eyes still bright with the light of the morning. One paw was torn and raw, ruined by the bite of a gin. He looked around but he was alone, the only witness to the sight of Scratcher the pine marten, cold and dead and nailed to the door of his cabin.

17

The long days of summer brought back something of that feeling Sarah thought she had lost at Rhyd-y-Benwch. Under blue and bright skies, she joined the weekly communings in the meadow, where buttercups had broken out in a yellow haze and where the stalks of grasses shivered with the passing of the breeze, and the meadowsweet raised bursts of creamy flowers towards the sun. Just to lie there feeling the warmth on her skin, watching a thrips struggling through the hairs on her arm, stirred something inside her she could not describe. When John asked her about it at work, she could not explain it. She had been training her mind for months now, and the discipline allowed her to slip more easily into that state, a state that was at once blissful, hopeful and alive, and yet more than that, as if she were close to something like God or creation.

She viewed the current crisis with a growing sense of detachment. Her encounters with the landscape were now almost exclusively within the wildland sites of the NWL and she was oblivious to the closing of the footpaths, where the crows and rooks had become the new masters, and where foxes, badgers and deer, now moved undisturbed. She drove past several pickets, including a large demonstration outside Marcherton town hall, and was followed once by one of the Land Rovers that had begun to patrol the roads by day and night, filled almost always with young men, armed and with dogs. Unbeknownst to her, and to Evan's bitter disappointment, for only the second time in its long history, the annual race from the clock tower at Hen Gaer was cancelled.

They were always looking for help at the Derwen Centre and Sarah was happy to volunteer. She helped to coppice the woods and to gather sheaves of grass for compost when the meadow was scythed. Ruth approached her directly to ask for her help in clearing out an old attic space at the rear of the chapel. It was an unpleasant job for a summer's day, hunched over in sour, muggy air, shifting boxes by torchlight. One of the boxes was full of what looked like old Welsh hymn books. They were tattered and yellowing and smelt quite strongly. Ruth told her to throw them out with the other rubbish they had removed, but it felt wrong to Sarah; the books were well-thumbed and must have been held by many hands in the past. She was more familiar with how the language looked now, with its fondness for the letter 'y', but there was no hope of her being able to read them. She slipped one into her bag regardless, before the rest were thrown away.

Ruth made them both a nettle tea afterwards and they drank it outside in the sun, where the sparrows waited expectantly around them. There was a shout from the direction of the chapel. A woman ran out from the open door Sarah recognised her as the woman with the shaved head she had seen crying in the canteen. Simon was following close behind her. The woman shouted something, ending with 'liar'. Simon shadowed her out onto the road. Ruth shook her head.

'Sasha,' she said. 'Many people are able to find healing here. It's just a case of cultivating the right mind. Sadly, that's not something Sasha has been able to do. I think this is the end of the road for her. Probably for the best.'

Simon left the woman to walk away and headed back towards the chapel. He stopped to speak with them as he passed.

'She's trashed the shop,' Simon said to Ruth.

'I'll help you in a moment,' she said.

'Sorry, Sarah,' Simon said. 'Some people just don't know how to let themselves be helped.' She smiled and he went back inside.

'Will she be alright?' Sarah said. Ruth nodded.

'So where are you living at the moment?' she said. Sarah told her about the cottage.

'Are you happy there?' Ruth asked.

'Yes,' she said. 'Mostly. The rent is very cheap.'

'You know there are rooms available here if you're interested?'

'Really?'

'I can show you around if you like.'

'What sort of rent do you charge?' Sarah asked. 'I'm not earning a lot at the moment.'

'We're very reasonable,' Ruth said. 'Residents only pay what they can afford, and we help each other out when necessary. There is no deposit as such, but we do ask for a contribution of two thousand prior to arrival.'

'I don't know that I'd be able to afford that,' Sarah said.

Ruth lowered her voice a little. 'Have you had an audience with Tamsin yet?' she said.

'No.'

'You know you can book an appointment to see her. I guarantee you it would be worthwhile.'

'She'd see me on her own?'

'Yes, of course she would. Would you like me to speak with her?'

Sarah was given an appointment with Tamsin the following week. She was asked to wait in the corridor outside Tamsin's room. This was in the roof space of the chapel, at the top of a steep staircase, scarred by woodworm. There were voices coming from inside the room. Sarah bent down to look out of the short window in the corridor, which only came up to her knees and which looked out over the courtyard below. The door opened behind her, and she stood up.

'Tamsin will see you now.' She recognised Julie, emerging from the room. Sarah thanked her and stepped inside. It was a lot smaller than she was expecting. There was little standing space, other than in the centre of the room, and what wall space there was available was stacked with books, at the top of which sprouted the ancient timbers of the roof which met directly above her head. Many of the books had foreign titles along the spine and displayed names like Shankara and Nāgārjuna. Tamsin was sitting on a mound of cushions at one end of a rag rug which covered almost the entire floor. She greeted Sarah and gestured for her to sit on the round cushion opposite her. Her silvery hair was lit from behind by the splendid circular window Sarah had seen from outside, set into the arch above the tall main windows.

'You must be Sarah,' Tamsin said.

'Yes,' Sarah said, sitting down. Tamsin had her feet folded beneath her. Though she was short, she was very broad, and Sarah felt small next to her now that they were both seated.

'I recognise you. You have a lovely face. Julie says you've been working hard here, so I'd like to say thank you very much.'

'It gives me something to do!' Sarah said. She felt shy in front of Tamsin and could not meet her eyes for very long.

'I'm just glad that you find it worthwhile. Do you like it here?'

'Very much.'

'Good. I'm glad.' There was a pause. It looked like she was waiting for Sarah to say something. 'Is there anything you wanted to ask me?'

'About the centre?' Sarah said.

'About anything.' There was a knock at the door and Tristan, the man with the ponytail from the canteen, came in, carrying a tray with tea for them both. He set the tea on a footstool next to Tamsin and poured it out as they spoke.

'I did want to ask something,' Sarah said. 'You talk a lot in your books about "natural monism". The way I understand it is that the spirit or essence of nature is kind of the same as us, deep down. Like we all have it inside us. And that's what people talk about when they talk about knowing God and God being inside of us.'

Tamsin nodded. 'You can call it God, or the absolute, or the supreme principle: the result is the same,' she said. 'That which underlies nature, underlies our true Selves and the state of true wisdom is to experience harmony between the basis of nature and the basis of our Selves.'

'Right,' Sarah said. 'So how does "raw consciousness"

fit in?' She thanked Tristan as he was leaving and picked up her tea.

'Let me see,' Tamsin said. 'What is it, to be the essence of something?'

'I don't know.'

'Are you your feet?' Tamsin asked.

'No.'

'Are you your arms, or your eyes? Are you your bones, or your hair pores? Are you the cells which make up your body? What about the particles which make up them? Or the atoms which make up the particles? Are any of these things you?'

'No.'

'Then what are you?'

'All of these together, I suppose.'

'But what if we took one of these things away? Would you still be you?'

'Yes.'

'Then what's the part that is really you then?'

Sarah thought for a while. 'I see what you mean,' she said. 'It's difficult.'

'Precisely,' Tamsin said. 'Truly you are none of these things. It is the same when you think about your mind. True, you cannot dissect your mind and examine it under a microscope in the same way, but are you your thoughts, your memories, your worries, your dreams? When you strip all of these things away, physically and mentally, what is left? Raw consciousness. That is the essence of what makes you you. A very old analogy is that it's like salt and water. If you think of the salt as being your true essence, or your Self, and you think of the water as being all of the things we've just discussed, dissolve the salt in the water and you can no longer see it anymore. It's like the salt has disappeared, but when you taste it, you know that it's there, and that it pervades all the water, even though you cannot see it. That is what your true Self is like; it is raw consciousness, prior to any thought, feeling, any body part you have. Your body may age, your mind may change, but beneath it all, your Self persists as raw consciousness.'

'I see. That kind of makes sense now,' Sarah said. She had already finished her tea. 'So how does that fit in with the rest of the universe?'

'What works for you, works for the universe and everything in it,' Tamsin said. She was as reassuring in person as she was during her sermons. 'When you strip anything down to its most fundamental principle then you get the same result. Raw consciousness is the fundamental nature of all things; it beats throughout all matter and expresses itself in the eruption of trees, the life of the soil and so on. If the ultimate reality of the universe is the same as the ultimate reality of ourselves, then it follows we must look to nature to better know our own Selves. My belief is that we have atrophied inwardly by placing a distance between ourselves and the land. We feel disconnected, unhappy. For us to experience true fulfilment in our lives, we need to return to the wild and surrender ourselves to it.'

'Do you mean like during the communings?'

'Yes, partly. But I think what a communing should be about is deepening our knowledge. You may have a pleasant experience during a communing and that's fine. Great. But pleasant experiences are not going to truly change anything. We can read about raw consciousness and so on in books, and we can talk about it but how much do we truly understand? We may understand intellectually but through communings we can begin to understand experientially, and those are two very different things. If we can *experience* understanding, true wisdom, then we will no longer see our lives as meaningless, we will no longer see ourselves just as blobs of flesh going around the world suffering without meaning. We can take that understanding down into our hearts and live with it with every breath, and truly we will be troubled no longer.'

'You mean we will stop worrying all the time?' Sarah said.

Tamsin laughed. 'Yes, precisely,' she said. 'We will stop worrying all the time. I'm not saying that all our cares will evaporate but they will cease to trouble us in the same way. Take even our most basic worry: death. We will be able to better accept death, understanding that our life has been part of all life. Raw consciousness cannot simply spring up from nowhere and disappear to nowhere. Everything exists in a chain of cause and effect. Take anything you like, any example at all and you will find that something came before it and something after it. It could be an object, or a thought, a planet or a star: anything. Now, I don't have all the answers and neither do these people.' She pointed to the books behind her. 'Whatever consciousness you have at death, I cannot say where that will go, or where it was before your birth for that matter, but I cannot see it just disappearing out of existence. That fundamental principle is certain to express itself elsewhere. And by being here, doing what we do, we can ensure that this is peaceful, and we can approach our own deaths with understanding and meaning, and most of all hope.'

'That's amazing,' Sarah said. She waited for Tamsin to finish her tea, which she drank carefully. She stared out of the round window when she had finished.

'So, what was it that led you here?' Tamsin asked eventually.

'I work with Emma,' Sarah said. 'She invited me to come.'

Tamsin nodded. 'You've come back since though,' she said. 'What I mean is, what do you hope to gain by being here?'

Sarah thought for a while. 'I don't know. Happiness, I guess.'

'There are often many old and ongoing obstacles in the way of happiness,' Tamsin said. 'Lots of the people who've arrived here have been deeply troubled in the past. Some have lived lives of unimaginable suffering. Here though, they've been able to overcome many of their difficulties and have moved on from the past. I count myself as one of them.' When Sarah did not respond, she continued. 'Whatever a person has been through, we can help each other here. We work hard to make it a place of togetherness and healing. Here we work to cut to the root of our suffering, in looking to our very Selves. So many here have suffered real trauma, and I'm glad to say they no longer see themselves as struggling around in a world of meaningless pain. Here we have a sanctuary and growth and healing at last.'

Again, Sarah could not meet her eyes, with their fine creases at the corners. Tamsin aplogised to her, as she had another appointment booked. Sarah thanked her, and Tamsin said she had enjoyed their conversation. She held out her arms and Sarah shuffled forward on her knees to meet her. It felt like Tamsin knew all about her; not that Emma had told her anything, just that she knew the sort of person Sarah was. With her face pushed up against Tamsin's coconut-smelling hair and arms pulling her close and tight, Sarah felt her throat harden with emotion.

She spent her drive home reliving the conversation. She had always felt deep down that she was 'damaged goods' with the background she had, and this separated her from normal people like Gill. What Tamsin had suggested was that there was a chance to change this finally. The Derwen Centre was actually a place for people like her, for people who had no other place. She imagined herself living there, surrounded by others like her, all of them working hard to heal and change, looking after each other, applying the teachings, moving forward together towards a life lived painlessly, amongst mountains and trees, besides hedgerows and rivers, under the sky and stars.

Evan looked down at the shotgun he was holding. His hands were white in the moonlight. It felt good, holding his twelve-bore with both hands. The moon shone along the barrels, glowing silver at the action and picking out the fine engraving. He looked ahead to the place where Richard had entered the woods. There was no sign of him, but it was dark, and Evan's eyes were not what they once were. He kept watching for movement at the tree line. The other lad waited away to his left, Richard's friend. He could just about make out the unlit cigarette jutting from the lad's lips. The dogs waited with him on their leads, the two of them poised, muscle flexed under fur, every sense fixed on the woods ahead. They were squat, mean-looking things, most likely used for badger baiting and the occasional two-legged vermin like today. Richard knew some rough people and this lad was one of them. He was thankful, though, that Richard had brought him along. They might no longer be Bowen woods, but he felt no less a duty to defend them. He was confident that Protheroe was wrong and that this was the place where they would cut off the trespasser. Protheroe and the other lads were away up on top of the hill, flushing the man out, whoever he was. Most of the lads were spoiling for a fight with the heat of the summer. He could see them fighting each other if they came back empty-handed. There was always the chance this trespasser might meet with a nasty accident, but that would weigh very little on Evan's conscience. Whoever it was had made a very big mistake.

There was hope now that the virus was slowing. Fewer cases were being reported and other areas of the country had ridded themselves of the disease. Though the wave might have finally broken and begun to retreat, nothing could be taken for granted. The farms had to be defended, and there were rumours of trespassers everywhere. He did not think much of many of them, but here he had seen the evidence with his own eyes. When they received the confirmation of a sighting over the CB, he had guessed that it would lead them here.

Evan spoke to his father under his breath, reassuring him, promising him it would all be fine. The race from the clock tower had been cancelled but the farm was all right. He was about to check his watch when Richard emerged again from the trees ahead. With the signal from Richard, the lad to Evan's left set his dogs loose and they pelted towards the woods. He was here. They had him. Gripping his shotgun and with one last word to his father, Evan began to run, moving away from the moonlight and into the trees.

Keeping himself very low, Rob stopped when he reached

the holly and took cover. He crouched down, trying to give himself time to think. Things were bad. He was a long way away from safety. He had passed through these woods before but only once in darkness. Using a torch was out of the question, so he closed his eyes and tried to recall the layout of the woods, where he might be and what possible escape routes he could use. He had to think several moves ahead or else they would trap him.

The data from the collars had been alarming. The pine marten project was now suspended and in danger of collapse. At this rate there would be no pine martens left to monitor. Sarah could have shared information about Scratcher and the others, but he did not believe that; he had enemies enough. He prided himself on his self-sufficiency, but thinking about her now in the darkness, crouched in hiding from these men, he felt miserably alone.

He knew he was being hunted. The lookouts had forced him miles off route. These men were not trackers and had twice shown themselves to him. They were careless in always choosing the higher ground, probably so they could get a clear shot, but this left them silhouetted against the moon. He was confident he could outwit them, even on their own land, but although the men troubled him little, he knew he could neither run nor hide from the dogs they kept.

He stood up carefully. There was no way he could find his way out now. He had to go back. Shortly after entering the woods, he had cut a waymark into the trunk of a birch, which stood alone amongst sycamores. He tried retracing his steps, moving as soundlessly as he could, but he was having to guess for most of it. He was relieved to recognise the birch ahead but as he drew nearer to it, he heard a sound, high above him on the wooded slope. His eye caught a flash of movement. Someone was there. Stealth was useless now; he had to assume he had been spotted, and he dashed over to the birch and ran his hand along the trunk for the waymark he had cut into the bark. There was nothing there. He looked back, only to be met with the fearful sight of a pair of dogs moving rapidly through the trees, running at speed down the slope towards him. He ran, every thought disappearing, thrashing wildly through branches, scuffing against roots, desperate only for distance. There was no time. Blindly, half falling down the slope, he crashed through the trees, bashing against them to steady himself, lungs roaring, eyes set to burst. He glanced behind him and there they were, right there, moving faster than any man, running him down, coming straight for him. He had three or four seconds before they would close. There was barely time to register the fence before he was upon it and at the last moment, just as he was about to collide with the barrier, he dove forwards, grasping the barbed wire in his hands, somersaulting upwards, his feet drawing an arc through empty space before crashing onto the ground beyond.

18

With summer drawing to a close, official opinion was that the virus too had run its course. There were fewer new cases and the restrictions on movement were relaxed, with the exception of those areas deemed most vulnerable. Farmers began to count the cost. An emergency fund had been set up which attracted some very generous donations, mostly from outside of Mid Wales, though it could manage no more than token payments to those affected. Farmers left unscathed by the crisis could ill afford to supply financial help to those stricken, though they helped in many other ways.

Rosebay willowherb crowded the verges on Sarah's journey to work, passing by her in a blur of lilac. In the fields, red-faced finches fed amongst the thistles left by the sheep, splitting open their downy heads and teasing out the shuttlecock seeds inside. Where she crossed the canal, dragonflies were hunting at speed, weaving through the Himalayan balsam that had worked its way along the banks, and at night the same water was haunted by the bats which came down from the woods around the castle to flit and feed along its length.

John had been taken ill with chickenpox and the running of the kitchen had fallen upon Sarah, whilst Malcolm managed to busy himself with things that were of little importance. It was hard work without John, but she and Emma made a quick and effective team. John always gave the impression that he hated the pub, but he was wedded to the kitchen, and telephoned in after less than a week away. He called during the afternoon lull, when Sarah was busy preparing a new round of baguettes. She had a list of questions collected for him which they ran through together, John moaning throughout.

'I don't feel well,' he said afterwards.

'I know,' Sarah said.

'I feel awful.'

'I know, John. Would you like me to bring you anything round?' she asked.

'Heroin.'

'I'm not bringing you heroin, John. Would you like some jelly sweets?'

'Are they going to get rid of my terrible pain?'

'No.'

'Oh, well. I'd like some anyway, please.'

'Okay, I'll bring them over this evening. You look after yourself and get well soon.'

When she came off the phone, Emma was waiting for her.

'There's someone here to see you,' she said. 'He's outside.' She gestured towards the open windows. Sarah could guess who it was.

'Give me a minute,' she said. 'Could you finish these for me please?'

She went out through the side door, still wearing her apron. The earlier rain had left a mackerel sky and the cool air irritated her lungs, so that when she saw Rob waiting and went over to him, she broke out in a fit of coughing.

'Are you okay?' he asked. He was noticeably thinner and his eyes were bruised with tiredness.

'I'm fine,' she said. 'So?' He looked away.

'Look, I'm sorry for being a dick,' he said. 'I get a little carried away sometimes. I'm sorry.' She nodded once in reply. He rubbed the back of his neck with his hand.

'What have you done to your hand?' she said. He looked down at it and she took him by the wrist and turned his hand over. His palm was healing from two deep lacerations. There were smaller cuts as well. The skin was pink and tight around the wounds and the gouged flesh had scabbed over, forming a rugged crust of black. 'How did you get these?' He lowered his hand without answering. 'Where have you been all this time? Have you stayed at the reserve during this virus? I hope you haven't carried on *illegally* across people's land.'

'There's work to be done. Important work. Virus or

no virus.'

'For God's sake, Rob. It's people's livelihoods!'

'I know and I've been very careful. I've been using disinfectant.'

'So you can do what, Rob?' Sarah said. 'What couldn't wait until the virus passed?'

'You know what I do,' he said. 'I check the camera traps. I remove snares. I disarm gins. There are plenty of things I come across which are illegal, but I don't hunt people down with guns and dogs. Anyway, it's pretty much over now. They'll be announcing the all clear soon.'

'Look, I'm working, Rob. I've got to go. What do you want?'

'Can I see you again?' he said. 'Please? When do you finish today?'

'I said I would look after Rachel this evening. I'm sorry, I can't see you.'

'Another time then?'

Sarah sighed.

'You don't look well,' she said. 'Go home. Get some sleep.'

'I can't sleep.'

'I don't have time for this, Rob. I've got to go.' He rubbed the back of his neck with his hand again. 'I'm sorry,' she said and went back through the kitchen door.

Sarah had signed up to the new study programme that was being trialled at the Derwen Centre. The course was broken down into three modules, with both practical and theoretical elements, and meant that Sarah spent almost all of her time outside of work at the centre. She had barely seen Sioned, so she had gone up to the farmhouse to offer to babysit Rachel again. She had bought Rachel a unicorn pencil case which was ready on the passenger seat next to her as she drove back from work. Coming into the farmyard, she was surprised to find so many vehicles she did not recognise. One of them was parked in her usual space, so she left the car near the cattle grid and used the disinfectant. She could hear voices coming from the direction of the old barn. Sioned was there, as was Evan and Richard and Ceri, but there were other men there she did not know. Ceri had hold of her mother, who was sobbing into her shoulder. The men looked round at her as she approached. Richard peeled off from the group and came towards her.

'What do you want?' he said.

'I was . . .' Sarah looked over to the rest of them. 'I was looking after Rachel this evening.' Richard shook his head. 'What's wrong?' she said. 'What's happened?'

'What does it look like's happened?' he said.

'Not the virus? Surely? We don't have it here?' Richard shook his head in response. 'Oh, phew,' she said. 'You frightened me for a moment.'

'It doesn't matter,' Richard said. 'Prosser's farm has it.'

'What? I don't understand,' Sarah said.

'It's a contiguous cull, isn't it. Don't you know that?'

'What does that mean?'

'It means Prosser has it at the farm on from this one, and that means they've got to slaughter here as well as there.'

'Oh, God! What, all of them?'

'Yes, all of them. So you'd better clear off hadn't you?' Sarah went to say something but could not think. 'Go on,' he said. 'You're not going to want to watch what happens.' Sioned came away from Ceri and approached them.

'I'm sorry, Sarah,' she said. Her face was bright pink. 'You need to be somewhere else for a few days. I'm sorry,' she sobbed. 'They're going to start today.'

'Oh! I'm sorry, Sioned,' she said. Sioned brought her hand to her mouth. A tear rolled across her fingers and landed just short of her shoe. 'I really am.' Ceri came over and held her mother again as she cried. Sarah looked from Sioned to Ceri, to Richard and then over to Evan and the other men. One of them placed a hand on Evan's shoulder.

'Okay,' Sarah said. 'I'll call . . . Okay . . .' she said again. 'Okay . . .'

In the months afterwards, Evan was dogged by the feeling that he was a coward. He was ashamed that he had not helped the men with the slaughter when they asked him. Sioned had made good excuses for him, but it was his farm, his animals, his responsibility. How could he though? The ewes carried the bloodlines of the farm, stretching back generations and generations, so that his animals were the direct descendants of those his father had tended and his father before him, going back beyond all memory, into the unreachable distance of the past.

He had entered the barns once after the farm had been cleared and had kept away from them ever since. The silence was obscene. Everything that was good and right and natural had gone, and a terrible nothingness had taken its place. The air that had always been heavy with the breath of the flock was now still and sterile. Even the birds had gone from the rafters above. It was an abomination. He came outside doubled over and retched into the yard.

There was the compensation and some very kind donations from elsewhere, but he and Sioned never had to speak about it. It would have been impossible to pretend that they could go on as they had before. They spoke even less together, and Evan found work flailing hedges with the tractor mower. Each day he watched the mower engage and disengage, checking his speed and distance, looking back along the hedgerow to survey his work. He paid no attention to the trauma in his wake, noticing neither the exposed bones of the twigs nor the birds' cries of alarm. He was oblivious to the ageing of the willowherb, whose white wisps danced in clouds around the tractor, and as autumn came, he saw neither the bead-like haws that broke out in their thousands, nor the lozenges of the rose hips that joined them, nor the sloes, round and fat as blueberries, nor even the butterflies that came flickering along the hedgerow to lap at the brambles' dying fruit. He saw only the flail working and heard nothing but the steady drone of the tractor. Though it was many hours alone, it was work, and they were hours spent away from his own thoughts.

Gwyneira died that autumn, though not before Brian had put the farm up for sale. She was buried in the chapel of her youth, in a village unknown to Evan, somewhere west of the middle mountains. He had attended her funeral, though he understood little of what was said, save for the Lord's Prayer in Welsh. What family she had thanked him in English. Then there was the pitiful spectacle of the auction, where the contents of Brian's farmhouse were carried out into a nearby field and arranged in rows to be sold. Those that knew Brian were kind and made him good offers for the family furniture. Others were professionals at this sort of thing and they beat him down until only a paltry sum was exchanged. He gave the shell of the grandfather clock away for nothing. Evan bought back the other clock his dad had given Brian, intending for it to hang in the hallway again, as it had done when Evan was a child. Though it had been left in the farmyard, away from the items being sold, a second cousin offered Brian a fair sum for his Land Rover and drove it away that afternoon. Evan offered to drive Brian back over the mountains to where he was staying with Gwyneira's relatives.

Coming home, he followed the meandering road that clung to the contours of the mountains, high above the valley below. The slopes were studded with the pinprick white of the grazing sheep, gathered in broad flocks close to the valley floor, then spread thinly as the land climbed steeply upwards and shed its greenness, until they were barely visible amongst the stiff brown grasses of the mountainside. On the far side of the valley, they were burning the bracken, the white smoke billowing upwards like a cloud anchored to the hillside. Evan checked the clock on the seat behind him and rolled down the window for some air. The car slowed and pulled into a lay-by, coming to a stop without him realising. He saw his hand opening the door, then looked down at his feet as they crossed the tarmac. It was as if he were outside of himself somehow, watching his own body making its way across the road and onto the verge opposite. The body that was no longer his stumbled through the grass towards the fence, then he saw his hands gripping the wire, pulling it together in his fists and shaking it as if it would break. Then there was a noise like none he had ever heard. He felt his ribcage would shatter, or his throat burst open. The sound echoed through his skull and drowned out the universe. The scream came from beyond, from the deepest well of hopelessness that lay cold and black inside of him, drawing strength from every cell of his body, bursting out from him in a dreadful howl that sent the valley quaking with its terrible power, so that the men burning the bracken looked up from their work and listened above the noise of the flames to the wind that carried his despair.

That evening the sickness began, starting with a sore throat before his skin became suddenly prickly and he could not bear the feeling of any pressure against it. He went to bed in Ceri's old room and slept. When he woke, he was hot and damp, and he thought for a moment that he must have fallen asleep in the bath, then he realised he had soaked the bed with sweat, and Sioned was standing over him and saying something he could not understand. Time passed and he woke up feeling on fire, throwing the sheets away from the bed in desperation, then woke again shivering uncontrollably, having no memory of ever actually going to sleep. Time went forwards, then backwards, then no direction at all. He remembered there being light at the window, but it was dark outside, and he looked again, and it was light once more. Someone held a cup to his lips and wiped him down, and then he was shivering in the bathroom, the light painfully bright on his pale thighs. He was back in bed, and then Nain was trying to feed him something that he did not like, and he was crying and asking for his dad. There was the wallpaper next to him in the bed and then eventually, he was no longer there himself, there were only thoughts, images, without anyone there to think them. Sometimes he was many people and sometimes none. Ceri was there and then a man he did not recognise. All around the bed there were men working on the clock tower at Hen Gaer, masons cutting the stone and men bent over under heavy loads. Somebody was crying and then there were men talking in Welsh, one of them holding a fish, and then there was the sea. Then the drovers arrived off the mountains with their thin cattle and the red dogs behind, and there was pipe smoke and ale and someone's hand holding three dirty shillings. Now there were other men and there was the smell of fire and the bones of the ancestors buried in the long barrow. They were clearing the woods for grazing and were speaking a language that was not Welsh but something older still. The men had brought antlers to trade, which were bundled together and carried on their backs. Then the measurer spoke and looked up to the sky. The sun and moon and stars were there, all of them and none.

He came to, still in bed in Ceri's room. There was a bowl and a jug and boxes of what looked like medicine, and a chair in place by the bed that he had no recollection of having been there before. He felt weak but his head had finally cleared. He drank thirstily from the jug, too desperate to bother with the cup next to it. When he set it down, the image of Sioned sitting in the chair came to him and he knew he had to go to her. With a thirst greater than that he had just quenched, he dragged his aching body out of the bed and fumbled with the door handle. It was dark on the landing, and he bumped into the other bedroom door before he could open it. He heard Sioned say something beyond the door, and he wrestled with both hands to turn the brass handle and push his way in. Sioned was sitting up in bed. Her long hair shone like twilight on the shoulders of her nightie.

'Evan?' she said. He moved towards her, whimpering childlike as he came, clawing back the bedsheets and clambering inside. 'Evan?' Sioned said again. He pulled her towards him, his arm around her shoulder, clutching her tightly, like a child starved of its mother, then still childlike, nuzzling into her, smelling her skin close to his face, bringing his legs up so they could be against her as well. She held him, and he pressed himself against her, running his hand over her back and thighs, wanting only this closeness, his body coming alive with feeling. He kissed her neck and cheek and her shoulders through the nightie. She cupped his head in her hand and kissed him back, then said his name again, softly. With their bodies remembering, they touched again, not daring to speak, stroking love into ageing limbs, mouths meeting, breath deepening, and the many years falling away, vanishing with heartbeats in the gloom, leaving nothing but this tenderness.

19

For the first time since coming to Wales, Sarah felt she had a vision of the future. The NWL gave her structure, companionship and above all purpose. There was no loneliness at the Derwen Centre; no one felt like an outsider. She had paid across the two thousand pounds initial contribution and had arranged to move in at the end of the month. She was practically living there anyway, staying in the guest room when she had no shifts the next morning. It felt like a homecoming. She was excited about living with her new friends and completing the next stage of the study programme. Most of all she looked forward to a time when she might feel rid of the doubt that had always afflicted her: that sense that she stood apart from everyone else. Tamsin taught that self-affirmation was not only possible for her but that the NWL practised the most direct way to individual fulfilment.

The older buildings were being touched up ready for winter and she helped to varnish the window frames and held the ladder whilst the eaves were repainted. Up close she could see the dried plugs where the masonry bees had entombed their young for the winter in the interstices of the walls. They took care to paint around the muddy half-bowls of the nests that the martins had recently abandoned. The day was cold but clear, and she did not want to go inside when they had finished, so she decided she would walk up through the woods where she had been on her very first communing.

The virus was over, for the most part. Though the rest of the country had been given the all-clear, in Mid Wales the virus lingered on, with several isolated cases still appearing. Reasonable use of footpaths was now permissible however, and Sarah picked up what looked like an old path through the woods. It could not have been walked much now the woods were used only for the directionless wandering of communings. The wood had yellowed with the wasting of the leaves. Some remained a defiant green, others ran with a coppery blood. Beneath the trees, the alien shapes of the fungi had appeared, breaking through the skin of shedded leaves or growing in strange formations from the fallen branches. The path climbed steeply and continued far longer than she had expected, and she was breathless when she emerged from the woods and found herself in a narrow cleft between two hills. She caught her breath leaning against a fencepost. Looking ahead, she could see the path became a road which followed the cleft between the hills and led away out of sight. There were no sheep around, so she thought she would push on a little further. When she drew close, she found that it was not a road but the beginnings of a deep tear in the landscape. As she rounded the corner, the fissure broadened, and a fine grey spoil began to bleed from its sides. She was now walking on loose stone, and as she pressed on, the land suddenly opened up like a leaden sea, and in the middle rose the ruin of an abandoned mine. The buildings were hardly recognisable as such, looking more like oversized gravestones set into the scree. Most were roofless, and one was little more than the suggestion given by a single remaining wall. She approached the nearest of them and entered tentatively through the cavity that would once have been a door. There was nothing inside but more grey stone. There was no sound save for the crunch of her own boots, and she felt afraid, as though she might disturb something best left asleep. She peered into the adjoining room, which was dark but for the narrow window space at its end. The light fell from the window space against the far wall and upon the orange and flaking remains of some ancient piece of equipment, rusted beyond recognition. The silence was broken with the sound of an engine, faintly audible in the distance. She went over to the window space and looked out across the rest of the mine complex. The noise was getting closer. Her instinct was to get straight back to the centre, but she told herself she was being silly and decided she would wait and see what arrived, just to prove to herself that she was not afraid. The roaring grew loader, until finally a Land Rover came tearing around the hill and sailed noisily between the mine works in a spray of stone. The vehicle pulled up outside one of the buildings. It was white and Sarah thought she remembered it from somewhere, then two men got out and she saw that one of them was Tristan and the other another man she recognised from the centre. She felt relieved and went to call out to them, but the pair disappeared around the building closest to them. Coming away from the window space, she went back out through the other room to go and meet them, but when she got to the doorway, she stopped. Tristan and the other man were carrying something out from the building. There was no mistaking it was a sheep, even from this distance, but the sight was so unexpected, she was struck dumb and unable to move. The two men bundled the sheep into the back of the Land Rover and closed the doors, then got back in themselves. She watched them pull away, driving out from the mine and away around the hill. She stood in the doorway confused. What were they doing there with that sheep? Where were they taking it?

The building from which they had emerged was the most intact of all the remaining structures. Approaching it, she found a door locked with a new-looking padlock and no other way inside. She listened at the door but could hear nothing. Not knowing what else to do, she walked away from the mine, slowly this time, back towards the woods. What had she seen? Why a mine? Why any of it? Coming down through the trees, she tried to think what possible purpose there could have been. Why would two NWL members keep a sheep in an old abandoned mine and come to collect it in a Land Rover? Where were they taking it?

When she arrived back at the Derwen Centre she tried searching for Tristan and the other man, but she could find neither, nor could she see the Land Rover anywhere near the centre. It was not parked along the road, nor was it amongst the residents' cars in the courtyard. She met Ruth on the way to her own vehicle.

'Sarah,' she said. 'How are you doing? Not long until you're here permanently, is it?'

'No. I'm fine thanks. Listen, I wanted to ask you something.'

'Of course.'

She told Ruth about everything she had seen. When she reached the part about the sheep, a visible change came over Ruth. She drew in a deep breath and pursed her mouth, saying nothing, even after Sarah finished talking. 'Well, what do you think?' Sarah asked.

'It sounds very unlikely.'

'I know, but that's what I saw.'

'It must have been someone else.'

'No, it was definitely Tristan and definitely the Land Rover from here.'

Ruth went to say something, then stopped.

'What do you want me to do about it, Sarah?' she said eventually. 'Even if it is true.'

'I don't know,' Sarah said. Ruth shrugged her shoulders.

'I can't go poking into people's private business,' she said. 'Now, if you'll excuse me, I'm very busy.' She opened the car door and got inside.

'It's not private business though,' Sarah said. 'The infection isn't over yet. It's illegal. And dangerous.'

Ruth snorted in response and started the car. 'Like I said, Sarah, I'm very busy.'

'But . . .'

'I don't want to hear about this again. We're a happy community and we don't need people coming here to stir up trouble. Goodbye.'

Sarah felt the rising heat of anger as Ruth drove away.

It was close to a week since Rob had last visited Rhodri. There had been a residential at the reserve, where teenagers from deprived backgrounds in the city would come to live and work with them from Monday to Friday. He welcomed anything that would help take his mind off Sarah and had done nothing but work since he last saw her, but the residential had put him in a bad mood. Sean had stopped him from supervising the attendees, as most were indifferent to the natural world, and this infuriated Rob who was liable to snap at them. Some were contemptuous of the reserve and complained about the food and the lack of Wi-Fi, and there was usually one at the back of the group who would imitate Rob's accent, to the amusement of the others. Apart from some encouraging signs seen in one or two of them, he was glad to see the back of them by the end of the week. Thinking about it made him angry as he made his way up to the clearing and Rhodri's bivouac. He mouthed his own thoughts as he walked, chopping the air with his hand as if he were in a real argument with someone. They needed these young people on side to fight the wealthy and powerful that continued to destroy this country, to push against those same people that go all dewy-eyed over the Queen's jubilee yet are happy to destroy swathes of ancient woodland with the laying down of a high-speed railway, all in the name of making themselves even richer. It was more than just class that was the problem though, and that was even more depressing. The reality of the landscape just did not exist for most people. It was far easier for them to get behind a premier league football team than it was to be persuaded of the value of an endangered habitat or species. People did not want to engage with their landscape; they wanted myths: simple tribal narratives of belonging and struggle against a perceived enemy. He had once seen a man in an England football shirt flinging his empty chip paper into a hedge. Rob had merely tried to point out to the man the contradiction between his actions and the love of country professed by his choice of clothing. That was how he got the dint in his nose. He rubbed at it with his finger as he ascended through the trees. Maybe Rhodri would get a punch on the nose if he asked what had happened to Sarah one more time.

When he reached the bivouac, Rhodri was not there. The fire was out. He sat and waited for him to return. He grew restless after a while and started gathering sticks to pass the time. Rhodri was never away for this long. He checked the hammock just to be sure, but the grubby sleeping bag was empty. He went a little way into the woods and called for him, moving around the camp in a circle, not wanting to be so loud as to draw unwanted attention. It was then that he saw the familiar green jumper sprawled across the tangled roots of an oak, one arm outstretched as if reaching for something and at the end of it, an open hand, with fingers white and rigid. It was Rhodri, lying prone and still. He approached slowly. Rhodri did not move. He bent down and turned him over at the shoulder, then jumped back quickly. The skin was blistered and the face frozen into a waxy rictus. Needing to vomit, Rob kicked the body back over then dashed away, retching.

Rob had feared this day would come, but he had not expected it so soon. Rhodri paid little attention to his own safety. Though he had saved him from a watery death in the Twymyn, Rob could never protect Rhodri from the threat of exposure, as he seldom wore more than that stupid jumper, preferring to warm himself through drink instead. Once he had collected himself, Rob recovered the binoculars he had lent Rhodri, as well as any other items that might look suspicious, and stowed them in his rucksack; the martens had to be protected. He had to walk a long way before he was able to get a good signal to call the authorities.

Afterwards, he waited near the gorge to meet with them. From where he was seated, he could see the footbridge across the gorge and would be able to signal to whomever it was the police were sending. He sat dejectedly amongst the mast that had fallen, his back resting against a tree. It was probably still illegal to be here but right now he was beyond caring. The stream prised the woods apart at the gorge and the water became bolder with the steepness of the land, cutting louder and deeper into the earth. He listened to the steady pulse of the stream and tried to concentrate on the sound, hoping to push away the thought of that lifeless face. There would be some difficult questions when the police arrived. For now, he would have a long wait. He closed his eyes but could not sleep, then remembering the bridge, looked out towards it. As expected, there was still no one. He lay back against the tree but then sat up; he thought he had seen movement. High above the bridge, in the woods on the other side of the gorge, there was a flash of colour. He stood up and stared into the trees until he made out the broken but undeniable shapes of two people, far from the footpath, moving without speaking. He reached for the binoculars, but when he had trained them on the woods beyond, the pair had disappeared from view.

20

Sarah wished she had never strayed from the woods and into the mine. There was no doubting what had taken place, and it angered her that Ruth had refused to take her seriously. She preferred not to think about it. Though it still niggled at her conscience, she was willing to drop the whole thing, as she wanted nothing to come in the way of her excitement at the future life she was to have with the NWL. Let it go, that was what the teachings said. Why worry about the mundane when the sacred was all around her, when all her petty worries could be dissolved through the bliss of union with nature? There was no drug, no therapy that could compare with the healing practices of the Derwen Centre. There was companionship, solidarity and freedom from life's sufferings. Here, beneath the trees, she had at last found peace.

She had enrolled on the intermediate course for which Tamsin ran the communings. The course focused on breaking down the mental barriers that distanced the Self from the natural world. Most exciting of all was the individual instruction given to those enrolled on the course. When the time came for their first session, Tamsin led her by the hand into the trees, where a light rain was falling on the canopy above. She whispered instructions to her as they walked, then they stopped at the foot of an impressive oak that grew deep within the woods, far from the trails left by previous communings.

'Try not to think of the tree as other,' Tamsin said softly. 'Don't think as you normally do, that there is a tree out there, separate from you. Instead, just concentrate on the experience alone. There is no Sarah, there is no tree; there is only this tree-like experience. Let the experience unfold by itself.

Sarah closed her eyes, then opened them, then closed them again. Rain dripped from the leaves, the droplets sounding as they struck her coat. The air was damp and fragrant. Soon she was conscious only of the tree that stood in front of her, yet it seemed to stand at the centre of her as well. She felt time melt away. She was conscious only of bark-skin and the fingers of branches, heavy boughs and questing roots, the taste of air and the flow of water, sunlight on hungry cells, the movement of insects. Then Tamsin's hand was in hers again, waking her, taking her back into the world she had left. Dazed and happy, she found herself saying goodbye to Tamsin outside the Old Chapel. Tamsin hugged her and Sarah drifted away into the canteen. A mug of rooibos tea and a meal of brown rice and vegetables brought her mind back to something like normal. It was the deepest she had ever gone, and it felt wonderful.

She spent the rest of the afternoon helping to clean down the canteen. Tristan was there, but she did not mention the mine. She thought she would go and visit what was soon to be her room again, before she left for the day. They had assigned her a spacious room in the house at the far end of the terrace, overlooking the market garden. She had fallen in love with it instantly. She let herself in through the rear entrance of the house and went upstairs. She was surprised this time to find the door open and two women inside, making up the bed.

'Hi,' she said.

'Hello,' said one of the women. They carried on fitting the bedding.

'Is someone staying here until I move in?' Sarah asked.

'No, Claire's moving in here today,' the woman said.

'But, I thought I was supposed to be moving in here?' Sarah said. The woman shrugged.

'We were told Claire was to move in today.'

'Oh.' The women continued. The one who had not spoken gave her a disapproving look before turning her back towards her and plumping up the pillows.

'Who told you that?' Sarah asked.

'Ruth did,' the other woman said. 'Today.'

Sarah came away from the door. It was so unfair. She had been so calm and happy earlier. She ran down the stairs and over to the Old Chapel. Ruth was not there but Simon was at his desk in the office at the back.

'Sarah!' Simon said. 'Lovely to see you.'

'I need to talk to you,' Sarah said.

'Certainly. Have a seat.' He gestured to the chair the other side of the desk. Sarah stood behind it.

'Ruth has given my room to someone else.'

'Yes, she did say something about that. Don't worry though, Sarah. We have another room for you.' He flicked through a notebook on the desk. 'Ruth's given you the room currently going spare in the old stables.'

'That's Sasha's old room.'

'Yes, I suppose it is.'

'It's the room furthest away from all the others. Why has Ruth changed her mind?'

'I don't know Sarah. I'm sure she has her reasons. Now, can I tempt you with a stuffed date?' He pushed the tray of dates on his desk towards her.

'I told Ruth what I'd seen,' Sarah said.

'Oh, right. What was that?' She could tell by his face that he knew.

'You know!' she said. 'You know already!'

'Know what?'

'I can tell that you know.'

'I'm very sure that I don't.'

'Tristan and someone else from the centre have been moving sheep about,' she said. She pointed a finger at him. 'It's illegal and dangerous and could spread the virus.'

'I beg your pardon?' Simon said.

'I've seen Tristan and someone else keeping and handling sheep and moving them around. Just what sort of business is this?' she said. 'What's in it for them?'

'Please sit down, Sarah.'

She sat down and he put his hands together and leant forward on the desk.

'Now I must admit, what you're saying sounds very

unlikely,' he said.

'Don't tell me that, that's just what Ruth said. I saw it with my own eyes. I'm not an idiot.'

'Of course you're not,' Simon said.

'You know something, don't you?' Sarah said. 'You know about this and so does Ruth.'

'Nonsense,' Simon said. He came out from behind the desk.

'Is everything all right? Are you a little apprehensive about moving into the centre? It's a big thing to do.'

'I'm not talking about that. I'm talking about the illegal moving of livestock being perpetrated by members of this community.'

'Perpetrated!' Simon laughed.

'It's not funny!' Sarah said, standing. 'Do you want this infection to spread? What if someone's animals get infected?'

'You seem very upset, Sarah, and I'm very busy. Why don't you go away and calm down and we can talk about it another time?'

'Don't patronise me! You do know something. That's clear. People could lose their entire way of living!'

'And what if they did?' Simon said. 'One fewer farmer, pointlessly taking up acres of land for their sad little animals. You of all people know the damage these people have done to this land and go on doing. What good are they doing? A way of life going out of the window. The land is for the people. We make far better use of it when it's in our hands. Why should a small number of stubborn people continue to hold this land and ruin it for no one's benefit?'

'It's their land!'

'Is it? We're doing people a favour, Sarah. The land is oppressed, and its people are oppressed. We are bringing freedom. We are the liberators of nature and the human spirit.'

'People have taken their own lives over this!' Sarah shouted.

'That is sad,' Simon said. 'But what value had their lives the way they were? Think how much happier these people would have been if they had come over to our way of thinking. But they won't. These people are intransigent. I saw you at the community meeting and you saw yourself how pig-headed they all were.'

'I'll tell the police,' Sarah said.

'And what are you going to tell them?'

'That a bunch of mad people are infecting their animals.'

'Think Sarah, just think. Imagine everything we could achieve here. Everything you could achieve here.'

'What else have you done?'

Simon came closer until he was standing over her. She looked up at his face.

'Nothing is more important than the work we do here,' he said softly. 'What does it matter how we help things along? Dogs, disease, depression; we're only speeding up a natural process. The time for sheep has passed and everyone knows it. They've had long enough, and it's our time now.'

'I'm telling Tamsin,' Sarah said.

'What?'

'Tamsin needs to know.' She moved quickly to the door. He tried to pin her against the doorframe, but he was too late, and she rolled away from him. She ran as fast as she could up the steps.

'Stop!' Simon called. 'Sarah, stop!' He caught up with her just as she flung open the door to Tamsin's room. Tamsin was at her spot by the window, with a book in her lap.

'I'm sorry, Tamsin,' Simon began, but Sarah was already halfway through what she had to say.

'. . . and Simon and Ruth know about it, and they've been doing it deliberately.'

'I tried to stop her, Tamsin, but she just pushed her way in here,' Simon said. Tamsin raised her hand.

'That's all right, Simon. If Sarah has something she needs to talk to me about this much, she can stay.'

'But she doesn't have an appointment!' Simon said.

'I don't care!' Sarah shouted.

'That's not a problem in this instance, Simon,'

Tamsin said. 'I will speak with you afterwards.' Simon glared at Sarah and slammed the door on his way out.

'Come and sit down, Sarah,' Tamsin said. She sat as she had done before, on a cushion in front of Tamsin, still in her boots and overcoat. 'What did you say was troubling you?'

Sarah recounted her story, adding that she had recognised the Land Rover number plate, which was not strictly true. Tamsin asked if that was everything. Sarah nodded. 'I'm sorry that this has upset you,' Tamsin said. 'But I'm not sure what I can do about it.'

'Can't you stop them? Have a word with them? They'll listen to you.'

Tamsin looked out of the round window.

'It's very difficult for me, Sarah. Ruth and Simon have done such a fantastic job here. From the vision we set out a little over ten years ago, we have come all this way. I could never have achieved all this on my own.'

'I know,' Sarah said. 'But don't you think they're taking this a step too far?'

'Think about this centre,' Tamsin said. 'About this movement. We have a chance to create something unique here. Can anything compare to the value we've been able to bring to people's lives?'

'But what about what they're doing?'

'I don't question Ruth and Simon's methods, as they always get results. That is what is important. We haven't revealed this yet to the rest of the members, but we've purchased a former farm, ready for a new centre. A further five potential sites have been identified, as well as more woodland and pasture. Isn't that amazing? On top of all the land we've been able to acquire and turn back to the wild. Think how many more people could find peace and happiness here. We could become an example to the whole world.'

'So you've approved this?' Sarah said coldly.

'I wouldn't exactly say that.'

'What would you say then?'

'Please Sarah, for all of our sakes, try to see the bigger picture. The land we hold is devoted not to profit but to the spiritual fulfilment of everyone. It's very difficult and expensive to purchase land, and it's virtually impossible to acquire land that's contiguous. There is no fairness here. We are a mere minnow compared to the powerful forces that have dominated this land for centuries. It is time to redress the balance, for the sake of everyone.'

'You have no idea of the suffering you've helped to cause,' Sarah said, shaking her head. Tamsin's gaze returned to the window.

'Sarah, please. From virtually nothing we are now poised to have a network of centres. People have worked so hard. These other landowners, they're fighting a tide; there's pressure enough as it is. I know it might seem callous, but in the long run everyone will benefit. History will judge us as having been right, and human happiness and fulfilment will be greater than it ever has been. And think about what comes after. When the world sees what we have built in Wales, the world will follow suit. Imagine that! Wildlands and communings and hedgerow sermons being held all across the globe. How wonderful! We are lucky to have such dedicated people here. People like Tristan and Ruth and Simon.'

'This is deranged. You can't take over the landscape just by causing as much misery as possible. It won't work.'

'Eventually our vision will come true. This virus, it's like the land expressing its need for change, for freedom at last.'

'I want my money back,' Sarah said. Tamsin shook her head.

'That money was a gift,' she said. 'We had hoped willingly given.'

'You're cheats! And liars. You torment people!'

'Sarah, think carefully,' Tamsin said. 'What is more important? Think what being here will mean for you and others.'

Sarah pressed her face into her hands.

'Would you like some tea?' Tamsin reached towards

a bell which was set on a pile of books close to her.

'Nothing is more important to me than the people I care about,' Sarah said, taking her hands away. 'And you cannot speak for them.'

'That is admirable, but we speak for people far better than many of them can for themselves. Countless people are floundering around in ignorance, not knowing any other way. We can finally help them to help themselves. We are creating a new beacon of hope, an example to the world. This is building the true Jerusalem, right here. More powerful than any religion.'

Sarah got up from the cushion and went towards the door.

'All of us speak for ourselves,' she said. 'And my religion is the people I love.'

Tamsin called after her but she left the room and the corridor beyond, then the chapel itself, without even a glance back towards the round window above.

Sarah pulled into a passing place along the narrow and high-hedged road on which she found herself, turned off the engine and drank from the water bottle that she kept in the car. Since leaving the centre immediately after her conversation with Tamsin, she had driven directionless across the countryside, taking arbitrary turns and twice going back on herself. She could not think anymore, nor did she want to. She was back where she started, driving aimlessly across this landscape, alone and miserable again. She got out and left the car behind, carrying on up the lane on foot before crossing a cattle grid and passing close to a farm. The lights were on in the farmhouse, and she could hear dogs barking in their kennels as she passed. She clambered over a gate and carried on up the hillside. Behind her, the swallowed sun had left its wake of embers above the hills; ahead lay a cold dusk. The grass turned sepia, and the wind blew colder and stronger as she made her way upwards.

Everything was ruined. She was lost again, having no one and nowhere once more. There was nothing for her in this landscape. She wandered on, alone and ashamed, oblivious to the disappearing path. Time evaporated as the valley disappeared and she trod purposelessly through the twilight, the monstrous towers of the turbines ahead looming black and terrible against the sky. She felt no comfort from the land, only a cold indifference. Alone in the gathering dark, there was only the pain of her own insignificance. The landscape stood apart from her, inhuman and uncaring.

21

Sarah burnt Tamsin's books in the cottage wood burner, along with every NWL leaflet and flyer she could find. It was too late; she had already given Sioned notice that she was leaving and saw no point in withdrawing it. Here she was, homeless again, directionless again, and alone again. She ran her hand over the walls she had painted. She had made a good job of this cottage. The work had been a distraction at the time, a way to take her mind off her own unhappiness. Now she felt proud of this place; the cottage had been in a dire state when she was handed the keys. Here was something good she had done by herself and for herself, without help from others, without looking to anyone else, and now she was leaving it, and for what? She could not stay on indefinitely at the farm without any prospects for the future. She feared it would absorb her and in time she would become little different from the dogs or the buildings or any other fixture. At least Sioned was someone with whom she could talk it over.

She set out for the farmhouse, passing under the pines that spoke to each other with the passage of the breeze, and she imagined them passing judgement on her, marking her out as the undesirable she was. Everything was broken. Though she had not returned Rob's calls, she still read the messages he sent and had learnt from him what had happened to Rhodri. Now Rhodri was dead, and all the animals were dead, and the pines knew she had brought her misfortune with her to this land.

Evan answered the door. Sioned was at her mother's, he said. The Renault was gone from the yard. He insisted she come in.

'So, we haven't got you for much longer?' Evan said. She shook her head. He pulled out her usual chair and sat the other side of the table from her. 'Sioned's gutted you know. She'll miss you. We both will.' Sarah looked away. There was a small statue on the shelf above the range which had not been there previously. It looked like one of Rhys's carvings. She had seen another in the hallway. 'I'll put the kettle on,' Evan said. 'Plans made then? Place to stay?'

Sarah shrugged. 'I suppose,' she said.

'You're welcome to stay here longer if you like.'

'Thank you, but no.'

'Alright then, forget about the tea,' Evan said, switching off the kettle. He left the room and came back holding the bottle of whisky she had given him. 'I haven't touched this since we opened it at Christmas. Let's have a goodbye drink, as you're leaving. Doesn't matter that it's three-thirty in the afternoon.'

He took out two glasses and poured a generous measure in each. He raised his glass and drank. Sarah did the same. It was quiet in the kitchen but for the ticking of the clock. The clock was a new addition and looked like an antique. It hung on the wall opposite the window. Sarah drank the whisky.

'What will happen with the farm?' she asked.

'Don't worry about the farm. You look after yourself,' Evan said.

'I feel responsible.'

'Don't be silly. It's nothing to do with you.'

'I know, but still.'

'These things happen,' he said. 'That's life. And you have your own life to lead.'

Sarah looked towards the window. She sipped her whisky.

'I don't know that I have,' she said eventually. 'A life to lead, that is.'

'Course you do. Everyone has. You have your own farm to look after, in a way. Even if it's not a real one. We all do.'

'I haven't,' she said. 'Other people might, but I haven't. Never have, never will.' She swilled the liquid around in her glass. Evan did the same. 'I'm just not that sort of person,' she said.

'Who's to say what sort of person anyone is,' Evan

said. 'Sioned thinks the world of you.'

'But I don't belong here, Evan. You've said as much yourself. I don't belong anywhere in fact. I should've got used to that by now.'

It was a while before Evan answered.

'If I did say that, then I'm sorry. This farm has been my life. It's everything I've ever known. I never dreamt what would happen would happen. I never imagined everything would be taken from me. I took it for granted that it would all go on forever, as it always had done. How could something like that be taken away from somebody?'

He finished his whisky and Sarah swallowed the last of hers. He poured them both another.

'Does the job, doesn't it!' he said. 'What I'm saying is, who says any of us belong anywhere? In a way, I don't belong here any more than you do. This place no longer belongs to me, and maybe I don't belong to it. I don't know how I'm supposed to go on now the farm has gone. But . . .' He shrugged. 'Sioned will think of something, always does. I'm not going to do what John Davies did. I couldn't do that to her.'

'Good,' Sarah said.

There was rarely a silence with Sioned, but Evan seemed comfortable with it. There was something different about him, but she could not think what. The clock ticked and they drank the second whisky.

'You still have a home here, though, in Mid Wales,' she said eventually. 'There's still a place for you, even if it's not the farm.'

Evan drank the last of his glass. He pointed his finger at her. 'Yes, but no more than you, not really,' he said. 'You say you're this sort of person, or that sort of person and you don't belong anywhere. Thing is, I'm no different from you. If it can all be taken away, then this home you're imagining doesn't really exist. There's no place for me anymore than there is for you. So I was wrong, Sarah. I was wrong to say what I said. We are the same, you and me.'

They finished the whisky in the darkening kitchen,

both looking out for Sioned and the lights of the car returning.

Sarah stopped at the edge of the clearing and unshouldered her rucksack. Ahead of her was the outcrop of rock, a familiar shape amongst unfamiliar trees. Her shoulders were sore from the weight of the rucksack. She set it down and walked around and up to the bivouac. There was the same ring of stones, in the centre of which was a grey cake of damp ash. Rhodri's tarpaulin was there, as was his hammock, but the rest of his belongings were gone. The bivouac was still littered with beer cans and other rubbish.

She had been worried she would take the wrong track and never find the place. The only real reference point she could remember was the stone circle and it had been a long walk from there. She was impressed by her own memory, especially as the trees had turned since she was last there. Relieved, she sat down to rest on one of the logs and listened as a robin sang.

'First things first, a fire,' she said. She was sorry she had spoken out loud. It sounded strange here and she decided she would not speak again. There was enough wood already gathered to start a fire. She had brought matches and paper in a sealed plastic bag to protect them from damp. There was nothing quite like a fire, she thought, as the flames began to pulse, the smoke rose and the powerful scent of burning filled the clearing. She fetched her rucksack and unpacked her belongings onto the tarpaulin, standing Rhys's carved hare on a ledge in the rock and carrying both her sleeping bags over to the hammock. Amongst the new items she had bought was a grill with folding legs. She stood it over the fire. There was a camping kettle as well, into which she poured water from her bottle and set it over the heat. She made tea in the cup from her flask, adding a little of the milk keeping cool inside. It was too hot, but she sipped at it regardless, delighted to have it between her hands.

The light was fading already, and the woods were chilled and damp. She found the new hatchet she had bought, its head wrapped in an old tea towel. Evan had shown her how to keep the edge keen, using a file and vice, neither of which she would have out here. She spent a long time between the trees gathering wood, sometimes hacking at fallen branches when they were too heavy to move on their own. Once she had picked up all the litter and pushed it into a crevice in the outcrop, she graded the wood, stoking the fire with some of the larger logs she had gathered. Her belly moaned loudly; she had forgotten her own hunger. There were plenty of tins of various foods, but she wanted to save them. Instead, she took the largest of the set of billy cans she had bought and filled it with water. She would have to find a stream, or other water source nearby. With the water heating on the fire, she emptied in the meat from the bloody plastic bag Sioned had given her. She cut an onion on the log with a folding knife and dropped it into the water, throwing the papery skin onto the fire. She chopped a carrot, a trimmed leek, and a few unpeeled potatoes and added them with a pinch of salt from a small container, skimming the surface of the soup and stirring in between. It was twilight now and the robin was quietening. She tasted the soup and added more salt. She wished she could remember what plants to forage for, like Rob. Perhaps there was wild thyme or garlic she could add. She sawed a clumsy slice of bread from the loaf she had brought, which had deformed in her rucksack along the way, and ate the soup from a mess tin, breaking off a chunk of the cheese she had had carried, wrapped in wax paper.

Full and satisfied, Sarah lay back on the ground next to the fire and looked up at the sky. The cloud of the day still lingered but where the shroud was broken, stars were just visible in the deep, blue-dark of space. Something moved in the distance through the trees, then it was silent once more. She was not afraid. Lying under the night sky, she smiled to herself. She did not care what people thought. Here, she sought neither approval nor acceptance. This landscape was her home now, and why should it not be? It was hers as much as anyone else's, meaning that really it was no one's. Everyone had it wrong about the land. Make a mirror out if it, and you will see your own reflection. You cannot defeat the land, nor can you really protect it. It cannot be owned, shared or reasoned with. It has neither head nor heart, no ears to hear, and when spoken to, cannot answer. It simply is: inhuman and unexplainable. The land stands apart from us, beyond our experience, unknowable and unreachable, closed forever to the human mind. She lay still, listening to the murmur of the fire and gazing upwards at the cold, incurious stars.

Acknowledgements

My thanks go first and foremost to Consuelo Rivera-Fuentes and all at Victorina Press. I would like to thank the Department of English and Creative Writing at Aberystwyth University for its continued support. In particular, I would like to thank my PhD supervisors Professor Matthew Francis and Dr Neal Alexander for their invaluable guidance, comments and other input. Thanks go to Claire Jones and family for consultation and experience of farming life.

Lastly, I would like to thank my wife Ailsa, without whose support this book would not have been written.

Biography

Morgan Davies is a writer interested in landscape, place and nature. He has a master's degree with distinction in Creative Writing from the University of Edinburgh and a PhD in Creative Writing from Aberystwyth University for which he was awarded a departmental postgraduate studentship. His short stories set in rural Wales have been published in winning anthologies and performed in London. He lives in Mid Wales with his wife and sons. *The Burning Bracken* is his first novel.